ATTACK!

The army patrol rode toward the post at Adobe Walls. Lieutenant Frank Baldwin was the first to hear the Indian war cries. Coming from the right, two buffalo hunters fled a large party of Indians. Ahead of the men, a wagon raced toward the corral gate. The Indians split ranks, trying to cut the two riders off.

"Pull your pistols and follow me!" Baldwin barked as he charged the war party.

Still out of firing range, the patrol saw two warriors pull ahead to ride beside the terrified men. One suddenly lunged forward and drove his lance into one of the men, sending him tumbling to the ground.

The Indian grabbed for the dead man's horse, missing the reins. He kicked his pony harder and reached again. His partner closed in on the remaining buffalo hunter.

"Fire!" Baldwin yelled.

Almost as one, the pistols boomed.

BOOK YOUR PLACE ON OUR WEBSITE AND MAKE THE READING CONNECTION!

We've created a customized website just for our very special readers, where you can get the inside scoop on everything that's going on with Zebra, Pinnacle and Kensington books.

When you come online, you'll have the exciting opportunity to:

- View covers of upcoming books
- Read sample chapters
- Learn about our future publishing schedule (listed by publication month *and author*)
- Find out when your favorite authors will be visiting a city near you
- Search for and order backlist books from our online catalog
- Check out author bios and background information
- Send e-mail to your favorite authors
- Meet the Kensington staff online
- Join us in weekly chats with authors, readers and other guests
- Get writing guidelines
- AND MUCH MORE!

**Visit our website at
http://www.kensingtonbooks.com**

BLOOD ON THE PLAINS

WALTER LUCAS

PINNACLE BOOKS
Kensington Publishing Corp.

http://www.pinnaclebooks.com

PINNACLE BOOKS are published by

Kensington Publishing Corp.
850 Third Avenue
New York, NY 10022

All Kensington Titles, Imprints, and Distributed Lines are available at special quantity discounts for bulk purchases for sales promotions, premiums, fund-raising, and educational or institutional use. Special book excerpts or customized printings can also be created to fit specific needs. For details, write or phone the office of the Kensington special sales manager: Kensington Publishing Corp., 850 Third Avenue, New York, NY 10022, attn: Special Sales Department, Phone: 1-800-221-2647.

Pinnacle and the P logo Reg. U.S. Pat. & TM Off.

First Printing: November 2001
10 9 8 7 6 5 4 3 2

Printed in the United States of America

This book is dedicated to my wife, Donna, and our children, who almost forgot what I look like, and to my editor, Karen Haas, who never had a doubt.

ACKNOWLEDGMENTS

I would like to offer a few words of appreciation to those who have made this novel possible.

To Jim Rementer of the Lenni Lenape (Delaware) tribe, thank you. You taught me that the Delaware are a kind, generous people with a great sense of humor. Without your help, Zachariah Cottontail (Chumumte) would not exist.

To the folks at the reference desk of Amarillo Public Library, thank you for helping me find the bits of information necessary to bring my characters to life.

Finally, a huge debt is owed to the Write Stuff Critique Group: Tom Allston, Debbie Bradley, Suzanne Dia, and Carol Smith. These guys stayed in the trenches and fought their way through the book one page at a time. What more could I want? Thank you.

ONE

Tall Elk stood atop the buffalo skull. He stared at the sinking sun as it set the western sky ablaze, and willed a vision.

He was on the rim of the canyon called Palo Duro, "hard wood," by the Comancheros. Its walls, normally painted with stripes of red, white, and orange, now were stained scarlet near the top and black at the bottom.

He had stood thus since before dawn, facing the sun as it made its daily journey. He'd watched the orb change from red to yellow to white and back again. Now it rode low on the edge of the world and bled across the sky.

Tall Elk gingerly stepped off the skull. He lifted it and gazed into its empty eye sockets.

"Tell me, Grandfather, why have I stayed on your head all day? I am hungry and thirsty, and I ache. All I wanted was a sign I would do well in battle. Is it so much to ask?"

The skull refused to answer.

Tall Elk sighed. Did it not understand the importance of his request? First, there was the fight with the buffalo hunters on the Canadian River, where so many Cheyenne had died, including Chief Stone Calf's son.

Now even more soldiers were coming to kill all the Cheyenne—and the Comanche and Kiowa.

Still he had no vision.

Frowning, he heaved the bone over the canyon rim and watched it tumble until it was swallowed by the darkness.

He climbed atop the nearest buffalo and crossed the herd toward his village. He saw tipis in the distance and his wife, Crow Woman, cooking dinner in a brass pot. The lodges of his wife's family formed a small camp circle, open to the northeast. Each lodge door faced east to catch the first rays of morning light.

His father-in-law stood amid the tipis, arms crossed. His face bore a look of concern. Tall Elk knew the failure of his vision quest was the talk of the village. Still, what more could he do?

Near the middle of the herd, a circle formed. In its center was an old bull, his pelt dusted white as though frosted with ice. Tall Elk approached. He and the buffalo calmly regarded each other.

"I should be angry with you," the bull said in a voice deepened with age. "You threw my head into the canyon."

"You would not answer my question, Grandfather, so I will ask again. Why did I not have a vision?"

The massive head rose, thick black lips curved in a smile. "Why are all my grandchildren in such a hurry? Have patience, *nixa*. The vision will appear when the time is right." The smile faded. "Now I have a question for you. Why must the Cheyenne kill me, strip away my hide, and pull the meat from my bones?"

"You are a gift to the People from Maiyun, the Medicine Spirit."

"How came this to be?"

"You know the story, as does every child in the village," Tall Elk said.

"Tell me again," the bull pleaded. "I am old and forgetful."

The warrior sat astride a cow who seemed not to notice him.

"Long ago there was famine among the People. There was no rain; the vegetation died, and the animals starved. From among the warriors came a young man called Standing On The Ground."

"I thought his name was Erect Horns," the bull said.

"Not then, Grandfather," Tall Elk replied. "Now, this young man took the wife of the chief and walked to a sacred mountain. They walked inside a cave, and he spoke of his people's plight to Maiyun and the Thunder Spirit. Maiyun taught them the Sun Dance and gave Standing On The Ground the sacred Buffalo Hat."

"Ah, yes. I remember now. It was made of buffalo skin and had horns that stood like mine. That is how he got the name 'Erect Horns.' "

"Yes, Grandfather. Erect Horns put on the cap, and as he left the mountain, the Roaring Thunder woke the sun and moon. The rain came, bringing forth fruit. All the animals followed the couple out of the mountain, and the People were given control of them.

"And now you know again. The buffalo must die for the People to live."

The old head nodded slowly. "You are right, Tall Elk. I know it all. I saw the first man hunt the first buffalo. I knew Erect Horns, and have been to the lodge of Maiyun many times."

"Then why did you ask me for the story?"

The bull said nothing.

Thunder rumbled in the distance, shaking the ground. Tall Elk scanned the red sky, but saw no clouds, no lightning on the horizon.

"He comes," the bull said.

"Who?"

Again the ground shook as thunder rolled across the land.

"He comes," the buffalo repeated. "We must be gone."

The bull unfurled huge black wings, as did the other members of the herd. Tall Elk was unceremoniously dumped on the ground as the cow took flight. The herd rose into the sky and disappeared over the canyon's edge.

A third clap of thunder, but different. Sharp, flat—a *thud!*

Tall Elk ran toward his village, dread filling his heart. He had no reason, but deep within him, he knew he must hurry.

A white giant appeared on the other side of the camp. As a massive foot raised, Tall Elk shouted a warning, but was too late. The foot crashed into a tipi, crushing all inside.

Tall Elk ran as fast as he could, but could come no closer. He watched helplessly as the giant walked through his village, destroying lodges and lives with each step.

Finally, the giant stopped in front of Tall Elk. It bent at the waist and peered at the warrior with blue eyes larger than Tall Elk's head. Its hair was long and golden and crackled like summer lightning, its yellow beard nothing more than prairie fire. It grunted, straightened, and lifted a foot over Tall Elk.

"Wait!" the warrior shouted. "Before you crush me, tell me why! Why do you kill us?"

The giant laughed, the sound rattling Tall Elk's teeth.

"You Cheyenne are a gift to me from my Great Spirit," it said in a guttural voice. "You must die that I may live!"

As the foot dropped, Tall Elk threw himself to one

side. He held his breath. When nothing happened, he slowly opened an eye.

All he saw was the vastness of Palo Duro Canyon. He glanced at the ground and saw he was within six inches of the rim. He quickly scrambled away.

Pain shot through his feet from standing on the skull. His thighs and calves cramped, and he cried out in agony. Yet the sky was blue, burned almost white by the midday sun. There was no herd of flying buffalo, no great white giant.

Tall Elk pulled himself to a sitting position. He leaned forward, peered over the edge of the canyon, and shuddered.

Tall Elk sat and stared across the fire at Gray Eagle. The old medicine man seemed lost in thought, and the very young warrior knew he was contemplating the story he'd just heard.

"You should talk this matter over with a priest," Gray Eagle said in a voice hoarse with age. "I deal with wounds of the body and illness. Visions belong to the shamans."

"I know, but you are also my grandfather. I did not want my vision spread through the camp. People will talk."

Gray Eagle nodded. "This is true. I don't believe what you saw will come to pass, but others may. There are those among the People whose tongues are sharper than their knives."

Tall Elk leaned forward. "Then you will help?"

"I will do what I can. Let's start with the most important part of your vision."

"The crushing of the village?"

"No," Gray Eagle answered. "You and Crow Woman. Have you feelings for this woman?"

Tall Elk squirmed. "I've seen her around the village."

"You know she comes from a very good family. Her father is on the Council of Forty-four. Her mother, a member of the Quilling Society. Any man who takes her as his wife would gain much prominence in the tribe."

"She is also very pretty, and speaks with a voice soft as a spring breeze." Tall Elk sighed. "I'm not blind or deaf."

"Then you have approached her."

"Of course not!" Tall Elk bristled at the statement. "That wouldn't be proper. Besides, what good would it do? I am barely a warrior. I've been on one raid and have only four ponies, all gifts from family. Why would she look at me? Especially with her sister married to Bull Buffalo. How can I compete? He has more horses than he can count and three lances—and a coup stick covered in scalps. I am nothing next to him."

Gray Eagle clucked. "You are young, that's all. Your father is a great warrior and will soon take his place on the council. Your mother has a very good reputation, and your sister married quite well. I believe you can claim Chief Stone Calf as a relative."

"Another uncle to give me a pony," Tall Elk said morosely.

Gray Eagle tossed a stick on the fire. "Let's deal with the rest of your vision."

Relief washed over Tall Elk. He didn't like talking about Crow Woman or the way she made him feel.

"The giant is the easiest to understand."

"He's the white men, right? The soldiers who come to kill us," Tall Elk said.

"Actually, he is one man. Think of the flaming hair and fiery whiskers. This is the man we call Yellow Hair. The whites know him as Custer. He is the soldier who killed our people at Sand Creek. Even now he pursues the Lakota in their sacred Black Hills."

"Do you think he will return here?"

"I don't know. You walked north across the buffalo herd."

Tall Elk nodded.

"Since the village was destroyed and you were not, Yellow Hair means to battle our cousins to the north, and we will escape." Gray Eagle paused. "Yet he walked up to you. I think we will fight the soldiers, too, but, like you, we will survive."

"And what of the buffalo?"

"They will go where the white hunters cannot get them and will return after they are gone."

Tall Elk sat a moment. "And if the white man stays?"

"Perhaps we will go the way of the buffalo."

TWO

As the train pulled into the Fort Leavenworth, Kansas, train station, Lieutenant Frank Baldwin carefully inspected the exterior of his shako for lint. As a recruiting officer for the U.S. Army, he was all too well aware of his image.

The shako was a curious-looking hat, much like its poor cousin, the forage cap, with stiffened sides. It was made of felt, covered in dark blue cloth, and lined in brown cotton. Like its relative, the infantry bugle was embroidered in gilt metal on the front. Inside the horn's loop was a golden 5 for the Fifth Infantry. But all this was overshadowed by a foot-high, white cock's feather attached to the cap's front.

Inspection done, he again pondered the whirlwind of events over the last few days. Stationed at Newport Barracks, Kentucky, as a recruiting officer, he'd received a telegram from his old friend George Baird instructing him to proceed at once to Fort Leavenworth per Colonel Nelson Miles's orders. Mystified as to why he would be summoned to regimental headquarters on such short notice, Baldwin worried until the following day when another wire arrived from Baird, this one informing him he was to be Miles's chief of scouts in the upcoming campaign.

Baldwin was elated. After eight years of mostly post-related jobs, he was finally to be back in the field again. Any form of combat meant a chance for promotion or decoration—or both.

He and his wife Allie danced around the parlor, laughing.

"Does this really mean a promotion, Frank?"

Baldwin gazed into Allie's brown eyes. "I can't say," he said, honestly. "But if there is ever an opportunity for me to advance, it is here."

She pulled away from him. "If you aren't getting a promotion, why are we dancing? What is there to celebrate? Your leaving?"

"No, not at all! I must go. To refuse this assignment would mean the end of my career."

Allie gripped his arms. "It's more than that, Frank. I can see it in your face."

"I have the chance to do what I do best—be a soldier. Any general store clerk can be a quartermaster; any salesman a recruiting officer, but the true soldier is a warrior."

"Yes, yes, he is, I suppose," Allie answered quietly. She let go of Baldwin's arms. "Then we shall make the best of it. You will be involved in many adventures, I suppose."

"I suppose, but, Allie, my job is to locate the Indians. I have no say in who I fight or where."

"Nonetheless, people will want to know what you've done. You are a great soldier, Frank. You will find glory among the savages. I want you to write down everything that happens."

"A journal? I'll not have time to write on the campaign!"

"Nonsense, you'll have the nights by the fire. Write it all down, Frank."

She pressed her body close to his. "Come back to me, Frank!" she whispered. "All of you."

Baldwin embraced his wife tightly. "I love you, Allie."

"Show me, Frank. Here and now!"

"But . . . but it's daylight. Really, Allie, what would—"

"The hell with them! It's not their man gone to war. Come with me, Lieutenant Baldwin, while I make the squaws and camp followers safe from Long Tom."

Baldwin put on the shako, adjusting the feather to keep it in front, but out of his face. He pictured himself as the ideal image of the soldier.

His dress coat was a double-breasted, dark blue, broadcloth frock coat with two rows of seven gilt buttons. Each button carried a large eagle and the letter *I* for Infantry. On his shoulders, he wore dress knots consisting of double rows of intertwined gold braid ending in a large oval. The inside of the oval was covered in dark blue cloth. Embroidered in its center was his regimental designation in silver metal flanked by two silver bars denoting his rank of first lieutenant. His trousers were sky blue with a one-and-a-half-inch dark blue stripe down each outer seam. The uniform had been tailored to fit him perfectly.

His only departure from regulation were his boots. Handmade Wellingtons of fine calfskin, dyed black and polished to a high luster.

He crossed the platform, quickly finding a porter and instructing him to have his luggage delivered to the fort's guest quarters. Feeling a hand on his shoulder, he turned to see the familiar face of George Baird.

"George!" he cried, as he took the lieutenant's hand. "It is so good to see you."

Baird smiled broadly. "I thought you'd like to see a friendly face. Ready?"

"Yes, I've already had my luggage sent to the fort. Am I to report to Colonel Miles now?"

"You are. You mustn't have heard he'd been breveted to major general."

"No. I take it he prefers to be called General."

"You take it right, my friend."

The pair boarded Baird's rig. They drove to the post talking about old times and mutual friends. Soon Baird drew the carriage to a halt outside a two-story white house.

"Here we are."

"Is this the general's home?"

Baird grinned. "Yup. He said for me to bring you here as soon as your train got in."

Baldwin climbed out of the rig. "How did you know when I was arriving? I sent no telegrams."

"Didn't. I've been meeting every train since the twenty-sixth."

"Oh. You coming in?"

"Nope. I'll just wait right here."

Baldwin frowned a moment, then shrugged. He quickly adjusted his hat and uniform coat. He rubbed the tops of his boots against his calves and examined the results. It would have to do.

If asked, he would have said he was a bit put out. After all, Miles could have allowed him time to prepare his appearance. Nevertheless, you don't keep a general waiting.

He opened the gate in the white picket fence and walked to the porch. As he reached the top step, he was met by an Irish setter. Baldwin and the dog eyed each other a moment; then the setter wagged its tail. Baldwin offered his hand to the animal, which sniffed it, then rubbed its head against his palm.

Baldwin chuckled. "You're a good dog. Aren't you, boy?" He scratched behind the setter's ears.

The lieutenant crossed the porch and knocked three times on the front door. As he waited for a servant to answer, he retrieved one of his cards.

"Whenever you first arrive at a new post, you must present your card to the commanding officer," he told the dog.

The man who answered the door wore an undress blouse, unbuttoned. Each shoulder bore a light blue, gold-edged strap and two stars.

"Miles!" Baldwin squeaked. The setter barked. "I-I-I mean Colonel Miles. No! No! No! *General* Miles!"

Miles drew on the large cigar he was smoking. He took it from his mouth, examined the ash, then slowly released the smoke, grinning. "Relax, son." He pointed the cigar at the dog. "I see you've met Jack." He looked back at the officer and shook his head. "I've got to stop answering the door. Next time I'll let Mary do it. That all right with you, Lieutenant?"

Baldwin gulped. "Yes, sir, General."

"Good," Miles replied. "I'm glad I have your approval. Now, who are you?"

"Baldwin, sir. First Lieutenant Frank D. Baldwin, Fifth Infantry, reporting as ordered, sir." He quickly threw a salute.

Miles responded with a wave of his cigar. "This is good." He looked over Baldwin's shoulder. "Is that my adjutant out there?"

"Yes, sir."

"Hmm. Well, Baldwin, you and I have a great deal to talk about. Why don't you get settled, then come to dinner here at seven. That suit you?"

"Yes, sir. Whatever the general wishes."

Miles looked Baldwin over closely. "I'd be careful

about granting a general's wish, son. I'd be damned careful."

Baldwin stood at Miles's front door and took a deep breath. He'd been cursing himself since his performance that afternoon. What Miles must think of him, acting like a nervous West Point shavetail.

He exhaled noisily, willing himself calmer. A stiff drink would be handy right now. Not enough to notice, just a healthy slug to cut the tension. Scuffing his hastily repolished boots against his calves, he readjusted the fit of his uniform coat and tried to ignore the thin stream of sweat running down his sides.

He slipped the white glove off his right hand and carefully removed the shako, holding it with his left hand in the crook of his arm. Then he rapped on the door with an air of much more confidence or authority than he had and waited.

His knock was answered by one of Miles's strikers, a young soldier whose duty it was to serve the general and his family. Baldwin fished a card from his coat pocket and handed it to the striker.

The young man glanced at the card and said, "Lieutenant Baldwin, the general's expecting you. Please come in."

Baldwin surrendered his hat and gloves. The striker led the lieutenant through the parlor and into the dining room.

The table was long, easily accommodating a dozen people or more. Seated at its head was Miles, Baldwin noting the general had changed into a dress uniform. He was pleasantly surprised to see George Baird and his wife sitting to Miles's right, while a woman he did not know sat to the left. He assumed the lady was Mrs. Miles.

As he stepped into the room, the general and his

adjutant rose to their feet. Miles walked around the table, hand extended.

"Baldwin," he said. "Welcome."

They shook briefly, and Miles ushered Baldwin to the table.

"I'd like you to meet my wife, Mary. Dear, this is Lieutenant Frank Baldwin, my new chief of scouts."

"Lieutenant, it is a pleasure to meet you."

Mary Miles was a pleasant-looking woman of indeterminate age with dark brown hair and eyes that sparkled as she smiled. She wore a forest-green gown of silk brocade and velvet. Baldwin offered her a small bow.

"Mrs. Miles, it is an honor," he said.

"Sit next to my wife, Baldwin," Miles boomed as he returned to his seat. "We don't stand on formality here."

Baldwin relaxed immediately and pulled back the chair. He started to plop down when he caught a warning look on Baird's face. Easing into the chair, he sat quietly, hands in his lap.

Miles rang a small silver bell, and dinner was served immediately. The soup was French onion accompanied by a white wine chilled from its stay in the cellar. The main course was roast pork and mushrooms, glazed in red wine and honey, then mashed potatoes with a rich brown sauce, field peas, and green beans. Hot bread and freshly churned butter topped the meal, all washed down with a French burgundy Miles had brought from the East. Dessert consisted of rhubarb pie and a sweet port.

Conversation during the meal stayed light, mostly centering on the differences of life in Kansas and that of Kentucky and points east. Dinner over, the women moved to the parlor, while the men retired to Miles's library for brandy and cigars.

"This room," Miles said, closing the heavy door, "is

my sanctuary from family and the army." He crossed to the desk and opened his humidor. "Help yourself, gentlemen."

Baird and Baldwin each chose a fat Havana from the box while Miles poured brandy into three snifters. Drinks distributed, the general unbuttoned his uniform coat and dropped it onto a large oxblood leather chair behind the desk. He indicated to the others to sit in similar, though not as plush chairs in front of the desk.

Baldwin looked over at Baird who had set his glass on the desktop and was trimming his cigar with a cigar cutter as was Miles. He set his brandy down and pulled out his pocketknife. Miles looked up as the knife's blade clicked open. He scowled and tossed the cutter to Baldwin.

"There are two things you need to remember, Lieutenant: the right tool for the right job . . ." He paused, struck a match, and puffed the cigar into life. ". . . And I like Cubans."

"Yes, sir," Baldwin mumbled.

The cutter worked like a small guillotine. Baldwin chopped off one end, then snipped the tip off the other end to allow for the passage of smoke. Satisfied and pleased with his efforts, he took a match from the desk's brass holder and struck it across the sole of his boot. He lit the cigar and drew smoke deep into his lungs, savoring the taste.

The general lived well. He ate well; he drank well; he smoked very well. Baldwin longed for the day when he would sit behind the desk with his own brandy and his own cigars.

Miles leaned back in his chair. "If I were you, I would be wondering, why me?" He looked at Baldwin.

Suddenly nervous, Baldwin blurted, "Uh . . . yes, sir, that had crossed my mind."

"And well it should, Lieutenant. Frankly, when

George recommended you for the job, I had my doubts—until I learned a couple of things.

"First, you were captured twice by the Rebels. Then you earned a Medal of Honor by capturing two Confederate officers with just your sword. I knew then that you had no fear of close contact with the enemy.

"Most officers believe that without West Point training, you'd lack proper education in wartime strategy. Bullshit! How many Indians do you think studied Clausewitz's *On War?*" Miles suddenly leaned forward and stared at Baldwin. "It is arrogance that will defeat them. Forsythe believed he was superior to his enemies, and the Indians killed him without trying. Custer believes it as well. Mark my words, he'll meet his Waterloo if he doesn't change his attitude.

"I, on the other hand, do not underestimate the capabilities of my enemy." He rose. "George, get the map."

Baird crossed the room and returned with a large map of the south central portion of the United States. He placed the easel in front of Baldwin, who rose for a closer look. Miles placed his hand on the area between Texas and Kansas officially known as Indian Territory.

"This, gentlemen, is where the enemy lives. His depredations range from central Kansas to the Mexican border. He is mostly Comanche, Kiowa, and Cheyenne. Already he has killed buffalo hunters on the Llano Estacado, attacked a trading post near old Adobe Walls, and ambushed a company of Texas Rangers.

"What Washington proposes is a multitiered attack. We are to proceed to Fort Dodge with four companies of Fifth Infantry. Eight companies of Sixth Cavalry will join us there, as well as a small detachment of light artillery. We will then march south pushing the Indians ahead of us.

"Meanwhile, Mackenzie's Fourth Cavalry will move

north from Fort Concho, Price and his Eighth Cavalry east from Fort Bascom, and Buell's Eleventh Cavalry northeast from Fort Griffin. All of the columns will merge with Davidson and his Tenth Cavalry at Fort Sill. This combined attack is designed to force all the Indians onto the reservation crushing any resistance as necessary."

Baldwin nodded. "It seems to be a well-planned campaign, sir."

"As far as it goes, I agree, but I have a few changes in mind, and that is where you and your scouts come in."

Miles's plan was simple. His units would leave Fort Dodge in early August, well ahead of the other four columns. The main bulk of the expeditionary force would travel southeast down the Fort Sill highway, but it was Baldwin and his scouts that Miles depended on.

"You will ride light, carrying subsistence rations only," he said. "I'd venture the men under your command would as soon live off the land. The only ammunition you'll carry will be for defense. I want nothing to slow you down."

Miles again turned to the map. "Here is Fort Sill," he continued, stabbing the area with his index finger. "To the northwest is Bent's old trading post where Carson fought the Comanches in sixty-four. About a mile north of it is Adobe Walls. Now, this post sits right on the edge of the Staked Plains. That, gentlemen, is where the enemy awaits."

"But, General," Baldwin said, "those plains extend west to Apache territory and south nearly to Fort Griffin. There's no way we can flush them out, even with ten times our number."

"And we won't. The peacemakers want time to allow the friendly Indians to register so we don't do what Chivington did. It is my opinion these hostiles will mix with their peaceful cousins attempting to avoid us. The most direct path from the plains to the reservation is due east along the north fork of the Red River."

Miles tucked the cigar into the corner of his mouth and talked around it, eyes alight with excitement.

"We will establish a supply camp midway between Dodge and Sill. This is our main base of operations. From there we drive south and west until we cross the enemy's path. Your job, Baldwin, is to find that point and track the hostiles to their camps."

"And if we find no tracks?"

"Then, Lieutenant, we will move west from Fort Sill until we catch him coming to us. Either way, I intend to have the Kiowas and Comanches safely tucked away on the reservation before Mackenzie sets foot on the plains."

THREE

Baldwin's train arrived in Coffeyville, Kansas, at 7:00 P.M. on July 30, 1874. Before leaving Fort Leavenworth, he'd wired the sheriff in Coffeyville to have an interpreter meet his train.

Baldwin looked at those around him on the platform. A derelict of a man dressed in patched buckskins hunkered near the end of the platform. His hair was black, long, and matted; his beard matched. He wore a dilapidated slouch hat sporting a long white eagle feather. As he sat with his chin nearly on his chest, the hat's crown effectively hid his face.

Baldwin approached the man and toed him. "Are you the interpreter?"

The hat brim lifted revealing rheumy brown eyes. The man nodded and unsteadily gained his feet. He was taller than Baldwin expected, and smelled of smoke, sweat, and whiskey.

"My God, man, are you drunk?"

"Gotta cold," the interpreter replied. For punctuation he hawked and deposited a glob of phlegm at Baldwin's feet. "Been drinking rum toddies. You Blaine?"

"The name's Baldwin. And you are?"

"Cottontail, Zachariah Cottontail."

"Zachariah? Was your father white?"

"Yup. Mother, too."

Baldwin was confused. "Then why the Indian name if you're not a half-breed?"

Cottontail grinned. "Married into the tribe. We was hunting one day, and I bet a friend that I could run down a rabbit on foot. When we got home, he started telling the story and he called me 'Chumumte,' saying I scurried like a rabbit."

"That means 'cottontail'?"

" 'Bout as close as a white man can call it. Lenape names don't always translate right."

"Lenape? I thought we were going to the Delaware reservation."

"We are. You call us Delaware, but we call ourselves Lenni Lenape, General. It means 'The People.' "

"I'm a lieutenant."

"Sure thing, General, whatever you say." Cottontail turned and stepped off the platform. "Now, I got you a room over at the Eldridge House, best hotel in town. I also got horses and gear waitin' at the livery. Come mornin', we'll ride out and meet."

Baldwin rose early, ate breakfast, and was met by the interpreter as he stepped through the hotel's front door.

"Good morning, Mr. Cottontail."

"How do, General?"

"That's Lieutenant," Baldwin muttered.

Cottontail absently scratched his chest, then under his left arm. "I reckon we ought to git."

"Lead on."

As they walked, Baldwin tried to think of how he would approach the old chief. Would it be better to appeal to the man's sense of honor? His hatred for the enemy? Flattery? He glanced up and noticed Cottontail regarding him closely.

"Question?"

"Sorta." Cottontail paused a moment, stroking his beard as he walked. "If you don't mind my askin', why you want a meet?"

"I'm recruiting scouts for an upcoming campaign against the Comanche and Kiowa. In particular, I was told to seek the services of one Black Beaver."

"Hmm. I'm not so sure Suctumakwe will parley. You got to understand that we Lenape lost most everything we had during the War between the States. Hell, what the Rebs didn't take, the Union government did after the war. Ol' Black Beaver gave his heart and soul to prove his loyalty, and all it got him was throwed off his own land."

"Damn!" Baldwin swore. "How am I to recruit willing trackers when . . ." He let the sentence drift off, then sighed. "There was another name. Falling Leaf, I believe."

"Cap'n Falleaf? Now there's a fighter."

"He's a captain? Did he gain rank in the army?"

"No, sir, he's a war chief, and a damn fine one. We call our war chiefs 'captain.' Anyway, Falleaf, his real name's Panipakuxwe, means somethin' like 'he who walks when the leaves fall,' he'd be a good 'un. Old man likes nothing better'n a good fight."

The two rode in companionable silence. Baldwin felt comfortable with Cottontail though he'd known the man for only a day. Perhaps he envied the interpreter, a white man who turned his back on his own people to live free and unfettered by civilization.

Baldwin also felt freed. He'd developed a taste for warfare in the sixties. He loved the thrill of the charge, thundering artillery, popping rifles, the sheer terror of counterattack, an enemy you could look in the eye. The horror was there as well, death and dismemberment at every hand, but beneath it—excitement. Blood-boiling, heart-pounding, light-headed exhilaration. It was a feeling no man could explain, much less conceive of, without being there.

"Too long," Baldwin muttered.

"What's too long?" Cottontail asked.

Startled, Baldwin didn't have time to lie. "Too long in forts, offices, and behind desks."

Cottontail grinned. "Tail sore?"

The lieutenant nodded, relieved not to have to explain his thoughts. Besides, the comment wasn't far from the truth. In the last nine years, he'd spent most of his time riding a chair.

"Well, won't be long now," the interpreter continued. "Yonder's Falleaf's house."

It was a neat, single-story log cabin. A porch protected the front door, and in its shadow sat two chairs. Chickens scratched in the yard, and cattle wandered the pastureland behind. It reminded Baldwin of small farms in his native Michigan.

"You live in houses," he said, awed.

"Yup. Shocking, ain't it?"

Baldwin blushed. "I . . . I," he stammered, then got mad. "Damn it, Cottontail, that is not what I meant!"

"Whatever you say, General."

As they neared the house, a man emerged from under the overhang. Baldwin thought him another white living among the Delaware. He was of average height with hair not overly long and streaked with white. Dark eyes sat on either side of a plain nose. His most striking features were his large, square jaw and chin. Their appearance gave his head a rectangular shape.

Cottontail reined to a halt. *"He, Ju!"* he called.

"He, Chumumte," the other replied. *"Weli Kishku."*

"Yes, my friend, it is a good day."

"*Who is the soldier?*"

"*He is Lieutenant Frank Baldwin. He comes from the Great Chief in Washington and wants to talk to you.*"

The man didn't respond. Baldwin leaned toward Cottontail. "Will he take us to Falleaf?" he whispered.

Cottontail raised a hand. "It's rude to talk while he's thinking."

The old man gazed from Cottontail to Baldwin, then back again. He nodded and walked back toward the porch.

Cottontail dismounted and waved to Baldwin. "All right, General, we can meet. When we get to the house, you take whatever chair he offers, and let me do the talkin'."

"Is he going to take us to Falleaf?"

"General, he *is* Falleaf."

As they approached the porch, Baldwin noticed the old man had taken the more comfortable of the two chairs. The other was straight-backed with no seat cushion.

"*Lematawpi,*" Falleaf said, pointing to the empty chair.

"He says 'Have a seat,' " Cottontail translated.

Baldwin sat. The old man looked unlike any Indian he'd ever seen. There was no painted face, no pierced ears or nose. His skin was tanned, but not coppery. If he had been dressed in European attire, Baldwin would have guessed him to be French or Basque.

"Cottontail, tell him I am honored to be in his presence and thank him for taking the time to talk to us."

"*Panipakuxwe, he says he's glad to be here.*"

"*I know. I heard. You think maybe they're going to try to make us move again?*"

"*No, not from what he's told me.*" Cottontail addressed Baldwin. "Falleaf says he's right honored to have you as his guest."

Baldwin grinned. "This is going quite well, isn't it?"

"Yes, sir."

"Good. Now tell him that General Nelson Miles is leading a campaign against his enemy the Comanche and Kiowa. The general needs his help and recognizes the Lenape as the best trackers in the world."

"See? The white men want you fight their battles again."

"It is not so bad, Chumumte. Ask him how much he will pay."

"Falleaf wants to know what the army will give him."

"We will supply horses, equipment, and food. He and his men will need to provide their own weapons. Besides that, we will pay him five dollars a day to lead and the rest one dollar."

"He is offering you much more than I thought he would, but I still don't trust the army." Cottontail frowned and bit his lip. *"I have nothing against Baldwin, but he has his own chiefs to answer to. These other men may not give us what he promises."*

"Ask him then."

"Falleaf says he hears what you promise, but will the general and those in Washington let us have them?"

Baldwin took a deep breath. He knew of the broken treaties and lies—the government's efforts to pen the Indians in one location or eradicate them.

"Cottontail, tell Falleaf that I will see to it that he and his men get everything I promised if I have to pay for it out of my own pocket."

"I think he is an honorable man, Panipakuxwe, but even an officer don't make enough money to pay that."

"True. Yet I can see that he is not lying. He will try. He may fail, but he will try. That is good enough for me. Tell him I will help."

"But why?" Cottontail cried. *"You fight for the white man and he moves you from your land! Maybe after this fight, he will make you move again."*

Falleaf raised a hand. *"No man wants to lose his home, but now we are here among the Cherokee in a land the white man does not want. Where will he move us to? Now, tell Baldwin what I said."*

Cottontail took several deep breaths, then faced the lieutenant. "Against my wishes, Falleaf has agreed to help you. What do you wish?"

Baldwin sighed with relief. He hadn't understood the last exchange, but from Cottontail's stance he had gathered there was disagreement.

"Very good." Baldwin faced Falleaf, but spoke to Cottontail. "Please tell him we need as many braves as he can gather. When he is ready, we will take the train to Fort Dodge and join the rest of the scouts."

Falleaf sat with pursed lips and looked Baldwin in the eye. He turned and looked at Cottontail.

Falleaf grinned. *"I think we will march down the main street near the station. Maybe some of those white men will think we're on the warpath. Be fun to scare them a little."*

Cottontail grinned in return. *"Then I will see you again, Panipakuxwe."*

"Soon again, Rabbit Butt," Falleaf answered in English.

Baldwin stared, mouth agape. "You speak English?"

"Some, but not so good as him," Falleaf said, jerking a thumb toward Cottontail.

The lieutenant faced his interpreter. "What did he call you?"

"Cottontail."

Falleaf laughed. "Him no tell you? Him name Chumumte; that mean 'rabbit butt.' "

"Rabbit butt?" Baldwin chuckled.

"Sure, him get wife. Good wife, cost lotsa money. I know father real good. After they married, him wife talk to mother, and say him all hairy like buffalo, but hair real soft. Mother say him more like rabbit then.

But wife say him's butt hairy, too. Mother laugh all day and name him Rabbit Butt. Good joke, better name."

Baldwin guffawed, a deep belly laugh that brought tears to his eyes. Every time he glanced at his red-faced interpreter, the laughter started over. Between bouts of gaiety, Falleaf sat down, holding his sides. Finally, Cottontail stalked off the porch and back to his horse.

Baldwin wiped his eyes and again shook the old man's hand.

"Thank you, Falleaf. I'll be in town if there is anything you need."

Waving, he walked back to his mount, still chuckling. He glanced at Cottontail.

"Rabbit Butt?"

Cottontail squirmed. "Listen, General, I'd be real appreciative if we'd keep this between the two of us. Most folks just plain wouldn't understand."

"I'll see what I can do," Baldwin said, climbing into the saddle.

"Thanks, General."

"That's Lieutenant, Rabbit Butt." Baldwin turned his horse and headed for town.

"Yes, sir, Lieutenant!" Cottontail called, swinging into the saddle. "Whatever you say, Lieutenant."

FOUR

Tall Elk had spent several days honing his hunting skills on the rabbit population. He'd leave each morning, scouring the countryside for game, and return that evening with his kill, which he presented to his mother.

Every day there were more tipis standing just to the west of the village, usually in groups of two or three. His father, Many Rivers, made no mention of the other camp, and Tall Elk decided to wait rather than ask. Camp gossips would soon tell him what he wanted to know.

This clear summer morning, he'd just left his village when he saw a large group in the distance. Certain he was still unseen, Tall Elk cautiously made his way toward the party, using the prairie's sparse vegetation for cover.

Were these Utes or Pawnees come to raid? Perhaps they were Lakota from the north looking for Cheyenne scalps. If they were enemy warriors, he'd have to warn the village.

He dismounted behind a large stand of mesquite trees and crept closer on foot. As he stole through the thick brush, four strong hands appeared from nowhere and grabbed his arms. Before he could utter a word, his vision was blocked by a blanket over his head.

"Let me go!" he shouted. "I am Tall Elk, a great

Cheyenne warrior. Let me go, or you'll pay with your life!"

In response, his assailants laughed and kicked his feet out from under him. Then they grabbed him under the arms and dragged him across the ground.

Tall Elk's mind raced. Who were these warriors? Would they kill him now? Maybe they'd save him for torture and a slow, agonizing death. Worse still, they might give him to the women!

He fought to pull the blanket from his head. Threats didn't work; maybe they'd listen to reason. "If you turn me loose," he said, "I'll let you live. You'll have to leave our lands, but I'll promise you safe passage."

One of the warriors laughed and kicked Tall Elk's legs again. The young Indian felt tears on his cheeks. What had he done to deserve this? He'd only been on one raid, hadn't stolen a horse or taken a scalp. Now it was over, and soon his hair would adorn another's coup stick.

Movement stopped, and he was hauled to his feet. He heard the sounds of shuffling horses but no voices.

"Behold the great warrior Tall Elk!"

Rough hands pulled the blanket from his head.

Tall Elk blinked against the light and the dirt in his eyes and found himself staring into the benign smile of Cheyenne Chief Stone Calf.

"F-Father?" he stuttered.

Stone Calf regarded the youth a moment, then nodded. "I know you. Your sister married my nephew. It is good to see you again, my son."

Anger drove out the terror as Tall Elk wiped tears from his face. "Is this how you treat all your sons? Throwing a blanket over their heads and dragging them through the dirt?"

"Only those who try to sneak up on me—and do it badly." Stone Calf laughed.

"Here is his horse," another warrior said, leading Tall Elk's pony.

"Good," the chief replied, then to Tall Elk, "Will you ride back to your village and tell them we are coming?"

Tall Elk took the offered reins and swung onto the horse's back. "I'll tell them," he said through gritted teeth.

As Tall Elk wheeled his horse, Stone Calf called after him, "And, Blanket, forget the anger. Remember the lesson."

Tall Elk galloped across the prairie followed by shouts of "Good-bye, Blanket" and "See you soon, Blanket."

Blanket, indeed, he thought bitterly. *Now everyone will call me by that name. What chance do I have with Crow Woman now?*

The next morning the camp hummed like a plucked bowstring. Tension in the air reminded Tall Elk of the heaviness before a great storm.

The men in Stone Calf's party made up the last of the Council of Forty-four. That they had come together without their bands was strange enough, but they had also kept themselves apart from Tall Elk's people.

Speculation, fed by gossip, floated from campfire to campfire as families discussed what the coming meeting would bring. Some believed the chiefs would demand a tribal-sized war party to avenge the deaths of Cheyennes at the hands of the whites. Others thought they would all flee to the lands of their northern cousins.

He'd brought the matter up to his father. Many Rivers had shrugged and said, "I don't know what is in the hearts of these men, but I do know they'll do what is best for all the People."

With that, the discussion had ended, and Tall Elk was left to himself. He wished he could sit patiently and wait for the old ones' decision, but that was not his nature. He was a warrior!

A warrior with no war. A hunter of rabbits and skunks, not buffalo. He longed to raid, yet feared death. He wanted Crow Woman for his wife, but was terrified to approach her. He felt like a piece of buffalo gristle caught between the jaws of two dogs, pulled this way, then that. Most days he just wanted to stay in his lodge, hidden beneath the buffalo robes. There, Crow Woman was his, and he was a great warrior and chief.

Tall Elk's reverie was broken by the arrival of Porcupine, his closest friend.

"Are you going?" Porcupine asked.

Tall Elk saw excitement in the other's shining black eyes, but shrugged.

"Why bother?" he replied.

Porcupine's eyes widened. "What? This is a *council* meeting. All the big chiefs are there. Stone Calf, Little Robe, even old Whirlwind. You have to go."

Tall Elk sighed. "I'll go, but we probably won't get close enough to see anything, much less hear."

As the young men strode through the camp, they saw only women and small children. Near the council lodge, Tall Elk spotted the two warriors who had captured him the previous day. One quickly pretended to hide behind his lance, peeking around the spear's shaft. The other stood with a blanket over his head.

People around the warriors laughed at their antics, as Tall Elk's ears burned with embarrassment. When he and Porcupine passed, the first pulled aside his lance and shouted, "Behold, I am the great warrior, Blanket!"

The second responded, his high falsetto muffled by

the blanket. "Please, please let me go! If you do, I'll let you live."

"They're pretty funny." Porcupine laughed. "Don't you think so?" He turned and discovered he was talking to himself. Tall Elk was already several strides away. Porcupine hurried after his friend.

"What's the matter with you?" he asked.

"Nothing," Tall Elk replied curtly. "I thought you wanted to go to this council meeting."

Not waiting for a reply, Tall Elk threaded his way through the men gathered around the meeting lodge. The sides of the huge tipi had been rolled up, both to allow air to pass through the structure and to afford a chance for those outside to hear and follow the proceedings. He found a seat next to a lodge pole, and peered under the rolled buffalo hide.

A shaft of sunlight fell through the open smoke hole and into this radiance stepped Chief Stone Calf. His face was calm, his movements slow, deliberate. He wore a single golden eagle feather in his scalp lock. His dress was a simple blanket wrapped around his waist and thrown over a bare shoulder. His hair hung loose, and seemed to glow in the light.

That Stone Calf had risen to speak told Tall Elk the opening ceremonies had already taken place. The Sweet Medicine Chief, as the council's leader, had begun the meeting by offering smoke to the four cardinal points and the gods who ruled them. He had then made his opening remarks, and offered the floor to his assistants. These four men represented the spirits of the cardinal points. After these men had spoken, it was the turn of the remaining thirty-nine chiefs.

Now Stone Calf stood quietly in the light, the center of attention. No one else would speak until he'd had his say, and none would hurry him.

"When I was riding here," he began slowly, "I had

many things go through my mind. I soon had a great talk put together filled with what I had to say." He paused, then sighed. "It is gone. My thoughts have become as butterflies carried away in the wind." He smiled. "I think my age is showing."

As the others chuckled, Stone Calf looked up at the smoke hole.

"Do you ever wonder," he asked quietly, "if the lodge poles get in the smoke's way? Can they? Even if they filled the hole, would not the smoke find a way through them, around them?"

He looked at his audience. "It is thus with the whites. They come into our land, and we ride to war, but as we fight, others come in from another trail. Like the smoke, the white man finds a way around us.

"I am of two hearts," he continued in a stronger voice. "One screams to avenge the death of my son at the hands of the buffalo hunters. The other weeps for the dead and begs for caution.

"I was at the hunters' camp. I saw the fight. We were ten times their number, yet we killed none but those caught asleep in a wagon." Stone Calf shook his head. "Think of it! These were not children. We had with us the finest warriors of the Comanche and Kiowa. Still we lost."

Stone Calf paused and allowed this bit of truth to sink in. He drew a deep breath and continued, "Some say we were cursed by the bad medicine of the Comanche shaman. Perhaps we were punished for not following *our* medicine as we should. I cannot say.

"But I know the enemy we face now is the white soldier, maybe even the buffalo soldiers. The hunters are smoke, painful to the eye, but avoidable. The Great White Chief's army is a wildfire racing across the plains. My greatest fear is that while we fight the flames and are blinded by the smoke, the fire will pass behind us and burn our villages, women, and children.

"Without them, what is there left to fight for? Who will pass on the stories of the Cheyenne? What will become of the People?"

Stone Calf sat, amid murmurs. Tall Elk scanned the faces around him. Some nodded in agreement, others scowled. The young warrior remembered his vision of the white giant crashing through the village.

Another Cheyenne rose and walked into the light. He was thinner than Stone Calf, his face masked in anger. He wore a breechclout and leggings. Silver bands circled his biceps and flashed in the sunlight. He was the war chief Medicine Water.

"I am no Stone Calf," he said in a harsh voice. "I don't know how to speak of butterflies and smoke. I am a warrior."

Medicine Water paced the floor, slipping in and out of the patch of light. He stopped in the glare.

"I, too, have thought to make the big speak, but there has been too much talk. The whites steal Little Robe's horses, but he cannot get them back." He pointed at Stone Calf. "They killed his son, yet he leads no revenge party."

Medicine Water paused.

"We took the peace road," he continued, "moved to the reservation. What has it gotten us? We cannot hunt the buffalo when the grass grows green because white hunters are already there. In the moon of the big freeze, the children cry with hunger because there is no food.

"And why? Because we have shown weakness to the Great White Chief! We crawl on our bellies to Washington and beg for food and blankets." He stared at Little Robe. "Are these the actions of warriors? Of men?" He faced Stone Calf. "Are we to allow another Sand Creek? Haven't enough of our people died?"

Medicine Water glanced around the lodge. "I say it is time to stop. Leave the white man's road and return to Cheyenne ways. We must gather our warriors and those of the Arapaho, Comanche, and Kiowa. Together we will drive the whites back into the great blue waters in the East!"

A roar erupted from those outside the lodge. As one, the males jumped to their feet with war cries. Old men, warriors, and boys brandished knives, tomahawks, or their fists.

Tall Elk glanced up and saw Porcupine standing next to him, his face fierce, eyes alight. Looking back under the lodge skin, he watched the faces of the council. Some frowned at the breach of decorum. Others were proud, even smug.

At one point, he saw a glance pass between Stone Calf and Little Robe. Eyebrows rose slightly, a gentle shrug, a terse nod. Then Stone Calf looked directly at Tall Elk as though the chief had known the young warrior was there all along. Tall Elk saw deep sadness in the chief's face, resignation in his eyes. Tall Elk then knew he was going to war.

FIVE

Baldwin stood at the bar nursing his third glass of whiskey. He wore his undress uniform—sky-blue trousers, dark blue broadcloth blouse, boots. His forage cap lay on the polished bar.

In the four days since visiting Falleaf, he'd become a regular at the saloon. He even knew the barkeep's name—Fred.

He quickly emptied the glass and signaled for a refill while fishing coins from his trousers pocket.

Fred produced an unlabeled bottle of amber liquid.

"You fixin' to leave, Lieutenant?" he asked, pouring the drink.

Baldwin shook his head and dropped money on the bar. "No, sir. Why?"

"Oh, nothing. Just you come in today in undress. Thought you might be headed home."

Baldwin raised his glass in salute and swallowed half the contents. "Actually, it's my concession to the heat."

Fred grinned. "I can imagine. I remember Vicksburg in July sixty-three."

"Which side?"

"Why, the right one, Lieutenant. Fourth Minnesota Regiment."

"You, Fred, are a blue belly! Yankee to the core. Me,

too. Nineteenth Michigan Infantry. Let me buy you a drink." Baldwin drained his glass.

"My pleasure."

Fred set another glass on the bar and filled both.

Baldwin raised his. "To the North, Fred."

"The North," the barkeep echoed.

Both drinks were emptied in one swallow.

Baldwin slapped the bar. "Another, my good man. Allow me to buy you another."

"Just one more, sir. I still have a job to do."

"Awright. Just one more."

The glasses again full, Fred raised his.

"If you don't mind, I'd like to salute all the soldiers, blue and gray. To fours years of hell and the waste of many a good man."

Baldwin nodded. "To all sojers anywhere."

The drinks finished, Fred returned to his other customers.

Baldwin regarded the bartender warmly. Now, there was a man. A good man. More: A comrade-in-arms. A brother bound by shared warfare and deprivation. A friend—his friend. He looked at the empty shot glass.

"Hey, Freddy. M'glass's empty. Lemme have another."

"You sure, Lieutenant? Maybe you ought to eat something."

Baldwin looked up.

"What?" he said thickly.

Who did this man think he was? Deny Lieutenant Frank D. Baldwin a drink? That lout! That ungrateful son of a bitch! Why, he even looked fuzzy around the edges.

Baldwin straightened and took a step back.

"You know what?" he asked. "You know what?"

Fred kept his face neutral. "What, sir?"

"Well, lemme jus' tell you . . ." Baldwin paused and

took a deep shuddering breath. He glanced around the room and noticed all eyes were on him. How long had he been standing at the bar? How many glasses of whiskey?

"Well, lemme just . . . You know what? I gonna go back to my room, that's what." He grinned at the barkeep. "But I'll be back."

Fred smiled back. "You do that, sir. After you've had some rest."

Baldwin picked up his cap and set it carefully on his head. He drew himself to attention, snapped the bartender a sharp salute, and faced about. As he approached the batwing doors, a stranger swung one side open, regarded the lieutenant briefly, then addressed Fred.

"You have got to see this. Looks like an Injun raiding party."

"Oh, shit!" Baldwin muttered.

He crossed the wooden sidewalk and leaned unsteadily on a horse hitch to watch the men walking down the street.

There were fifteen to twenty men in the party. Falleaf strode proudly at the head, followed closely by Cottontail. The others were all ages and descriptions. Most wore white men's clothing. A few wore brightly colored cotton shirts with bandannas tied around their heads. Surprisingly, many had facial hair, a distinct difference from those Indians Baldwin had known before. Their armament was as varied as their dress. He saw rifles, pistols, shotguns, hand axes, tomahawks, clubs, and many knives.

Cottontail spotted the lieutenant and walked over to the saloon accompanied by Falleaf.

"Howdy, Mr. Baldwin."

"Zachariah." Baldwin waved a hand toward the scouts. "Captain Falleaf, I see you have brought many good men. This is much better than I had hoped. As soon as I can gather my belongings from the hotel, we shall leave."

Falleaf muttered something to Cottontail, who shrugged.

"The captain wants to know how long," the interpreter asked.

"Have the men move to the station. I shall join you in fifteen minutes or less. Is that soon enough?"

Falleaf nodded and shouted orders to his men. The group went down the street ignoring the stares from the townspeople.

"Where the hell they think they're goin'?" the stranger at the saloon door asked.

"To war," Baldwin replied, irritated at the man's attitude. "They are going to risk their lives so men like you won't have to."

He stepped into the street and hurried to the hotel, sobering rapidly as he walked. Inside, he quickly settled his bill and packed his gear. Back into the street, he marched briskly to the station. He found the Delawares behind the depot, away from the main platform.

"Mr. Cottontail," he shouted.

The interpreter hurried over. "Yes, sir, Lieutenant."

"Precisely, how many men are with you?"

"Twenty, counting me."

"You sure?"

Cottontail grinned. "Counted 'em myself. Figured you might need to know."

"And did you inquire about the next—"

"Forty minutes."

Baldwin smiled and clapped Cottontail on the back. "Good job. I admire an efficient man. Now, will you ask Falleaf to join us?"

At Cottontail's signal, the Delaware chief approached.

"Captain Falleaf," Baldwin said, "before we begin this adventure, we need to establish a chain of command. That is, who's in charge."

Falleaf shrugged. "Easy. You give me order. Me give all hims order." He then said something to Cottontail in Lenape.

At Baldwin's glance, the interpreter began, "We have worked with the white soldiers many times and for many years. It is always the same. The captain receives his orders from the white soldiers, then instructs the rest of the scouts. He also says that if you think your Lenape's good enough, you can order them yourself."

Baldwin grinned ruefully. "Falleaf, I don't think the word 'Chumumte' will get me very far."

Falleaf laughed and pointed at the interpreter. "Him Cottontail."

Baldwin also laughed at the inside joke. Cottontail looked from one man to the other and shook his head.

"I just shoulda stayed home," he said.

Baldwin grabbed his arm. "Come along, Zachariah. Falleaf, have the men move to the platform. I'll meet you there with the tickets."

The lieutenant and Cottontail walked to the depot. Peering through the window was a small man, balding and myopic.

He stared at the officer, his interpreter, then the Indians gathered near the rails.

"You with them?" he asked Baldwin.

The ticket agent's voice was both high-pitched and hoarse, a combination that grated on Baldwin's nerves.

"Actually, they are with me. I need twenty-one seats on the next train to Fort Dodge, which I believe arrives within the half hour."

The agent consulted a gold railroader's watch. "Close enough, I reckon. Won't do you no good, though. Them Injuns ain't riding on my train."

"Excuse me? Those men are employees of the United States Army and, as such, are entitled to all that brings, including transportation on your railroad."

"I ain't allowin' a bunch of redskins to ride in the same car as decent white folk."

Baldwin glared through the window, the agent's thick lenses, and into his watery blue eyes.

"Then I suggest you find the decent white folk other accommodations."

The agent's face reddened, and a vein began to visibly throb in his forehead. "Like hell I will! I ain't about to pull people off a train so red niggers can ride and stink up the car!"

Baldwin leaned as close to the man as the window would allow. "I will have those seats, even if I have to confiscate them," he said quietly.

"You, sir, are drunk!" the agent replied with a wrinkled nose.

"And you, sir, are an asshole. I, however, shall be sober by morning." He stepped back and bellowed. "Mr. Cottontail!"

The interpreter jumped. "Yes, sir."

"Do the Lenape participate in the time-honored practice of taking scalps?"

"Yes, sir, Lieutenant. That is, when we ain't raping white women."

"Very well, I want you to enter this building, kill this bat-blind son of a bitch, and bring me his hair." Baldwin handed a piece of paper to Cottontail. "Afterward, you will count out twenty-one tickets and leave this voucher in their place."

The agent's eyes went from narrow to wide to bulging. He rushed to the depot's door and threw the bolt. Cottontail ran to the side and pounded on the door with the butt of his pistol.

"Let me in, little man," the interpreter called. "Me wantum scalp for squaw. Me needum glasses, too."

"Goddam you, soldier boy!" the agent shrieked. He grabbed a handful of tickets and tossed them out the window. "Take them and begone. But this isn't over, by God! Just wait until I tell the sheriff what you done. He'll have your balls—all of ya!"

Baldwin retrieved the tickets, counted what he needed, and passed the rest, along with the pay voucher, back through the window. The agent regarded the materials as though they were poisonous.

"Why, thank you, sir," the lieutenant said softly. "We do intend to have a pleasant journey. By the way, should we run into, shall we say, undo difficulty during our journey, my friends will have to return here and discuss the issue with you at some length." Louder, he said, "Come, Zachariah, we have a train to catch."

"What? You promised me a scalp! Here I got my Injun blood all riled up—"

"You have no Indian blood. You're as white as fresh-fallen snow."

"Now, I am wounded, cut to the quick. Broken promises, that's what it is. You whites can never keep a promise."

Baldwin rubbed throbbing temples. "Would you settle for a bottle of whiskey and a Cuban cigar?"

Cottontail drew a deep breath. "Well, I wouldn't want it said that I wasn't a reasonable man. I believe that would help to heal my Lenape pride and bruised confidence." He grinned. "That's what I like about you, Lieutenant. You know how to inspire loyalty among your men, whatever the cost."

"My God," Baldwin muttered as he walked across the platform. "Is *this* going to be a long war!"

SIX

Travel bag in hand, Baldwin stepped from the train amid the general confusion of disembarking passengers. He noted with satisfaction the large military presence and knew each day brought more soldiers into Dodge City.

Looking over his shoulder, he watched the Indian warriors step from the train into a widening pool of silence. Baldwin tried to imagine what people thought of these men, armed to the teeth and dressed in every manner from farmer to half-naked savage.

Baldwin signaled for Cottontail to follow him to the three empty wagons across the street. A small knot of soldiers stood nearby, a sergeant among them.

"Sergeant," Baldwin called.

The noncommissioned officer broke from the group, and offered a casual salute. "Lieutenant," he said. "Z.T. Woodall, Sixth Cavalry."

Baldwin returned the salute. "I'm Frank Baldwin, Fifth Infantry, and the gentleman behind me is Cottontail, one of my Delaware scouts."

Cottontail raised his hand as though to take an oath and intoned deeply, "Howdy, paleface."

Woodall took a long look at the scout. "Yes, sir, if you say so."

Baldwin glared at Cottontail a moment, then returned his attention to Woodall. "Yes, well, Sergeant, I gather you're the answer to my telegram."

"Yes, sir, just like you ordered: three wagons and troopers to drive them."

"Very good," Baldwin said, then called over his shoulder, "Cottontail, would you be so good as to ask Captain Falleaf to bring his men here?"

"Me go get-um now, Lieutenant."

"Mighty peculiar Injun," Woodall commented, watching the scout walk away.

Baldwin sighed. "He's no more Indian than you or I. You have a mount for me, Sergeant?"

"Yes, sir, tied to the last wagon."

"In that case, I shall ride to Fort Dodge and report to General Miles." He smiled at the sergeant. "The Delaware I will leave in your care. Their leader is an old chief named Falleaf. Listen to him; ignore Cottontail."

"Yes, sir." Woodall threw a salute. "I'll take good care of 'em."

Baldwin returned the gesture.

"Oh, and, Sergeant Woodall, have your men watch what they say. I imagine most of the scouts speak English quite well."

"Noted, sir. Do not upset the Indians."

Fort Dodge was strung along the Arkansas River, a large corral with long, low buildings beyond. As Baldwin approached the corral, two rifle-carrying privates stepped forward. One raised his hand and Baldwin stopped.

"Good morning, Lieutenant," the guard said.

"Good morning, Private. I'm here to see General

Miles. I've been told he has established his headquarters here."

"Yes, sir. Ride to the flagpole, then turn right. The commanding officer's house is just on the other side of the parade ground. It's the only two-story building."

"Thank you, Private," Baldwin replied.

The guard came to attention and saluted.

The enclosure to Baldwin's right was actually three corrals joined together. The overall length of the structure looked to be about three hundred feet. A series of small buildings sat directly across from the corrals. He guessed the civilians lounging near them were teamsters hired to drive the supply wagons. The low buildings had the look of enlisted men's barracks, a suspicion confirmed when he saw several women carrying baskets of clothing toward the river. These were the post laundresses who were paid to wash the men's clothing. Some also offered other services. Baldwin didn't have to be told of what took place between the soldiers and laundresses. He'd served on enough frontier posts to know the arrangement.

The parade ground was a large open area surrounded by the fort's buildings. Normally empty except when the troops drilled, it now was covered in the white two-man shelters of the newly arrived soldiers. Unit flags and guidons separated the infantry from the cavalry and identified the company camps.

At the end of the parade ground stood a group of houses with a two-story structure in the middle—Miles's new headquarters. The rest would belong to the post staff officers.

Baldwin walked his horse between the barracks and parade ground, returning the salutes of several infantrymen. When cavalry troopers spotted the blue stripe on his uniform trousers, they ignored him. The disrespect disturbed him, but he did nothing. This was neither the time nor the place to pick a fight with horse soldiers.

As he approached the house, a private walked forward to take Baldwin's horse. As Baldwin opened the front gate, Jack bounded down the porch steps, his coat flashing coppery in the sunlight.

"Hello, Jack." Baldwin bent to scratch behind the dog's ears before entering the house.

"Why, hello, Frank," George Baird said warmly, rising from a small desk to shake Baldwin's hand. "How was your trip?"

"Fine, George. You settled in?"

Baird nodded. "More or less. The general came, kicked out Dodge and his sergeant major, and moved us in. I've been billeted in worse."

Baldwin nodded. Like Baird, he had been in the military long enough to have served at forts with tents for offices and dugouts for homes. Dirt floors were nothing new to the two officers. Comparatively speaking, Fort Dodge was a paradise with wooden buildings, sidewalks, and glass windows. Though not as lavish as regimental headquarters at Fort Leavenworth, the accommodations were nonetheless clean and functional.

"General in?" he asked.

"Yep. And he's chompin' at the bit. Said to send you right in."

Baird rapped sharply on a closed door, then opened it to announce Baldwin.

Miles sat at the post commandant's desk reading dispatches and smoking a cigar. As Baldwin came in the room, he waved to a chair.

The general's eyes shone with excitement. He worried his cigar, alternately smoking and chewing on it. He slammed his hand onto the desktop.

"Goddammit!" he shouted with a piratical grin. "Do you know what we've done, Lieutenant?" he asked, then continued before an answer could be given. "We've beat them, that's what!"

"Yes, sir."

Miles gaped at Baldwin. "Did you hear me? We've beat them, beat them all! Don't you see?"

Baldwin squirmed. "Uh, beat who, General? The Indians?"

"Hell, no!" Miles gestured with his cigar. "Think about this: Mackenzie hasn't left Concho, Buell and Price have barely moved, and Davidson's stuck at Sill with Indian agent woes. On the other hand, we have scouts, cavalry, infantry, and an artillery unit all but ready to go."

Baldwin saw what he meant. Of the five columns designated by the War Department, Miles's expeditionary force was the only one moving forward rapidly. At the rate troops were arriving, the column could expect to move out by the middle of August.

"We've beat them, sir."

"Damn right, Lieutenant! Now tell me about the Delawares."

Baldwin described his trip to Coffeyville and his meeting with Falleaf. Miles listened attentively, then rummaged through the papers on his desk.

"Ah," he said, picking up a telegram. "What about the Coffeyville train station? It says here you threatened to have one of your scouts scalp the stationmaster."

Baldwin suppressed a smile. "Actually, sir, the stationmaster wasn't going to allow us to ride on the train. I merely used whatever means necessary to persuade him otherwise. Failing that would have delayed my arrival here and moved back the beginning of our campaign."

"Uh-hunh." Miles chewed his cigar. "The Coffeyville mayor wants your butt in a sling." He rolled the smoke from one side of his mouth to the other. "Not allow you to ride, eh? Delayed the campaign . . . Well, Lieutenant, you know what I say?" He dropped the message on the desk. "Screw 'em! The whole damn town! No one, and I mean no one short of God or the President, is going to slow us down. Got that?"

"Yes, sir!"

"Good. As I see it, the Delawares are quite self-sufficient. We'll see to it they get outfitted. I would think those that wanted saddles probably brought their own, but they can have army issue if they so desire.

"Now I need you to find me some white scouts, preferably men intimately familiar with the Llano Estacado. I talked to a few men myself, including a couple who fought at Adobe Walls. One of them was that fellow with the long shot. I think his name was Dixon."

"Yes, sir. Anything else?"

"No, go on and find your quarters. Baird has all the assignments, and he'll get you fixed up." Miles stood. "You did good, Baldwin. I appreciate the effort."

Baldwin rose to attention and saluted. "Thank you, sir."

Miles returned the salute with a wave of his cigar, and Baldwin turned to leave.

"By the way, Lieutenant, there is a man I want you to take on. His name is Marshall, and he's a newspaperman for the Kansas *Daily Commonwealth*. He's offered his services as both scout and as chronicler of this expedition. We could use some good publicity, and the *Commonwealth* has proven to be our friend, so sign him up."

Baldwin did not like the idea of taking on a scout whose primary duty was to paint a vivid picture of Miles in command, but this was not a request.

"Yes, sir," he said quietly. "If that's what you wish."

Miles grinned. "Cheer up, Baldwin! Play your cards

right, and it'll be your name you see in the newspaper stories."

Moving was nothing new. Each change of the seasons brought movement. Sometimes it was to follow the buffalo, other times to meet for the Arrow Renewal ceremony. Enemy attacks, bad weather, even an ominous omen meant packing up and going somewhere.

Tall Elk and Porcupine sat on their ponies atop a small bluff, watching the campsite disappear as one tipi after another fell.

"There goes your lodge," Tall Elk said.

Porcupine nodded. "It won't be long now." He looked at his friend. "Are you excited?"

Tall Elk had to think before answering. All his life he'd been taught and prepared for war. His destiny was to face his enemies, to protect his people.

Yet beneath it all was the vision of the riderless horse, the fallen warrior.

"I suppose," he said slowly. "And maybe a little scared."

Porcupine snorted. "Scared? Scared?" He raised his hands high. "We are Cheyenne, the People. We are the greatest of warriors!" He gazed at Tall Elk through narrowed eyes, but spoke evenly. "Fright is for babies and white men."

Porcupine kicked his pony and took off at a gallop. He reined in sharply, then wheeled the horse in two tight right-hand turns, finally charging back at Tall Elk.

"Who are the best horsemen on the plains?" he shouted as he rode past.

"The Cheyenne," Tall Elk replied.

The horse slid to a stop, and Porcupine cupped his hand around his ear. "Who? Did you say the Kiowa?"

Tall Elk grinned. "The Cheyenne!" he said, more loudly.

"That's right," Porcupine said, walking the horse back. "We can outride and outfight any enemy. We can go a whole moon without food and water. We will catch the soldier's bullets in our teeth and spit them back into his face as we take his scalp! We are Cheyenne!"

"We *are* Cheyenne!" Tall Elk shouted.

"I am Porcupine!" he announced to the camp below. "I will shoot my quills into my enemy and laugh as he dies." He pointed to Tall Elk. "And he is Tall Elk, who will . . . who will . . ."

"Bugle?" Tall Elk offered weakly.

"Bugle? Yes, bugle. Tall Elk will bugle so loudly as to split the eardrums of the soldiers, and they won't hear the war party attack!"

Porcupine kicked his horse and started down the bluff.

"Follow me, Tall Elk. The enemy is below!"

Sounding war cries, the pair charged down the bluff and through the village. A dog ran out in front of them, and they chased the animal until it veered off. They weaved as close as possible around the lodges, at times touching the skins with their knees. Rounding one tipi, Tall Elk, who had taken the lead, saw a drying rack covered with meat too late to avoid crashing through it. Half-cured jerky scattered in the air to fall and be gobbled up by the camp dogs.

They charged through dying fires, showering people with ash and embers. They knocked over water buckets, frightened children and old women, drawing curses from mothers and toothless threats from the old men. They finally exited the camp, leaving behind chaos, crying babies, and an array of vexed villagers.

The two young warriors galloped around a hillock. Tall Elk almost lay on his horse's neck. He'd never felt more alive. Heart pounding, blood racing through his veins, he was giddy with adrenalin. Was this what it was like to charge the enemy, face masked in war paint? He imagined himself wearing one of the great war bonnets, its feathers trailing behind him. He saw his horse painted with medicine and war honors. His shield, covered in buffalo rawhide, edged in the scalps of his enemies, would be painted with his personal medicine.

They rode across the plain, through belly-deep grass that swayed in the wind. Their path flushed quail, dove, rabbits, and their predators. A startled hawk squawked indignantly and hastily pumped upward to avoid the charging horsemen. The boys rode hard, pushing their animals, until finally, his horse flecked with foam, Porcupine drew to a stop.

Tall Elk followed suit, feeling almost as winded as his horse. He reached down and patted the animal's neck with affection.

Porcupine chuckled.

"Did you see that?" he said. "Did you see their faces? They were falling down trying to get out of our way!"

Tall Elk nodded, then grinned sheepishly. "They sure were scared. The women will probably throw buffalo shit at us when we go back."

"They wouldn't dare." Porcupine snorted, then kicked his horse into a slow walk. "We're warriors, men who demand respect."

Tall Elk followed without comment, allowing his mount to cool. Glancing across the prairie, he saw a glint of sunlight at the base of a bluff.

"Porcupine," he said. "Look at that bluff. Do you see anything?"

"No, just rocks and brush. Why?"

"I thought I saw something shiny, like sun on metal."

Suddenly alert, Porcupine reined in and stared intently across the land. "Was it on the ground or on top? Did you see anything move?"

The questions came quickly, leaving no time for response. Porcupine's change in demeanor made Tall Elk nervous.

"I saw it near the base, maybe by that stand of cottonwood."

A line of trees meant water. Tall Elk knew a stream ran near there. The flash of light could have been anything—or anyone.

"Do you think—"

"I don't know," Porcupine interrupted. "It could be one of us. But when the soldiers watch us, they sometimes use a long metal tube that lets them see a great distance."

"Can they see us now?"

Porcupine shrugged. "Let's ride back toward the village. Then we'll circle behind the bluff and see who's there."

Easing the horses into a lope, the boys crossed the flat land until they came to an arroyo. They rode into the gully, then changed direction back toward the bluff.

"What if it's a white man stopping for a drink?"

"Then we'll kill him, Tall Elk. We'll kill him if he's an enemy of any sort."

"What if there's more than one?"

Porcupine grinned. "Then you can fight them while I run for help."

Riding out of the arroyo, the boys found themselves near the bluff. They tethered their horses and set off on foot. Tall Elk unsheathed his knife; Porcupine carried a war ax.

Tall Elk's heart pounded, but not with the same feeling as when he was riding. His nostrils flared, and his breath came in short gasps. His knees almost buckled when his friend suddenly grabbed his arm.

"Voices," Porcupine whispered.

Tall Elk listened intently, then heard faint sounds of talking. The voices drifted away and returned with the breeze. He nodded, then crept forward alone. Near the end of the bluff, he dropped on all fours and crawled through the waist-deep grass. Finally, he dared to rise high enough to take a quick glance.

The first thing he saw were long black braids and a golden eagle feather hanging in a scalp lock. He ducked back down and scurried back to Porcupine.

"I saw an Indian," he whispered hoarsely.

"What?" Porcupine's voice sounded like a gunshot.

"Shh! I didn't see enough to know who he was. He might have been a Navaho or Blackfoot."

"Was there more than one?" Porcupine whispered back.

Tall Elk shrugged.

Porcupine made a disgusted face and crawled back to the spot Tall Elk had vacated. He raised his head cautiously, then stood and waved.

"Come on out, Tall Elk," he called. "They're Cheyenne."

Tall Elk's body went limp with relief. He realized he hadn't breathed since Porcupine left him. He hurried to his friend's side, and the two of them approached the group of warriors.

As they drew near, curious stares came their way, but no comments were made. Tall Elk saw most of the attention was directed to a small group of men under one of the cottonwoods. He looked closely and recognized Kiowa among his own people. He and Porcupine moved closer until they could hear clearly.

Beneath the tree, a circle of men sat on blankets. He saw Stone Calf, Medicine Water, and several of the Council of Forty-four. He didn't know their guests, but one had a great hawklike nose and a bitter face. Another was older, with white in his hair. Still a third was huge. He could easily have made two of Tall Elk. He'd heard of this Kiowa. He was Bear Mountain—lieutenant to Lone Wolf, war chief for all the Kiowa.

Stone Calf lifted a pipe and smoked slowly. He passed it to Medicine Water, taking care that the bowl did not touch the ground. Medicine Water smoked and passed the instrument on. No one spoke during this ceremony. The smoking of the pipe was sacred, and all who partook swore to tell the truth.

As the pipe was finally passed back to Stone Calf, he gently cradled it in the crook of his arm. He took a deep breath.

"It is good to see our friends the Kiowa again."

Bitter Face nodded. "We, too, are pleased to see our Cheyenne brothers. It has been too many moons since we hunted together."

Stone Calf grunted. "If the whites have their way, we'll hunt no more. At least not the old way."

"What you say is true. That is why we choose to ride here. Have you heard what the soldiers are doing?"

Stone Calf shook his head.

"They are counting us." Bitter Face said. "Counting us like the cattle they slaughter. I tell you now the truth, for I have heard the words from Striking Eagle. First they let us in the fort; then they say we cannot come in. Then they say we must live by the stinking waters and wait to be counted. Never! That is what I say. Never will they count me for the slaughter."

A low buzz ran through the spectators. Could this be possible? Were they to be counted, penned, and killed like so many cattle?

Stone Calf sighed. "It is as I feared, but we have decided to stay out here where we belong. Soon the rain will come again, then the snow. We will have to hunt many buffalo."

Bitter Face's laughter chilled Tall Elk.

"Come with us, then. The white man is handing out food at the reservation. He has said if we come in and let him count us, we can get food, blankets, bullets for the guns. Striking Eagle says we will be given a piece of paper that says we are the white man's friend."

"But you have to be counted?"

"Yes," Bitter Face said. "But I will not enter the fort nor give up my weapons. They can count me and give me the paper, but then I will take my goods and my people and come back here."

"Are you not afraid the soldiers will try to stop you?"

Again the mirthless laugh.

"What soldiers? The man at the agency does not believe in fighting. He is weak and will give me what I want. Then I will let him count me. This you can do, too. Ride with me and my warriors. Together we'll take what we want—live free again!"

"It is a good idea, but I have many mouths to feed. All the Cheyenne are to be free, so I must gather food for everyone. I think it is good for us to go to the reservation. Let them count us and give us the peace paper. Then we will take our food and come back to the Palo Duro."

Stone Calf said, "But I do not trust the soldiers, so I say we stay on the plains and move north toward where the buffalo hunters lived. Then we go east to the reservation. If the White Chief's soldiers seek us, they will come from the north and pass us to the south."

Murmurs of approval sounded from the crowd, and Tall Elk nodded. It was only right the white man should give them food and blankets in return for the buffalo they stole.

Bitter Face rose. "We will ride through the canyon, then north to the reservation. If all goes well, we will see your people at the agency."

The Kiowa mounted their horses and rode away without a wave or backward look. Tall Elk turned and saw Stone Calf regarding him.

"Hello again, Father," he said, crossing to the chief.

"Blanket, it is good to see you."

"Will we ride soon?"

"Perhaps. The council still has to vote on my plan, but I don't think they'll disapprove." He clapped Tall Elk on the back. "When we leave, I'll need some brave warriors to ride ahead and look for enemies. I hope you are in the party."

Tall Elk was elated. He'd feared he might be forced to ride with the old ones and babies.

"Of course I will," he said. "And Porcupine, too?"

Stone Calf smiled. "By all means, bring your friend. We need all the sharp young eyes we can get." The smile faded. "But listen, Blanket, this is going to be a long war, and we have many enemies. Do not do anything foolish. Listen to the older men and follow their lead."

Sobered, Tall Elk nodded. "I will, Father."

"That is good. I do not want to be the last of the Cheyenne."

SEVEN

Baldwin found it difficult to breathe in the small, hot room. The air was blue with smoke from cigars and pipes and a few cigarettes. The atmosphere was also scorched by words. Officers packed together cheek to jowl swore at the Indians, the army, the heat, and the lack of rain.

The higher ranks sat closer to the front. Lieutenants found themselves against the back wall.

Hard wooden chairs provided little comfort; the open windows, curtains limp in the swelter, offered none.

A cramped and decidedly uncomfortable Baldwin squirmed as sweat trickled down his sides beneath his woolen dress coat. He was convinced the windows actually invited more heat into the room.

While he waited, he observed his surroundings and companions. Two staff-grade officers occupied the prized chairs near the door. These majors would be the first to realize any advantage from a breeze.

Field-grade officers in the first and second rows were a mix of cavalry and infantry commanders. The lowly lieutenants were intermingled as to service and grade, as though a first lieutenant were indistinguishable from his junior counterpart.

A large map of Kansas, Indian Territory, and most of the state of Texas dominated the front wall.

George Baird stepped into the room, calling the men to attention. Miles strode through the open doorway, accompanied by the scrape and screech of sliding wooden chairs. He motioned the men to sit, and positioned himself directly in front of the wall-sized map.

Miles looked clean and freshly shaven, his uniform immaculate. His mustache was trimmed to perfection, not a hair out of place. His appearance and demeanor gave the illusion of a man walking on a brisk autumn day.

My God, thought an awed Baldwin. *Is the man incapable of sweat?*

"Gentlemen," Miles said crisply, "the time for action is at hand. We have the distinction of being the first into the field, and as such, we have a golden opportunity to conclude this campaign in a successful and most satisfying way."

He turned to the map and placed his hand on the Texas plains.

"It has always been my contention that the Indians will be met and defeated here, the Llano Estacado. Our enemy is as familiar with these grasslands as any man is with his own house. He has vast areas for concealment and for observing our movements. Arroyos and canyons dot the land. He has gulches, gullies, bluffs, breaks, and any manner of tree and valley to hide in and behind." Miles paused a moment, then continued. "He knows we're coming.

"What do we have? We have Lieutenant Baldwin and his scouts. His Delaware are among the finest trackers in the country. More importantly, they've worked with us before and understand the mission. His white scouts are veteran hunters and trappers, men who have lived in this land and know it as well as the Indians. These men will ride light and fast, locating the camps and leading the main force to them."

Baldwin shifted in his seat, acutely aware of the responsibility just placed on him. If the Indians were not found, the blame would rest squarely on his shoulders.

"Our goal," Miles said, "is to drive the Indians onto the reservation. This campaign is not about retribution or eradication."

He lowered his hand and gazed levelly at his men.

"Make no mistake in this. We will chase the Indian to hell and back if necessary to make him surrender, but when he does, he is to be treated as a prisoner of war. I'll not suffer a Chivington in my ranks, nor will I allow such actions to stain my record."

Miles looked from man to man as he paused to let his words sink in. Several men wore scowls indicating what they thought of the announcement, but no one spoke. Miles's reputation as an iron-fisted leader was well known. He would as soon horsewhip a major as a private.

Satisfied his point had been made, Miles relaxed.

"Cheer up. We're the only column prepared to advance. Buell and Price have hardly moved. Mackenzie's still trying to gather his troops, and Davidson's too busy counting Indians to start. If we're lucky, we can wrap up this campaign before the others are mobilized. Think of what such a victory can do for your careers. I may be standing in front of a room full of generals.

"Lieutenant Baird has your assignments, and I'll yield the floor to him. Lieutenant."

Baird cleared his throat and began listing the assignments, referring to his notes.

"The command is to be broken up into five separate units and three columns as noted: First Battalion is composed of Sixth Cavalry Companies D, F, G, and L under the command of Major Compton, Sixth Cavalry.

The Second Battalion, under Major Biddle, also Sixth, consists of Troops A, H, I, and M. A third battalion will consist of four companies of Fifth Infantry under Captain Bristol of the same. The artillery detachment with its ten-pound Parrot and two Gatlings will be commanded by Lieutenant Pope, Fifth Infantry. The final unit is Lieutenant Baldwin and his scouts.

"On or about August eleventh, the Second Battalion and scouts will depart Fort Dodge and head south toward the Cimarron River. Upon arrival, they will separate, with Second Battalion moving to Camp Supply. Lieutenant Baldwin's people are then to perform an extensive scout, ranging south to Adobe Walls and thence east to Antelope Hills, finally rejoining the command at Camp Supply. A few days after the initial units' departure, the remaining units and the supply train will march directly to Camp Supply."

"And that, gentlemen," Miles said from across the room, "is all there is, to this point." He walked back to the map and pointed with his cigar. "Depending on what Baldwin finds, we can move in any of the cardinal directions. We have free rein and no boundaries to worry about. Wherever our friends are hiding, we will find them and root them out."

Miles clamped the cigar between his teeth and walked out of the room. Baird called the men to attention again as the general left. The other officers filed out the door and to their units to prepare for the march.

Outside, Baird caught Baldwin's arm.

"Listen, Frank, tomorrow's the old man's birthday. Headquarters staff is standing drinks for him in town. You're welcome to join us, if you'd like."

"Why, why certainly!" a startled Baldwin stammered. "I'd be honored."

Baird smiled. "Good. He'd like that, you know. You've found a warm spot in the general's heart."

Baldwin hurried away, head spinning. Being invited to Miles's birthday celebration was one thing, but for the adjutant to tell him he was favored was something else. He felt as though he could walk on clouds. The oppressive heat of the day drained away, replaced with thoughts of promotion and glory alongside General Nelson A. Miles.

Nothing, he thought furiously. *Nothing must ruin the opportunity. Count the drinks, three or four at most. Then switch to beer. Better yet, just go home.*

Freshly shaven and full of breakfast, Baldwin rode out of Fort Dodge, south toward the Arkansas River, thinking about the men he'd met just a few days ago.

He'd called them together just outside the enlisted men's quarters. The scouts had separated into two groups—one Indian, one white. Each group regarded the other closely, some with curiosity, others with open hostility.

The oddest sight was Falleaf and Cottontail. The old chief wore a clean white shirt, its sleeves rolled up against the heat. He had on black twill pants, brogans, and a derby hat. Baldwin thought he looked more like a banker than a warrior chieftain. Cottontail wore his fringed buckskin suit and moccasins. His face was buried under enough war paint to make him unrecognizable, and he had an assortment of feathers tied in his hair.

"Is that you, Zachariah?" Baldwin asked.

Cottontail's reply was a curt nod.

Baldwin turned to Falleaf. "Is he always like this?"

Falleaf shook his head. "Chumumte has been on vision quest seeking medicine for fight. Him say this is what him saw." He looked Cottontail over from head to foot, then faced the officer again. "Sometimes I think him don't see so good."

Baldwin laughed and turned his attention to the white scouts.

"Gentlemen, my name is Lieutenant Frank Baldwin, and I am in command of this detachment. The distinguished man in the derby is Captain Falleaf. He's war chief for the Delaware and in command of the Indian part of our group. Under all that paint is our interpreter, Zachariah Cottontail. He's white, believe it or not. Many of these men speak English. I'd keep that in mind.

"If any of you cannot work closely with the Delaware, leave now. I will not brook a lack of discipline. I don't expect you to act like soldiers, but you're riding army horses, eating army chow, and drawing army pay. Until you no longer do any of these, you will take orders from me, my superiors, and anyone I tell you to take orders from.

"Any questions?"

Baldwin waited and let the silence grow. A few of the faces he saw hardened while he was speaking, but no one left the group.

"Good," he continued, grinning. "Now that we got the official horseshit out of the way, let's get to know each other. Like I said, my name's Baldwin. I've been in the army since the war, when I fought with the Michigan Nineteenth. Since then, I've been assigned to the Fifth Infantry."

"Infantry?" a voice from the scout side said. "You're a goddamn foot soldier? What're you doing with the cavalry?"

"What's your name?"

A man of average height and looks stepped from the group.

"Plummer. Joe Plummer."

"Well, Mr. Plummer, I go where the army says. I asked for the cavalry, but they had other plans. Now they've instructed me to lead the scouts on this campaign. What do you do?"

Plummer's face drew into a deep frown.

"Nothing," he said dourly. "Not anymore. Not since them red niggers killed my partners. Before then, we was huntin' buffalo."

"I see," Baldwin replied. He pointed to a tall thin man. "Who are you?"

"My name's Charles Jones," the scout replied in a reedy voice, "and I've been working as a teamster for Mr. Myers. Folks call me C. E."

"Bullshit!" a new voice rang out. "You been Dirty Face Ed as long I knowed ya."

"Why do you call him Dirty Face Ed?"

" 'Cause he never washes it. Leastways, not while driving a team."

Jones had a pained look on his face.

"There wasn't much reason to," he said. "Man'd just get dirty all over again."

"Yeah? What was your excuse in town?"

The speaker strode forward. He was of medium height, but powerfully built, and sported a handlebar mustache that covered his upper lip.

"I'm Thompson McFadden. I've scouted for Carr, Crook, and Little Phil Sheridan. I can lead a man to hell and back, if I've a mind."

"That may be necessary during this campaign. Thank you, Mr. McFadden."

The next man Baldwin pointed to was smaller than any of the others save one. His build was solid, though not bulky like McFadden's. He had dark skin, black eyes, and long brown hair.

"What's your name?"

"Billy Dixon," came the reply.

Like the man, the voice was solid. Baldwin's eyes widened.

"I've heard you mentioned," he said. "Buffalo hunter, right? You were one of those at Adobe Walls."

"Me and Bat both," Dixon answered, pointing a thumb at the man who stood at his side.

"As I recall, they said you killed a man a mile away."

Dixon shrugged and put his hands in his pockets. "Lots been said about that shot."

"Did you mean to shoot him?"

"Well, I meant to shoot *at* him."

"Why?"

"I dunno. Guess he riled me."

Baldwin laughed. "Remind me to keep on your good side." He looked at Dixon's companion. "And you, sir. You were at the trading post as well?"

"Yes, sir."

The latest speaker looked very young. Though probably not much older, Dixon and the others had a hard edge to them that this man didn't possess. He was tall with fair hair and clear, blue eyes.

"And your name is Bat?" Baldwin asked.

"Yes, sir. Bat Masterson. I've hunted, worked as a teamster, and was employed at the Myers and Leonard store during the attack."

Baldwin nodded absently. Masterson's speech and deportment showed he was well educated and brought up in a decent family. Why would he want to scout for the army? Perhaps like many young men, he looked for adventure on the frontier.

"Thank you," Baldwin said, then gestured at the smallest man in the outfit. "And who are you?"

"*Mein* name ist Wilhelm Schmalsle."

Unlike his name, Schmalsle was a short man with a thin body, pinched face, and small mustache.

"And what did you do?"

"Hunt ze buffalo," he replied, then drew himself up straight. "Wiss ze Big Fifty."

Baldwin was impressed. The famous Sharps .50-caliber rifle had a recoil known to knock down men much bigger than this scout.

"I'm amazed, Mr. Schmalsle."

The remaining scouts came forward to introduce themselves and state their qualifications. They ranged from grizzled veterans like A. J. Martin and John Kirly to the newspaperman, J. T. Marshall. All together, Baldwin was in charge of thirty-seven men.

Now, he saw the men had once again segregated themselves, but more along the lines of preference. Some men had erected shelters varying from brush arbors to old army tents, and the rest slept on bedrolls. Most of the scouts had found shade in one form or another, preparing for the hot afternoon sun. A few sat around a campfire, sipping coffee or cleaning weapons.

Baldwin stopped and dismounted, acknowledging greetings from his detachment. As he walked to the fire, he waved his men in. He pulled his watch from its pocket. It read 9:45.

"I guess you've heard General Miles intends on testing your marksmanship skills," he said, tucking the watch away. "The one thing I'm not worried about is your ability to shoot. However, he is my commander . . ."

"Can you tell me when we're leavin'?"

Baldwin glanced at the speaker.

"Plummer, right? We pull out at first light day after tomorrow. The troopers camped over to the west are members of Major Compton's battalion. We'll ride with them, then strike out on our own."

"Pardon, Lieutenant," McFadden said. "Are we all going?"

"No, sir, you're not. About a dozen of you and the Delaware will ride with me. The remaining scouts will be part of the general's force.

"When we all get to Antelope Hills, though, we will work as a single unit running patrols wherever needed. Does that answer your question, Mr. McFadden."

McFadden nodded and spat tobacco juice into the dirt. "Yes, sir, I believe it do."

The men turned at the sound of horses. Miles was leading a small group of men—all officers, Baldwin noted, except for the regimental sergeant major.

"Here he comes, boys. Do me proud."

Baldwin stood at attention and saluted as Miles and the others drew near. The general reined to a halt and returned the salute. Unlike earlier, Miles seemed to be all business.

"For those of you who don't know me," he began, "I am General Nelson A. Miles, regimental commander of the Fifth Infantry. I only expect two things from the men under my command: competence and discipline. The competence to do their job well, and the discipline to follow my orders."

He dismounted. The members of his party quickly followed suit.

"Now, I've heard many stories about the legendary shooting ability of the buffalo hunters," Miles said. "Frankly, I have my doubts. On the other hand, I know that skilled shooting, particularly on the level I've heard, requires both the traits I look for in a good soldier. I have never been one to make snap judgments, so I will allow you gentlemen to demonstrate your abilities. Who will go first?"

McFadden stepped forward. "Well, General, I ain't

no sharpshooter, but I reckon I can hit most of what I aim at. Pick your target."

Miles turned toward the river. "Across the river, about one hundred yards out, is a cottonwood tree. That's your target."

"The whole tree?"

Miles nodded.

McFadden pulled his rifle to his shoulder, and fired. Bark flew from one side.

"There is a limb coming from the west side of that tree, near the bottom."

The scout nodded and reloaded. He shouldered his weapon, then lowered it again and spit into the dirt.

"Fresh chaw," he said. "Lotsa spit."

Again he raised the rifle, aimed, and fired. About three feet of branch fell.

"Try one of the smaller branches."

Again the rifle boomed, but nothing moved on the tree.

"Damn!" McFadden muttered.

Miles grinned. "Who's next?"

Dixon stepped up. "I'll give it a try."

"Gentlemen, this is the famous long shooter, Billy Dixon. Well, Mr. Dixon, do you think you can hit that limb?"

Dixon raised his Sharps and fired in what seemed one fluid motion. The twig flew from the tree before the echos of the rifle died.

As Dixon reloaded, Miles pointed downriver. "Along the line of my nose is a dead tree about a quarter of a mile out. Can you hit that?"

"Tree or branch, General?"

Miles looked sharply at the scout. He was about to rebuke the man, but the look on Dixon's face bore no insolence.

"Whichever you wish."

Dixon drew his bead. He took a long slow breath in and squeezed the trigger. A thunderclap, and one of the tree's branches spun away.

"Very good," Miles said. "Now, in the middle of the river is a snagged log."

"You mean that one about a thousand yards out with one branch stuck straight up?"

"That's the one."

Dixon whistled. "Long way," he said, as he chambered another round. "Long way, indeed."

Baldwin saw a smug look on Miles's face. *Damn him,* he thought. *He just wants the man to miss. Can't wait for it.*

Dixon looked around at the trees, checked the sun, then dropped to one knee. He propped his elbow on the other, firmly tucked the rifle's butt into his shoulder, and froze. He drew one long breath, blew it out. Then he drew another, and blew it out. A third. He held it and squeezed the trigger.

The recoil nearly knocked him over, but a half mile away the branch tumbled through the air until it splashed into the water. The scouts cheered the shot. Dixon grinned, opened the block, and loaded another round.

Once again he sighted downriver and fired. Chunks of wood flew from the partially submerged trunk. The scout loaded again and fired into the dead tree a third time, sending splinters in every direction.

He lowered the rifle and stood.

"Good enough, General?" he asked quietly.

Miles nodded, and turned to Baldwin.

The lieutenant beamed like a brand-new father.

Members of the Council of Forty-four and tribal elders led the procession of families. The chieftains rode with heads held high and backs straight. Each wore his best clothes and war bonnet, some with trains of eagle feathers almost touching the ground. Behind them were the warriors with weapons ready to repel any threat to the women and children who followed.

Lack of rain had yellowed the prairie grass and dried out the soil. The passing horse herd loosened the dirt, which was picked up by a southerly wind and carried aloft. It drifted back to settle on anyone unfortunate enough to be downwind. But even those upwind could not escape the blowing dirt, and soon all the people looked like tan ghosts of themselves.

The Cheyenne scouting party waited upwind. They had nothing to do until their leaders arrived, so they watched their families leave, hoping for a glimpse of a loved one.

The sight of so many Cheyenne covered in soil bothered Tall Elk. He imagined them as ghosts wandering the plains forever. He shook off the image and concentrated on the great brown cloud drifting to the north.

"How can we get by the soldiers with that following us?" he asked Porcupine.

"The whites will think it comes from buffalo. Besides, we will know where they are long before they can find us."

Six warriors broke from the main column and rode toward them.

"Here come the cradle boards," Porcupine muttered.

The scouting party included young men who had at least been on a horse-stealing raid. Tall Elk knew all the youths around him; most were from his own band. When he had first asked Stone Calf if he could ride with the advance party, he'd imagined himself among seasoned warriors.

The youngest members had given themselves over

completely to being warriors. They covered their faces in paint, brightly decorated their horses, and carried as many weapons as possible.

A pudgy boy name Bear Killer, whom everyone called Moonface for his round, open countenance, was dressed in leggings and a breechclout. His face, covered in layers of green, black, and red paint, looked as if he'd fallen into the paint dishes headfirst. He carried a stone ax and had three tomahawks and two knives tucked into his girdle. With each step his belly wobbled, and he had to hitch up the girdle to keep his clothes on.

When he spied the warriors, he hurried to the front of the pack.

Talk Elk looked away to keep from laughing aloud at Moonface.

The older warriors stopped close to the party, and one rode forward. Tall Elk recognized him as a Dog Soldier named Red Wolf. The warrior wore nothing other than his breechclout and moccasins. Two white stripes had been painted under each eye.

"You young men, listen," he shouted in a strained voice. "This is *not* a war party. Most of you have never looked the enemy in the eye. Your time to fight will come, but first we must get our women and children to safety.

"Do not go anywhere without one of the Dog Soldiers with you, and never go off alone. We are not only fighting the whites—our old enemies are still around.

"I want you to separate into six groups. One group will go with each warrior. He will be your leader. Stay with him; listen closely to what he tells you."

Red Wolf wheeled his mount and ordered his men to disperse.

As Tall Elk turned to get his horse, he caught the angry look on Porcupine's face.

"See?" Porcupine said bitterly. "We are bound hand and foot like babies!"

He spun on his heel and almost collided with Moonface. The younger boy quickly stepped back, eyes wide and belly aquiver.

"Outta my way, Moon Butt!" Porcupine growled.

EIGHT

Baldwin awoke the morning of August 11 to the sound of birds and hushed voices outside his tent. Donning his boots, he ran his fingers through sleep-scrambled hair and stepped out of the tent.

To his surprise, he seemed to be the last man up. The others had gathered in small groups, cleaning weapons and speaking quietly. Cottontail sat on a log by the fire, coffee cup in one hand, a sack of sugar at his feet.

"Good morning, Zachariah," Baldwin said as he approached the fire.

Cottontail smiled and waved at a log. " 'Light, Lieutenant. Cuppa coffee?"

Baldwin nodded absently, squinting at the morning sun. He felt for his pocket watch and decided he must have left it in the tent.

"Do you have the time?" he asked.

Cottontail glanced at the sky, then the ground. "I make it 'bout ten past nine o'clock."

"You can tell that by the sun?" Baldwin asked, mouth agape.

"Yessir. That and my shiny silver watch I checked just 'fore you woked up."

Baldwin grinned. "I should have known better. I

don't believe I'll—" He stopped, then stared at the interpreter. "Did you say *nine?* My God, man, why didn't someone wake me up? What are we doing just sitting here? Compton will have my ass for sure! No telling where's he's gotten to."

"Hold your horses, sir!" Cottontail said, motioning to Baldwin to stop. "Them pony soldiers ain't gone. Fact is, they ain't near ready."

"How do you know?"

"Well, they ain't struck their tipis, the wagons ain't loaded, and the horses are grazing near the river. Don't take a Injun to see that." He grinned up at Baldwin. "Now, how 'bout that coffee?"

Baldwin nodded and sat on the log. Cottontail filled a cup with boiling black liquid, handed it to him, then picked up a sack.

"Sugar?"

"No, thank you. I like it black."

"Not me. I like the Injun way. Lotsa sugar. Milk, too, sometimes."

"Really? You know, Zachariah, I really ought—"

"It can wait, Lieutenant," Cottontail interrupted. He picked up the pot and refilled his cup. "Way I see it, we ain't leaving 'til past noon. That camp's been quieter'n a whorehouse on Sunday morning. Hell, they didn't even do their wake-up buglin'. No, sir, we got more'n enough time to enjoy this fine army refreshment."

Baldwin sipped his coffee without comment. Not even properly in the field yet, and the cavalry was already ignoring camp protocol. There would be hell to pay if Miles ever found out. But Baldwin wouldn't tell him. His life depended on the support of the mounted soldiers, and he would give them no excuse to abandon him in a tight spot. Besides, their slipshod ways would be apparent to the general soon enough.

After coffee and a breakfast of bacon and biscuits, Baldwin retired to his tent to change. He'd decided to dress for comfort in the saddle.

He donned sky-blue kersey trousers and a dark blue cotton shirt with his rank sewn onto the shoulders. Over the shirt was his undress blouse. He pulled on his kid leather boots and finished with a wide-brimmed campaign hat. From a distance, he was indistinguishable from his cavalry counterparts.

Previous service on the plains had taught him how hot the flatlands could get, so he'd had the shirt made to mimic his undress blouse. Once on the trail he could shed the woolen garment and ride in relative comfort while still looking like a soldier.

He opted to walk to the cavalry camp, knowing he would be stuck in the saddle for the next several weeks. His path took him along the river, and he listened to the morning birdcalls. The summer's drought had killed most of the vegetation, and the usually green banks of the river were brown and yellow.

Baldwin refocused on his mission. "Mission" was probably too strong a word, but he felt he must learn why they were delayed. General Miles had expected them to be on the move at daybreak.

Major Compton had the largest tent in the battalion, erected in the middle of the camp. As Baldwin made his way there, he returned the few salutes casually offered him. He said nothing, just gritted his teeth and continued walking. Near Compton's quarters, he heard voices.

"I wish to God this campaign were already over."

"Amen to that, brother," a deeper voice answered. "I'm not looking forward to sweating my ass off for Miles's glory."

"I, for one, don't understand how we got put under the command of a slog-foot." The third voice was high and flat, almost shrill. "After all, is it not the cavalry who will be expected to chase down the heathens?"

"Now, now, gentlemen," said a smooth baritone voice. "Colonel Miles has no more choice about his command than we do about our commander."

"Major," the first voice said, "I thought Miles was a general. That's all you hear the foot soldiers call him."

"That's true, Captain McLellan, but he's only been breveted a general. Congress still has the final say, and I think it'll be Mackenzie who gets the nod."

"Do you really?"

"Miles has used his political abilities to get where he is. My God, the man's not even from the academy. Mac is not only West Point, but he's single-handedly cleaned up most of the border trash in Texas. Mark my words, Mackenzie will be the next brigadier."

"Unless Miles settles the Indian question," a new voice said quietly.

"Bite your tongue, Lieutenant Henely!" Compton snapped. "I want rank and glory as much as the next soldier, but I'll not get it riding the coattails of some goddamn infantry martinet. When the Indians are found, *we* will attack them, *we* will defeat them, and *we* will make sure Marshall reports it right!"

"Speaking of which," McLellan said, "what do you think of our scouts and their leader?"

Before Compton could reply, the high voice cut in. "What I want to know is, how did *he* get command of the scouts? Another cavalry position given to the infantry."

"Do you want command of the scouts, Tupper? Think about it. Just who are these trailers?"

"I don't know, Major. Hunters? Trappers, maybe."

"That's right, Captain. They're buffalo hunters, who started this mess by breaking the Medicine Lodge Treaty. They're trappers who trap in Indian lands, horse thieves, bummers, old men who can find no other work, and Indians. So, tell me, just who are these men?"

After a pause, Tupper offered, "Undesirables?"

Compton laughed. "Very good, Tupper! They're niggers. Red and white, and who knows what mix, niggers. Is that what you want? As for Baldwin, he's nothing more than a recruiting officer sent to the field. Again, an appropriate choice."

"I heard he'd applied to the cavalry," the second voice said.

"Well, he didn't get it, did he?"

Baldwin could hear the sneer in Tupper's voice.

"After this campaign, let him apply again," Compton said. "After all, he'll have plenty of experience in the saddle. Better yet, let him go to the Tenth. The brunettes are always looking for good officers."

Baldwin's ears burned as laughter came through the tent. The lack of respect smarted. Still, he knew his capabilities and believed in his men. He'd find the renegade Indians. He'd find them, and he and his scouts would show the pony soldiers a thing or two about Indian fighting.

Major C. E. Compton raised his right hand and bellowed, "First Battalion!"

The echoing roll call followed like ripples in a pond.

"D Company!"

"F Company!"

"G Company!"

"L Company!"

Baldwin took a deep breath as his turn came and shouted, "Scouts!"

Behind him Lieutenant Henely yelled, "Company H Detachment!"

Almost overlapping Henely's call, Compton barked the next order.

"Prepare to mount!"

On the word "mount" the other commanders again repeated the order. Two hundred soldiers placed their left feet in their left stirrups, hands on saddle pommels in anticipation of the final command.

"Mount!"

Almost as one, the column stepped into the saddle, accompanied by creaking leather and clanking gear. Men and horses grunted as both tried to find a comfortable position.

Then came the final preparatory command: "Column of twos, forward!"

Again the echo rippled down the line. Baldwin never heard the order of execution. It was lost in the sudden rumbling of twenty supply wagons and hundreds of horses' hoofbeats.

Baldwin's position in the column was behind the supply wagons, but in front of Henely's detachment. Why the young officer had been separated from his home company in the second battalion, Baldwin couldn't guess. Furthermore, he wasn't interested. Command level decision rarely seemed sensible at company level.

"Rider comin' down the line, Lieutenant."

"Thank you, Mr. Dixon."

Baldwin saw the battalion sergeant major riding along the column in his direction. As the ranking non-commissioned officer drew near, he wheeled his horse and fell in beside Baldwin. He offered a salute.

"Compliments of Major Compton, Lieutenant. He'd like you to deploy your trackers now."

Baldwin returned the salute. "Very good, Sergeant Major."

The soldier nodded, then galloped back to the head

of the column to reclaim his position near the commander. As he rode away, Baldwin turned in his saddle.

"Chumumte," he called.

"Yes, sir, Lieutenant," Cottontail replied, riding nearer.

"Please have Captain Falleaf send out the first group of scouts. Then come back, and we'll take a ride."

"Will do," Cottontail said, and wheeled his horse.

Baldwin faced the front again. He heard Falleaf's voice as the old chief shouted orders and the first set of teams peeled away from the column to ride in different directions.

Baldwin's planned scout was simple. He'd divided his unit into two sections. Each section had five teams, each comprising two Indian trackers and a white scout. They would ride between five and ten miles away, depending on terrain, conduct a brief examination of their locale, and report back.

"Ready, Lieutenant?"

Baldwin glanced at Cottontail, now alongside him, and nodded. The pair broke formation and kicked their mounts into a ground-eating lope. As they reached each company commander, Baldwin offered a salute. He didn't care whether the gesture was returned or even noted.

As they neared the head of the column, Baldwin turned his horse east and rode toward a formation of bluffs he'd seen earlier. They rode in silence until reaching the location Baldwin wanted. He led Cottontail along the base of the bluff until they found a way up.

At the top, Baldwin sat silently looking over the land they'd just crossed. It was a river valley with trees and thick vegetation. He could see the column in the distance, less than three miles away by his reckoning. Dust rose in a pale cloud above the soldiers. As they reached drier territory, the dust cloud would become more pronounced, making the unit's progress easier to track.

Baldwin glanced at his scout. "Somewhere out there are those Cheyenne, Comanche, and Kiowa Indians who refused to submit to Sherman's orders." He returned his gaze to the approaching column. "And we're going to find them."

"Yes, sir." Cottontail answered, watching the dust cloud. "If'n they don't find us first."

He had pictured something different when he was allowed to join the scouting party. He wanted adventure, discovery, maybe even a scalp. At the very least, he'd hoped for sight of the enemy. Instead, he watched horse rears.

Bear Tooth, his group leader, had assured him that watching over the horses was a very important job. He made sure there were always fresh mounts available. The scouts needed speed to seek the enemy.

Tall Elk looked through the flying dirt and saw his horse herd companion, Moonface. The boy rode on the downwind side of the herd and was covered in dust. Apparently sensing he was being watched, Moonface looked over to Tall Elk. The elder youth waved him over, then dropped farther behind the herd.

Moonface pulled away from the horses with the practiced ease of one who'd spent his entire life on horseback. He circled around behind Tall Elk and moved up beside him. The two rode together quietly.

Tall Elk regarded his partner in misery closer. Moonface and his horse were the same color of tan. Sweat had mingled with his war paint and rolled down his neck and across his body, leaving behind grayish green streaks and mud trails. Additional drops fell from his nose and chin. They splattered on his chest and belly, only to be covered in dirt until his skin was as mottled as a bobcat's coat.

"I hate this," Moonface said glumly. "I had on paint and carried my medicine and had my weapons and . . . I really hate this."

Tall Elk shrugged. "It's not so bad." He wished he had more to say.

"Oh, no? We're Cheyenne wolves in a scouting party, but what if we have to fight? Who'd be afraid of me?" Moonface flung his arms wide. "Look at me!"

"Maybe you could say you have bobcat medicine."

Moonface offered a lopsided grin. "Maybe they'd laugh so hard, they'd fall off their horses and break their necks."

"If they did, we'd have to change your name to 'Kills At A Distance.' "

"Instead of Bear Killer, I could be 'Long Killer.' "

"Maybe so, Moonface."

The silence grew comfortably between the boys. Then Moonface spoke again.

"To be honest, I'd just as soon not have to fight the white man."

Surprised, Tall Elk stared at Moonface.

"Why not? Do you want the buffalo gone? Do you want to see our way of life ended?"

"You sound like the old men. How many whites have you seen?"

Tall Elk paused. Actually, he'd never seen a white man, except once when an old trapper passed through his village. The aged man had a Cheyenne wife, and they were traveling to see her people. But he didn't seem white. He wore Cheyenne clothes and spoke the language as well as Tall Elk did.

"Not many," Tall Elk confessed. "Still, what about the white soldiers and what happened at Sand Creek?"

Moonface nodded. "I know. I lost family there. At

least that is what my grandfather says. All I know is that I don't want to go to war."

"What *do* you want?"

"To be a medicine man," Moonface answered, leaning forward to rub his horse's neck. "That's what I want, and it's what my mother wants. I'm going to have two or three fat wives and raise many fat children. I will cure the sick and make the rain. I will have a good life. That is what my mother says, and she would not lie."

"Some medicine men fight."

"Some do; others don't."

"The only ones I know who don't are old or wear dresses."

Moonface glared at Tall Elk.

"I am not like that!" he shouted. "I will have wives and children. Good strong children! And I will be a great medicine man no matter what you or my fath—" He clamped his mouth shut.

Tall Elk could say nothing. He knew what was happening now. Moonface's father was a famous warrior. Many coups, scalps, and horses. It was only natural for the father to wish his son to follow in his tracks. But Moonface was not so strong, and he sided with his mother.

The arguments would end with Moonface being accused of being less than a man, that he should wear a dress and live with those who preferred the company of men. These celibate priests had much medicine because they would not lie with a woman and could not lie with a man. To do so was death. While held in great respect and no little awe by the warriors, no one wanted to live like them.

"I did not mean to say that—"

"I'm not," Moonface interrupted.

He wheeled his horse and rode back to the side of the herd.

"You'll see," he called over his shoulder. "One day, you'll see."

Watching Moonface's back, Tall Elk felt bad. He had never intended to hurt his feelings. On the other hand, how was he to know? He and Moonface weren't friends. Where was he on the hunts and horse raids? With his mother. Where was he during the dances? With his mother.

Tall Elk reined to a halt as a sudden thought struck him. Moonface never did anything the other boys did. He didn't know how to act like a warrior. He didn't talk like one or look like one. Maybe Moonface's father was right. Maybe he would be wearing a dress one day.

Tall Elk kicked his pony into a lope and caught up to the herd. Whatever happened to Moonface wasn't his problem. What he needed to do was to get someone to take his place on the horse herd. There were trails to scout, enemy to chase, and scalps to collect. Tall Elk intended to get his share.

Throughout the day, Baldwin and his men had raced through and around the countryside surrounding the column. The only real excitement had come late in the afternoon when a team of scouts rode in with news they had seen fresh tracks on top of a bluff. He accompanied his men back to where they'd found the tracks taking Cottontail as interpreter.

As they arrived, one of the Delaware trackers pointed at the ground and started talking rapidly.

"He says that there were three, maybe four horses up here," Cottontail translated. "That they was Injun horses 'cause they had no shoes."

Baldwin nodded, then asked, "Could they have been wild horses?"

Cottontail repeated the question and listened intently to the answer.

"He says the prints are too deep for riderless animals. He also says that near the base of this hill he found fresh horse apples where they'd been tethered for a while."

"Hmm. Does he think they're Comanche or Cheyenne?"

Cottontail's translation of the question drew a sharp laugh from the scouts and a brief answer.

"What did he say, Chumumte?"

"He says 'Shit, we're good, but not *that* good.' Or words to that effect."

Baldwin regarded Cottontail quietly. He finally said, "I don't suppose it would do any good to follow the tracks."

"No, sir, I wouldn't recommend it. Hell, you know how us Injuns are. There might be four sets of tracks here, but a war party with a hundred warriors just over the rise eyeballin' us as we speak."

"Very well, we'll return to the column. When we get back, I want the Delawares to tell Falleaf everything they've seen."

The scouts rode back to the main unit, which had since bivouacked for the night. Baldwin found Compton's tent and reported his activities for the day, including the discovery of the fresh tracks. Compton seemed bored by the report, but did manage to say that Baldwin's refusal to follow the tracks was not the action of a *real* soldier, but since they were just scouts, he supposed it was the best they could do.

Baldwin bristled, but bit his lip, saluted, and left the major's tent.

"Next time I'll bring him a head in a tow sack," he muttered. "Maybe that'll be soldierly enough for the son of a bitch!"

He rode to his unit's camp area and slowly dismounted. He ached from the waist down, his legs from gripping the horse, his butt from pounding the saddle. Unlike most of the men, he'd spent the last two years riding a desk. He unsaddled, watered and fed his horse, then dropped his saddle and bedroll next to the fire, disdaining the use of the tent.

As his men began to turn in, he finally admitted he could avoid the issue no longer and went to his bed. He took his time, unrolling the bedroll and adjusting the blanket just so, in an attempt to delay the inevitable. Then he gingerly rested his weight on one cheek, winced, and rolled to the other side. With a sigh, he lay on his stomach, ignoring the grins around him.

NINE

The Journal of Frank D. Baldwin, Lieutenant, Fifth Infantry, July 14, 1874.

This is the end of our fourth day on the campaign. I report precious little, for it seems we combat heat and thirst rather than the elusive Indian. Another day's scouting has brought no enemy in sight and no sign since finding tracks the first day out.

All is not hardship. Today my Delaware trackers brought fresh buffalo meat to camp. They espied two hunters skinning a kill. Apparently, the hunters spotted the trackers, and believing them to be hostile, fired. My men, fearing for their lives, retreated. I find it odd that those who are pillaging the land tried to shoot the very men charged with their protection. I fear neither white man has his nose still attached. To return to the tale, when the hunters quit their kill, my men returned. They then butchered the animal, saving the special tidbits for the scouts. That they were willing to share with the rest of command attests to the generous nature of the Delaware. Had the situation been reversed, I am confident the Indians would have had no meat tonight.

At dawn we separate from the First Battalion and continue our scout to Adobe Walls and Antelope Hills.

Baldwin stared at the page of text and sighed. Less than a page of writing. He could write volumes about his loathing for Compton and his staff, listing in small detail every act of incompetence and action unbecoming an officer. On the other hand, should his journal fall into Compton's hands . . .

He snapped the book closed. Some things were better saved. When he was old and writing his memoirs, he would reveal the sort of soldier he had to serve with in the Indian Campaign of 1874.

Tucking the book back into his saddlebags, Baldwin walked to the campfire for another cup of coffee. After almost a week in the saddle, he found much of his soreness gone. He felt stronger and believed the hard days of riding were reshaping the recruiting officer into a soldier again. For Baldwin, the change seemed a godsend.

He had just filled his cup when he saw Cottontail walking his way. The scout was frowning.

"*He*, Chumumte," Baldwin said in Delaware. "You look like a man with a problem."

"Ain't me, Lieutenant," Cottontail replied, with a shake of his head. "Seems Captain Falleaf's horse come up lame today."

"Get him another from the herd."

"Did that." Cottontail offered a sideways grin. "Least, I tried to do that."

Baldwin knew he was in for a story and sat on a log near the fire. "Have a seat, and tell me what happened."

"All righty, I just will." Cottontail started to sit, then

moved to the fire. "Mind if I get me a cup of coffee first?" he asked.

"Help yourself."

Cottontail filled the cup about half full. He then added a heaping handful of sugar. He took a long drink and closed his eyes.

"That's a cup of coffee." He smiled at Baldwin. " 'Bout the only thing I found worth a damn in the army—present company excepted."

Baldwin said nothing. To answer Cottontail would be to further delay the telling of the original story.

"Well," the interpreter said, "like I was saying. I went to the man who handles the herd and told him my chief needed a new horse 'cause his come up lame. He looks me over a minute, then hollers at some other soldier, only this other man don't have stripes on his sleeves. The second man brings over a horse like the first feller told him. Only problem was this second horse was worse than the one that went lame."

"Did you say anything?"

"Hell, yes, I said something. I told him the horse was plumb wored out! He says to me it's good enough. So I answer back that it was maybe good enough for wolf bait, but it ain't a fit animal for a Lenape war chief. Well, sir, he gets all red-faced and such, and tells me that horse is plenty fine for a Injun, and if'n I don't like it, I can just walk."

Baldwin silently prayed for strength. "So," he said, "what did you do?"

"What could I do?" Cottontail answered. "I took the horse. Course, I ain't no army officer or such, so I had to make the best of it. A man in a better position might—"

"I can try," Baldwin interrupted, "but I can't promise you anything. General Miles is the only man they fear, and he's not here."

Cottontail sat silently, sipping his coffee. Finally, he dumped the last half cup in the fire and stood.

"Well," he said, "if I have to make do, I reckon I'll take that critter for a ride. I'll make camp out yonder, sing a few songs, make a few prayers. Maybe get him some sweet grass to eat."

"Will that help?"

Cottontail laughed. "Cain't hurt, Lieutenant. I'll be seeing you tomorrow."

As the interpreter rose to leave he said, "You mind if Falleaf and me get a early start?"

Breakfast over, Baldwin was carrying his saddle when he first heard the horses. Leading a dozen or so men, Captain Tupper approached the camp. As the group reined to a halt, the soldiers spread out on either side of Tupper. Baldwin dropped the saddle and saluted.

Tupper walked his horse forward until he was directly in front of Baldwin.

"Well, where is it?" Tupper asked, ignoring the salute.

Baldwin lowered his hand. "Where's what, sir?"

"You know what!" Tupper snapped. "My horse! *My* horse that *your* half-breed interpreter stole!"

Baldwin frowned. "Cottontail? He's not a half-breed. Actually, he's a white—"

"What he *is*, Lieutenant, is a horse thief."

"I'm afraid I don't understand, Captain. I understood Cottontail was given a horse to replace one of the lame animals."

"He was, Baldwin, but the horse he was issued was not the animal he took."

Baldwin said nothing, waiting for further explanation. In the growing silence, Tupper's face reddened.

"Sergeant Ames!" Tupper shouted. His shrill voice

cracked, making the officer's command sound like an elk's bugle.

A rider broke ranks and rode forward. He was sloppy, his uniform wrinkled and stained with horse manure. He wore three chevrons on his sleeves.

"Yes, sir, Captain Tupper," the sergeant said.

"Did you or did you not issue a mount to one of the Indian scouts yesterday?"

"Yes, sir."

"And did this same individual make any comments?"

"Yes, sir! He said that horse weren't worth a fig."

"And?"

Ames looked blank a moment. Then he broke into a smile. "Oh. And I told him he could take what was issued or walk."

"And did he?"

"No, sir."

"What?" Tupper shouted, looking directly at the sergeant.

Ames panicked when he saw the murderous look on Tupper's face.

"Honest, sir! That Injun didn't walk nowhere. He just took that pony and rode off real quietlike."

"And tell me, Sergeant Ames, where is that horse now?" he asked, looking directly at Baldwin.

"Well, hell, sir. You know where it—" He stopped as Tupper started to turn in the saddle. "It's back with the herd, sir," he said quickly.

"So you see, Baldwin, it is really quite simple." Tupper's voice was mild. "My horse is gone; therefore, your man returned with the horse he was issued and switched one for the other."

Baldwin addressed Ames. "Excuse me, Sergeant, but how do you know Cottontail returned the horse?"

Ames snorted. "Hell, that's easy! Just look at him. We got horses set aside for the Injuns."

"Special horses?" Baldwin asked.

"Hell, yes, Lieutenant." Ames giggled. "They's special all—"

"That's enough, Sergeant," Tupper interrupted. "Return to your duties!"

Ames shut his mouth, offered a weak salute, and rode off. Baldwin didn't need to hear the rest of his explanation to know that Compton had instructed the herdsmen to save the worst, most worn-out animals for the scouts and trackers. He looked up at Tupper.

"Well, Captain, I guess I'll send Cottontail over to you when he reports in."

"Yes, Baldwin, you do that."

"Of course, this is such a breach of army regulations, he'll no doubt be court-martialed."

Tupper yawned. "Of course. I'm sure Major Compton will insist."

"Oh, no, Captain Tupper. A crime of this magnitude deserves a high tribunal, and I am sure General Miles will insist on acting as judge."

"Miles?" Tupper asked.

"Yes, indeed. You know how the general is a stickler for military regulations. It'll have to be a proper trial with you testifying about how it was your horse stolen. And Ames will have to explain how he knew which animal was returned and how Major Compton's selection criteria worked. . . ." Baldwin paused as he saw Tupper's face pale. "You feel all right, Captain?"

Without a word, Tupper turned his horse and rode back toward First Battalion's campsite. His detachment followed closely behind.

Baldwin stood on a small hill with Lieutenant Henely where they had a commanding view of the North Canadian River. First Battalion was heading downstream ably led by scout David Campbell. The column was to follow the Canadian until it arrived at Camp Supply. There it would link with General Miles.

"Well, Lieutenant, we're on our own now," Baldwin said.

"Yes, sir."

"It's just going to be silly for us to keep calling each other 'lieutenant' on this trip." He offered his hand. "I'm Frank."

Henely shook it. "Austin," he replied.

The men rode back to their unit in silence. Henely's sergeant had formed the troops into two columns of nine, with himself and a guidon at the head. The scouts gathered loosely to one side. The wagon that carried their sleeping gear and supplies waited on the other side. A black man sat in the driver's box.

"Nigger Clark," Baldwin said to Henely, pointing out the driver. "The cook's name is Nigger Clark, like 'nigger' was the man's Christian name."

He shook his head and reined to a halt. Looking over the group, he waited until he knew he had their full attention.

"Gentlemen," he said, "I want four Delaware trackers at the head of the column. I will be behind them with Lieutenant Henely's detachment, followed by Mr. Clark and the wagon. The remaining scouts are to ride as trailers and flankers."

As the men began to position themselves, Baldwin called to Billy Dixon. "I gather you know the way to Adobe Walls."

"Yes, sir."

"Good. Then will you please lead the column. We are to follow the Canadian to Palo Duro Creek."

TEN

Baldwin fished his watch from its pocket, opened the case, and steadied the timepiece against the rocking of his horse.

Ten o'clock. The column had been on the march since daybreak in heat that grew steadily more oppressive. He felt sweat run down his sides and longed for a breeze.

"What a way to start the week," he muttered.

He briefly scanned the distant bluffs. The day before, August 16, a pair of his flankers had ridden in to report signs of Indians. When he'd asked where, they pointed to the west, where he saw a lone brave on a hilltop.

The Indian sat atop his pony, both silhouetted against the bright blue sky. He held a staff or spear in one hand. As the column approached, he slowly turned his mount and rode out of sight.

Baldwin didn't bother sending riders after him. No matter what tribe he was from, his intent was clear—to watch the column. They spotted ten more such watchers during the course of the day as Baldwin ordered his command across dry washes and gullies. He doubled the guard that night, but no one attacked or threatened the livestock.

Now as he regarded the horizon, he wondered how

many times his scouts would find their scouts. His thoughts were interrupted by the arrival of Dixon and Masterson.

"We're coming to Palo Duro Creek," Masterson said. "If we follow it, it'll take us right to the Canadian and Adobe Walls."

Baldwin closed the case on the watch and pocketed it.

"Any reason not to?" he asked.

"Well, Billy says there's sand, lots of it. Not like quick-sand, but hills loose enough to slow a wagon."

Baldwin paused a moment, contemplating his choices. "Very well," he said, decision made. "Let's push on. I'm sure Mr. Clark's mules will get him through."

Both men nodded their agreement, waved, and rode back to their positions.

Baldwin liked these men. Despite General Miles's opinion of their morals and fitness for duty within the army, they had proven themselves both willing and able to fulfil their tasks. No more could be asked of a regular.

Two hours later the sun was at its zenith, and a hot and thirsty Baldwin would have sworn they'd pro-gressed less than a mile. The land wasn't so much hilly as broken by arroyos and dry washes. The soft soil gave way under the weight of the wagon. The sand seemed to grab at the wheels as though it resented the intrusion of man and animal.

On a particularly difficult ascent, Baldwin had taken hold of one of the lead mules' halters to encourage the animal to pull harder. As they neared the crest, he was surprised to see his men dismounted and ranged along the hilltop. He released the mule and rode up.

"Oh my God!" The words escaped Baldwin's mouth unnoticed.

The plains were covered by an ocean of buffalo. The

herd stretched as far as he could see in either direction and to the horizon before him. Baldwin stood on the hill in mouth-open awe.

"Hell of a sight, huh, Lieutenant?" said Dixon.

"Indeed, it is. I had heard of such, but have never had the privilege of viewing it."

"Well, sir, you're fixin' to get an eyeful."

"Why?" Baldwin asked.

Dixon grinned. " 'Cause Adobe Walls lies on the *other* side of the herd."

How many hours they traveled through the herd, Baldwin couldn't guess. He didn't check his watch, but the steady movement of the sun toward the western horizon told him enough. He'd closed ranks on the patrol, moved to firmer ground farther from the creek, and brought in all but four scouts. Now in two columns with the wagon trailing, they snaked their way across the plain.

At first glance, the herd looked like a solid mass of animals, but once inside, they found the buffalo moved in small groups. As they approached each group, the buffalo walked away, eyeing them closely.

The animals followed the Palo Duro as the soldiers did, splashing through the shallow creek. After watching several groups cross, Baldwin decided to forgo drinking from the creek. Occasionally a cow threatened to charge as the men neared her calf. Baldwin turned his scouts away, giving the mother a wide berth.

The distance between groups ranged from a few to several hundred yards. During these brief gaps, Baldwin hurried his command. He didn't dare charge through the animals, because the hunters had told him they might stampede. He shuddered at the thought of being trapped inside a swirling, dusty, raging herd of millions of buffalo.

Baldwin used the time for reflection. He'd been in the field for almost five days, each day's advance made in sweltering heat with the only real sign of Indians the day before. He wondered what his outriders had found today, but he'd have to wait to learn that. His last order to them was to avoid the herd unless an attack was imminent.

He reckoned they'd be at Adobe Walls in another day, perhaps two. The long ride to the Antelope Hills and Miles's command was still to come. Would they see any Indians, or was the occasional, elusive scout to be their only contact?

As he mulled things over, the heat and the gentle rocking motion made him drowsy. He shook himself awake and nudged his horse with his heels to move faster until they caught up to Dixon at the head of the column.

"Do you have any idea how far away we are from Adobe Walls?"

"Oh, I reckon forty, fifty miles," Dixon said. "A hard day's march, but doable. Land's not much different." He looked down. "But there's sure a lot less buffalo shit."

Baldwin nodded. "I'm sure, but what of the Indians?"

"Hell, Lieutenant, Indians'll find *us* when they want to."

"Was that the way it was at Adobe Walls?"

Dixon sighed. "No, sir. We'd had a couple of killings, but then we had us a couple every year. Course, some of your soldiers come by and tried to warn us off. Most of the men there called 'em liars. There was even talk of a hanging."

Baldwin grimaced.

"And then the Indians came," Dixon continued. "Seeing them charge across the valley was a magnificent sight, even if it did scare the shit outta me."

"I can imagine. I've seen the same sight, only the enemy was dressed in gray, not feathers. Sometimes it amazes me, the things we face and live to tell about."

"No doubt," Dixon replied with a chuckle.

Baldwin slowly turned his horse and started back down the column.

"When we get there, Mr. Dixon," he called over his shoulder, "I'd like you to show me around."

The number of buffalo dropped as the shadows lengthened. Once clear of the herd, Baldwin called a halt for the horses to be rested and watered. Less than a mile away, he saw a grove of trees.

"Mr. Dixon," he called, "ride to that stand of trees, and if it's suitable, we'll camp there tonight." As Dixon rode off, Baldwin shouted, "Two shots for yes!" He turned to another scout. "Mr. McGinty, I'd like you to take two of the trackers and find our outriders. Tell them where we plan to stop."

"Yes, sir, Lieutenant."

McGinty climbed into the saddle and started across the prairie, calling two of the Delaware. The Indians kicked their horses into a gallop and chased the scout. Within moments, the trio was out of sight.

Baldwin heard the sharp bark of a pistol, followed closely by another, come from the direction Dixon had ridden. He took off his campaign hat and ran his sleeve across his sweaty forehead.

"Well, that's it, boys. Form a column of twos and make for the trees."

The unit bivouacked for the night. Clark had just started a cook fire when a bull suddenly appeared in the middle of camp, then another.

McGinty rode in behind four more head, trailed by the two trackers and the outriders.

"Looky here, Lieutenant," McGinty said with a grin. "We found these beeves just wandering around."

He reined to a halt and dismounted. The cattle stopped and started to graze.

"What are we to do with these?" Baldwin asked.

McGinty pulled his pistol, walked to the nearest bull, and shot it between the eyes.

As the animal fell, he looked at Baldwin.

"Have steaks," he said.

Baldwin stared at McGinty, then slowly nodded his head. "Why not?"

Clark and his helpers quickly dressed out the animal, wrapping several large cuts in burlap for another meal. He immediately pan-fried the best cuts in lard. While the meat cooked, Clark made a Dutch oven full of cornbread.

Each man ate as much beef as he could hold. Huge bites of bloody steak took turns with handfuls of hot cornbread, all liberally washed down with the bitter alkaline water of Palo Duro Creek.

Finally satisfied, the men turned in with the sun barely on the horizon. Some immediately fell asleep. Others spoke to each other in low tones or smoked quietly. Baldwin felt especially well. The day had been long but uneventful, save for the herd of buffalo. They had made good distance, almost thirty miles by his reckoning. His belly was full, and he was pleasantly tired.

The wind was a constant companion on the plains. As Baldwin watched the tree boughs swing gently, he saw a change. The wind blew harder, and the movement of the foliage became more animated. He looked into the darkening sky for a sign of an approaching storm and felt dirt brush his cheek.

Baldwin rose to his feet, to see a pale wall in the distance—a moving wall.

"Boys, I think we're in for it."

The sandstorm hit suddenly and with full fury. The air filled with choking dust and dirt, darkening the night further. He stood with his back to the wind, his shirt flapping madly at his sides. Sand stung his skin, piled up in his hair, and poured down his shirt collar.

He heard the horses whinny.

"To the horses!" he shouted above the storm. "Get to the horses before they bolt."

Bodies slowly materialized from bedrolls as the men rose. Baldwin ran around the camp, kicking at men, shouting for them to see to the animals. Making his way back toward the horses, he saw two bedrolls were still occupied, their owners' heads covered.

"Get up!" he screamed, kicking the nearest prostrate form. "Get up, goddammit! If those horses pull their pegs, we'll be afoot."

When neither moved, Baldwin grabbed one man's covers and yanked. The scout rolled out of his bedroll and into his companion. Baldwin looked closer.

"Get off your ass, Plummer!" he yelled. "When I give an order, I expect it to be followed."

As Plummer slowly got to his feet, he angrily shook the other man. Dirty Face Ed Jones peeked from beneath his blanket. Seeing the look on Baldwin's face, he quickly gained his feet. Together, the scouts trudged through the blinding storm to the horses, Baldwin close behind.

Reaching the horses, the men did what they could to calm the animals. Baldwin placed his neckerchief over his horse's nose to help it breathe. Inwardly he fumed.

Plummer and Jones, he thought angrily. *I'll remember*

them. As soon as we reach Miles, they're finished as army scouts.

Tall Elk spotted it first—a quick flash in the sunlight. He pointed it out to Porcupine, and the two rushed down the hill to get a closer look. The object of their attention was a metal container, round, about the size of a large man's fist, with a hole in one end. It bore drawings of what looked like a fruit or vegetable and strange markings. Neither young man could guess its purpose.

"Let's take it to Bear Tooth," Porcupine suggested. "Maybe he can tell us what it is."

Tall Elk retrieved the object, and the pair rode back to their leader.

"Bear Tooth!" Tall Elk shouted, waving the container. "Look what we found."

He reined to a stop and handed the container to the elder warrior. Bear Tooth turned it over, examined the outside, and sniffed at the opening.

"It's food," he said.

The rest of their group had gathered around them. Bear Tooth handed the container to one of the other youths and nodded.

"Yes," he replied. "This is what the agency man gives you to eat when you live on the reservation. It is what *veho* calls food. They take meat and fruit and pack them in there."

"Like a parfleche," Porcupine offered.

"Yes, something like that, only you don't have to cut the top off the parfleche to get to eat," Bear Tooth replied with a laugh.

Passing the white man's parfleche from warrior to warrior, each looked it over. Finally, it was back in Bear

Tooth's hands. The old Dog Soldier pursed his lips and regarded it closely.

"Have you warriors not noticed something?" he said, slowly turning the parfleche.

The boys looked at each other, but none spoke.

"There is no rust," Bear Tooth said. "Our knives will rust, our black metal pots and rifles, but this has not." He dropped the container on the ground and faced Tall Elk. "Can you show me where you found this?"

Tall Elk nodded.

"Good." Bear Tooth mounted his pony. "Come, follow Tall Elk and Porcupine. Perhaps we will learn a new lesson."

Leading the seven-member scouting party, Tall Elk rode across the prairie to the hill where he'd first seen the object. As they halted, he pointed.

"Down there, Bear Tooth," he said, "at the edge of the tall grass."

Bear Tooth nodded. "I want each of you to take a separate direction. Ride out about an arrow-shot away, then come back. Look for signs of a horse or wagon."

The group scattered. Tall Elk continued on his original course. He turned around and surveyed the land before him. Bear Tooth had dismounted close to the original site and walked circles through the tall grass. Porcupine was atop a hillock. Coyote walked his horse slowly, head down, scanning the ground.

A shout came from the distance. Tall Elk saw Bear Tooth trot toward one of the Cheyenne wolves, so kicked his horse into a gallop. He saw the others riding in, Porcupine with a large grin on his face.

Tall Elk reined in beside Bear Tooth, who was looking at the ground.

"Look here," the elder said. "This is the trail left by a white man's wagons. The grooves are made by the wheels, and you can see where they run over the horse prints." He slid from his pony's back and knelt. "I see the tracks of two . . . maybe three horses. And one from a mule." He waved his arms. "Look around. If he has companions, the signs will be here."

The young men scattered again looking for more trails. Finally Bear Tooth called them together. He stood between the wagon tracks and faced the tall grass.

"We know that we seek one wagon, perhaps only one man." Bear Tooth pointed up-trail. "These lead through the place Tall Elk found the parfleche. Down there, the grass is tall and hides the sign of his passing, but up here, there is less grass and soft soil. The wagon marks the ground easily, the trail plain. And since there is no rust on the parfleche, our white man must be close."

Bear Tooth remounted.

"Tall Elk, you and Porcupine follow the wagon. Take Coyote with you; he has good eyes. The rest of us are going to ride ahead and see what we can find."

As Bear Tooth rode away, Tall Elk felt excitement wash over him like a cold rain. He shivered, then grinned at Porcupine and Coyote, kicking his horse into motion.

Exhilaration gave way to boredom as the minutes turned to hours. Tall Elk's neck and shoulders ached from his constant bending to watch the trail. The unrelenting sun beat down on him, and the dry wind whipped grit into his eyes and mouth. The tracks seemed to lead nowhere and constantly disappeared as the terrain changed. Conversation died after Porcupine made the comment they might be trailing this wagon for days.

Bear Tooth and the others rode back and forth across the prairie. They searched canyons and arroyos, bluffs and stands of trees—anywhere a man might hide a wagon and team.

In fading sunlight, Tall Elk strained to see the wagon tracks. He was worried they might lose the trail altogether. As he turned to ask Porcupine his opinion, he heard approaching horses.

"We have found him!" Bear Tooth called, as he and the other wolves hurried back toward them.

Tall Elk was surprised to hear the excitement in the old warrior's voice. Surely he'd been on so many raids the discovery of one wagon didn't mean much.

"What will we do?" Coyote asked quietly.

"Why do you whisper?" Bear Tooth said. "Are you afraid he might hear us? We are much too far away. White men only hear a buffalo stampede when they are in the middle of it."

The insult brought laughter from the rest of the scouting party, and the mood relaxed.

Bear Tooth pointed toward a distant high bluff, now only a silhouette in the darkening night.

"I saw the light of a fire near that bluff."

"How do you know it is a white man?" Tall Elk asked.

"Because no Indian fire is so bright that it is easily seen."

Tall Elk felt his cheeks redden and was glad the sun was almost set. A foolish question had once again shown his inexperience.

"Now, here is what we will do," Bear Tooth said. "We will divide into two groups and approach the wagon from the north and the east. When you get close, get off your horse. Remember, do not let *veho*'s horses know you are there, or they will warn him. When we are all near enough, I will signal, and we will attack. If he is alone, do not kill him, but if there are many, shoot first. If we can, we'll try to take one of them alive."

Tall Elk, Porcupine, Coyote, and Bear Tooth rode as one party. They circled the bluff to the north and approached cautiously. Tall Elk's heart pounded, harder as they drew closer. His palms were sweaty; his breath came in short, sharp rasps.

He glanced at Porcupine. His friend seemed cool and comfortable, as though he were hunting rabbits. Tall Elk envied Porcupine his confidence, his certainty that all would go as planned. How could that be? The man sitting next to that blaze was surely armed. Did none fear the white man's bullets? Was he the only one who realized they might die?

The time for speculation passed as Bear Tooth stopped his horse and slid from its back. He dropped the reins, knowing the well-trained pony would stay put, and crept forward. Tall Elk and the rest followed suit, but kept a discreet distance behind.

As they moved nearer the fire, Tall Elk could almost feel its heat. He could see the white man sitting next to the flames. Tall Elk wondered why he didn't shoot. Surely, he'd seen them by now. Bear Tooth walked up from behind.

"He is alone. This is very good!" the elder said with a low chuckle. "I am going to the other side. I want to take him alive. You move up closer and wait for my signal."

Tall Elk watched his leader disappear into the gloom. He wiped his hands on his breechclout and hoped he could keep a grip on his tomahawk. The young warriors crept closer, then dropped to all fours and crawled to within feet of the camp. They hid among bushes and peeked through the leaves at their quarry.

Tall Elk looked across the small clearing and saw Bear Tooth emerge from behind the wagon. Was it possible this white man did not know they were there? How could he not?

When Bear Tooth signals, he thought, veho *will leap to his feet, pistol blazing, and there will be six dead young men and one old one.*

Bear Tooth gave the sign. Warriors exploded from both sides of the brush. The look on the white man's face told Tall Elk surprise had been complete. Suddenly, the youth was filled with joy. He screamed his war cry, and clutching his tomahawk, charged across the camp.

The terrified white man also screamed, and clawed for his pistol. Just as the weapon came free, Coyote charged past Tall Elk. With one swift movement, he buried his tomahawk in the white man's head. Without a sound, the man collapsed, blood gushing from the wound.

Bear Tooth grabbed Coyote and threw him aside, then bent and checked the wagoner.

"Dead!" he shouted. "Dead!"

He stood and kicked the corpse, then spun and glared at Coyote.

"I told you I wanted him alive!"

"But he had a gun!" Coyote protested in a shaky voice.

Coyote was ashen, his body covered in the blood of the man he'd just slain. Suddenly, he vomited. Tall Elk turned away.

The look of rage on Bear Tooth's face softened. He pulled out his knife and handed it to Coyote.

"Take his scalp," he ordered. "You earned it."

Coyote stared at the white man's ruined head. "But . . . but . . . I've—"

"Watch!"

Bear Tooth bent and grasped the dead man's hair near his forehead. With a quick slicing motion, he cut through the skin. He tugged and the scalp came away with a soft sucking sound.

"Here, Coyote, take it."

After Coyote took the bloody trophy, Bear Tooth turned to the rest of the party.

"Coyote has killed an enemy and taken his scalp. That is good—for him. But at what cost? If we had taken this man alive, each of us could have counted coup on him. Then we could have staked him over a fire and taken his medicine." He paused and looked at Coyote. "After that, you would have had his scalp."

Tall Elk was shaken. He'd expected Coyote to be honored for his actions. The shame and tears on Coyote's face were enough to make Tall Elk wonder if he could ever kill a man.

Tall Elk stood among the other young men near the campfire. Opposite them, four Dog Soldiers stood behind Red Wolf. Bear Tooth alone faced his leader's wrath.

"Is it not enough that we take children with us," Red Wolf said, "that you must lead them into danger?"

Bear Tooth stared at the ground, tight-lipped.

"How am I to teach them proper behavior if their elders act with foolish abandon? Tell me, Bear Tooth, if one of these young men had died, would you want to be the one to tell his father, his mother?"

No reply.

Red Wolf grunted. "I thought not." He turned toward the boys. "I should be angry with you, but the fault lies with the one who was to lead, and since I lead all, the fault is mine." He walked past the fire and stared into the night sky. "The stars are bright and clear and of a number like the Cheyenne who once covered these plains."

Tall Elk stole a glance at Bear Tooth. The older warrior had joined his peers and was watching Red Wolf. What was he thinking? Did he regret leading his group on the raid? Tall Elk didn't think so. Bear Tooth was not the sort of man to waste time on regrets.

Red Wolf again faced his men.

"What has happened tonight may be a good thing. It certainly was for Coyote. He has been blooded, has counted coup, and has a scalp and a captured horse. Those with him have been part of a war party. They have seen the enemy die.

"Perhaps I have been too cautious," he said, his voice growing stronger. "After all, are we not warriors? From now on, if the enemy force is small, we will attack. Every *veho* we kill now is one less we will have to face later."

He began to dance around the fire, singing a victory song for Coyote.

"Coyote has a big surprise for his mother. He has a scalp."

He repeated the line over and over and was soon joined by the rest of the Dog Soldiers. The young men gathered around Coyote, asking to see his trophy. Shyly he pulled the scalp from his saddlebag and held it up.

"It's not very big," one said.

Porcupine laughed. "That's because Coyote almost split the man's head in two."

"My father told me that if you don't stretch them, they shrivel up," said another.

"That's what I heard, too," a new voice rang out. "Coyote, you better stretch it pretty quick."

Coyote looked at the faces surrounding him. "I don't know how."

"Get Red Wolf or Bear Tooth to show you," Tall Elk suggested. "I bet they've seen plenty of scalps."

"Yes, Coyote, ask the Dog Soldiers," Porcupine said; then he snatched the scalp from Coyote's grasp. "But first we dance!"

ELEVEN

The scouting party now rode as a single unit. Occasionally Red Wolf ordered one group or another to follow trails in search of prey. The returning wolves would then fall in behind the horses, relieving the herders.

Earlier that morning Moonface got his chance, and as he rode by, he offered Tall Elk a wide grin. Whooping and screaming, he kicked his pony into a gallop and charged across the land. It was good to see Moonface happy, to see him act as a warrior.

Coyote had stretched his trophy on a small frame made from green twigs. He then bound it to a stick that he said was to become his coup stick. He rode with his head held high, his earlier shame replaced by pride. Soon Coyote would get his adult name.

Tall Elk was anxious to receive his new name, but he had yet to earn it. Riding with the wolves would gain him nothing. He must face an enemy as Coyote had done. He needed to count coup.

Porcupine slowed his horse and drifted back to Tall Elk.

He said, "I wish Red Wolf would let us scatter as before. We can wander through the grass for days and see nothing."

Tall Elk offered his friend a lazy smile. "I have been

thinking the same, but he still sees us as children. Besides, fighting is hot work, and I'm hot enough."

He reached for his water gourd. As he drank deeply, he tried to remember the last rain. The days grew hotter, the ground drier. Water, when it could be found, was sharp with alkali.

"But you know what I want more?" he said, replacing the stopper in the gourd. "Fresh meat!"

Game had been sparse. Each meal was jerky and water. Tall Elk longed for the taste of fresh buffalo hump or kidneys. Bear Tooth had told them of a river near the village of the hunters. He said the war party had stopped there the day before the battle and shot buffalo. He said the water was sweet and cold in nearby springs.

To Tall Elk it seemed far away. Perhaps they'd find water before then. Maybe there would be antelope or deer or even some juicy berries. Anything would be better than another night of dried buffalo and warm water.

"I will eat anything that won't eat me first."

Moonface's voice from behind broke his reverie.

"How can I fight when I may die from hunger?" the youth continued.

Porcupine laughed. "Moon Butt, you will still be here long after the rest of us are reduced to skeletons."

"My name is Bear Killer," Moonface said quietly.

"What?" Porcupine asked, turning to look behind.

Moonface stared stonily at Porcupine. "I said I am called Bear Killer. The blood of my father is my blood, and he is one of the greatest warriors among the Cheyenne. I, too, will be a great fighter."

Porcupine regarded the other youth narrowly. "Perhaps your first fight will come sooner than you think."

"Porcupine," Red Wolf called from the front, "if it is a battle you wish, perhaps you will find us an enemy.

Gather Bear Tooth and the rest of your group and ride north. We are nearing where we fought the white buffalo hunters. I'm sure Bear Tooth remembers the way."

Tall Elk urged his horse into a trot, followed by Porcupine, who glared at Moonface as the pair rode off. The remainder of their group soon joined them.

"Tall Elk," Moonface called, "if you can't find an enemy, maybe you can find some nice fresh meat."

"Yes, sir, that's what done it," Cottontail said. "Nice fresh meat. You see, you white folks ain't got the stomach for eatin' half-raw beef and drinking gyp water. Now, you take us Delaware and the white scouts, we been livin' like this. Rotten, maggoty meat and pond water with an inch of scum—"

Baldwin groaned. "Please, Cottontail, enough," he said thickly.

"I'm sorry, Lieutenant, but it's got to work its way through."

"I'm sure it will—as soon as I've shat my guts out." He bent over his saddle pommel. "Christ, I've got to stop! Tell the men."

Baldwin jumped from his still-walking horse and ran for the nearest bush. His bowels had been in an uproar since dinner the night before. The first attack occurred shortly after the sandstorm quit. Since then, he'd spent most of the night squatting over a hole. The worst of it was there was no other kind of water to be had. As thirsty as he was, he chose to abstain.

On more than one occasion, he crossed paths with a pale Henely, apparently affected by the same malady. The two passed with only a nod and a knowing look. Other men suffered as well, except the scouts. They spent the morning commenting on the "fine feed" and the weaknesses of the soldiers' digestive systems.

Stomach trouble was nothing new to Baldwin or any other veteran of the Civil War. Dysentery had run rampant through both armies. He'd seen more men disabled by disease than wounded by enemy bullets.

Finally purged again, Baldwin cautiously straightened. He waited for the telltale cramp and clutch in the gut that foretold another round, but nothing happened. His stomach was sore, deep in the muscle. Rubbing his belly, he walked back to the column.

"Where's Henely?" he asked, failing to locate his second-in-command.

"He went the other way, sir," Cottontail said. "Said something about if'n he don't come back soon, follow the buzzards."

"Very well." Baldwin remounted his horse with a grunt. "Cottontail, get Dixon for me."

"Sure thing, Lieutenant."

Baldwin squirmed in the saddle, trying in vain to find a comfortable position. He was wishing he could find something soft to sit on, when Dixon arrived.

"I am sure you are well aware of our current situation."

"If you mean the reason we've been stopping every five miles," Dixon replied with a smile, "the answer is yes."

"Good." Baldwin paused and took a deep breath. "Then bearing that in mind, can you tell me how long before we reach the post?"

Dixon thought a moment, then removed his hat and ran fingers through long, sweat-soaked hair. "If we can pick up the pace, 'nother six hours or so. If not, we'll have to camp on the trail and make the Walls tomorrow." Dixon replaced the hat. "Course, your biggest problem's gonna be water. There ain't much between Palo Duro Creek and Adobe Walls Creek in a good year. Way things been this summer, I don't hold there'll be any."

"All right, here's what we'll do. Mr. Dixon, tell McGinty to lead on at a canter; then you and Masterson ride to the Walls and warn them we're coming. The last thing I want is a bunch of jumpy hunters shooting into the ranks." As Dixon rode off, Baldwin turned to his interpreter. "Cottontail, wait here for Lieutenant Henely; then bring him along."

The sun rode low on the horizon. Valleys and thickets were already dark. Bear Tooth and his six men rode quietly. He'd told the wolves they weren't close to the village, but they were very near a large herd of buffalo. If they stumbled on any hunters' camps, they were to avoid them.

They crossed a narrow stream and Bear Tooth called a stop.

"This is good water. Drink as much as you can, your horses, too. Then fill your gourds." He looked at the land around them. "I remember this place. We passed it after leaving the fight."

"Bear Tooth?"

"Yes, Porcupine."

"It is said that we lost the battle with the *veho* buffalo hunters."

"It's true." Bear Tooth nodded. "But it was not our fault. The Comanche brought with them a medicine man who said he had spells to keep the hunters asleep. He also had a yellow paint that he said the Great Spirit gave him to make us bulletproof." He shook his head sadly. "It was lies, all lies."

Tall Elk had heard parts of the story before, but he wanted to know it all.

"What happened?" he asked.

Bear Tooth laughed, not a joyful sound, but one that rang ruefully.

"We all painted ourselves," he began. "All except one Kiowa, a chief named Lone Wolf. He never trusted the Comanche shaman, and would only offer one arm to his paint. Then we charged. We attacked the lodges with little more than color and knives. Many warriors rode naked, their bodies protected by ochre.

"*Veho* saw us and fired with the big guns he uses to kill the buffalo." He pantomimed a man holding a rifle. "He killed us everywhere, but still we attacked." He lowered his arms and shifted in his saddle. "Soon we tried to get into one lodge, then another, but it was too late. There was no surprise, no sleeping whites."

Bear Tooth paused and gently stroked his horse's neck.

"We hid behind the trees and over the hills," he continued, "but he killed in sight and out of sight. Many believed that the Great Spirit gave medicine to the hunters because we had abandoned our medicine for that of the Comanche shaman. We wanted to kill that Comanche after Stone Calf's son was shot. Stone Calf challenged the medicine man to prove his magic worked, but nothing came of it. We said the shaman had skunk medicine and went home."

No one spoke for several moments. The boys gathered their animals and prepared to move off.

"If I had been there," Porcupine said angrily, "I would have killed the Comanche!"

Bear Tooth nodded. "I suppose you would have, but that is in the past. It is now to be told as stories and lessons for young warriors like yourself."

The group rode into the gathering gloom. Bear Tooth signaled for a stop.

"There, in the distance, can you see it?"

Tall Elk strained his eyes and saw a faint light.

"Is it a camp?" he asked.

"Worse," Bear Tooth answered. "It is the village of the white hunters. I had hoped they would be gone, but as you can see, there is still someone there."

"Why don't we sneak up on him like we did the man with the wagon?" Porcupine asked impatiently. "I want a scalp for myself."

"No, we won't do that," the older warrior replied. "We will go back to the little stream and make camp. Red Wolf and the others cannot be far behind. Tomorrow the whole scouting party will visit the lodges of *veho*."

The sun had long set, and the column advanced slowly under clear, starry skies. The transition to full darkness had been gradual, and Baldwin had little trouble seeing his way. His stomach still roiled and gurgled, but otherwise the trip was uneventful.

A rider appeared from the shadows.

"We're here, Lieutenant," Masterson's voice said.

"And where exactly is that?"

"Less than a mile from the Walls; maybe a hundred yards from Adobe Walls Creek."

"Thank God," Baldwin said. He leaned toward Henely. "We'll camp here, Austin. I don't know about you, but my butt's like a raw piece of meat."

"I understand all too well, Frank. Shall I have the men bivouac at the creek?"

"Yes, sir, please do."

"Begging the lieutenant's pardon," Masterson said, "but the water's too low in Adobe Walls Creek for this many animals."

"What do you suggest?"

"Well, just south of the post, there's Bent's Creek.

It's full of water. It also runs next to a mesquite flat with plenty of room for the tents."

Baldwin sighed. "Very well, we'll take your advice." He turned to Henely. "Sorry, Austin, but we're not through yet. Have the men follow Mr. Masterson to our new campsite."

They rode to a huge structure, a stockade fence at least ten feet in height with a watchtower on the corner. A building ran down part of the fence line, and a lantern hung behind a shuttered window.

As the soldiers approached, a door opened and bright yellow light spilled onto the ground. A dozen men emerged to line the front of the store silently.

One man stepped forward. "Welcome to Adobe Walls, Lieutenant."

"Thank you, Mr. Dixon," Baldwin replied, recognizing his scout's voice. "I suppose you know where we're headed."

"Yes, sir. Just keep heading south. You'll come across the flat, and the creek lies just beyond. All told maybe a mile, mile and a half."

"Very good." Baldwin turned in his saddle. "Mr. Henely, take the column and proceed to the south. There should be water and a suitable bivouac site within the next mile."

"Yes, sir," Henely's voice called from the dark.

"Mr. Dixon, I'll be expecting my tour first thing in the morning. Gentlemen, I bid you all a good night."

Amid a chorus of replies, Baldwin slowly turned his horse and followed his command into the night.

TWELVE

"Well, Mr. Clark, it seems we're having beans and biscuits this morning," Baldwin said, holding out his plate.

The cook nodded and dipped a ladle in a large black kettle. "Yassuh," he replied, filling the plate. "We's havin' breakfast beans."

Breakfast beans consisted of canned white beans, molasses, fatback, and chili powder. For dinner, Clark left out the molasses and made cornbread.

"Coffee, suh?" Clark asked, holding up a pot.

Baldwin nodded, shifted his plate to one hand, and accepted the proffered cup with the other. He held it aloft in a salute. "Thank you, sir."

"You most welcome, Lieutenant. 'Joy the meal."

Baldwin joined his men who sat around one of the campfires. He exchanged greetings with the scouts, noting that those who had been ill the last two days looked better. Even Henely seemed to have some color back in his face, though he had no food, only a cup of coffee.

"You should eat something, Austin," Baldwin said as he helped himself to a heaping spoonful of beans.

Henely smiled weakly. "Maybe later, Frank. I managed to stay in my tent all night. I'd like to be able to sit the saddle awhile."

Baldwin attacked breakfast with relish. After not eating the night before, he'd awoken famished. He'd lain on his bedroll, waiting for the pain to start, followed by the cramp and desperate dash for a slit trench. But this morning there had been none of that, just an emptiness that cried for food.

"Too bad," he said around a mouthful of beans. "Cook's done a right fine job today."

He took the last half of his biscuit and sopped the bean juice in his plate, then sipped at his hot coffee, savoring its warmth and taste.

"Mmm," he moaned with pleasure. "Nothing like a good cup of coffee."

"Ain't it the truth?"

Baldwin looked across the fire at Cottontail, who sat with his sugar bag in his lap.

"How the hell would you know?" he asked. "You got so much sugar in there, you can't even taste the coffee."

Cottontail grinned. "That's another problem with you *vehos,* you got no appreciation for the better things in life."

Baldwin laughed. "What was that word you called me? Vay-hoes? Is that Lenape?"

"Nope," Cottontail answered, shaking his head. "It's a Cheyenne word Young Marten learned. It's what they call you. Means spider, I think. They use it because the whites spin a web of lies to trap the Indians." He grinned. "Their words, not mine."

"Indeed? I wonder what the Delaware call us." Baldwin drained his cup. "I'm taking a ride to Adobe Walls. I want to see what condition the post is in, and how many men are still there. Cottontail, you will join me, as well as Mr. Masterson. Austin, I want your guidon and one sergeant."

"Me, too?" Henely asked.

"No, I need you here. I don't anticipate trouble, but one never can tell."

Tall Elk watched the warriors prepare for battle. Each quietly groomed his warhorse, saved just for this purpose. The animal needed stamina rather than speed and mustn't be frightened by the noise of battle. Some horses were painted, others had medicine tied in their manes or tails.

The men prepared themselves as well. They wore their best leggings and shirts and fanciest moccasins. They carefully braided their hair and adorned it with ornaments.

Face paint varied as to medicine and taste. A warrior with eagle medicine painted himself to look like an eagle. Another had slashes of red across his forehead like streaks of the enemy's blood. Still another covered one side of his face with black and the other white.

Tall Elk also noticed two of the Dog Soldiers were dog men. Each wore a sash with a stake attached to one end. During a battle, they drove the stake into the ground and wore the sash over one shoulder. Then the warrior announced he would not move from that spot until he was either dead or the battle was won. Tall Elk doubted either man would use his dog rope, but if the war party was being pursued, they might stake themselves out to buy time for the others to escape. Such was the nature of dog men.

Red Wolf had forbidden the younger men to paint themselves.

"If we are separated and you are caught," he'd said, "the soldiers might not kill you if you don't look like you're ready for war."

The younger men had argued, especially Porcupine

and Moonface, but Red Wolf's order stood, much to Tall Elk's relief.

Now, as the older men mounted their war horses, Tall Elk and the rest rose.

Red Wolf moved forward. His face was a vision of horror to remind the enemy whom they faced. He'd painted his lower jaw black with white streaks like the fangs of a wolf, his eyes large and yellow. Red streaks crossed the rest of his face like slashes from a wolf's teeth.

"Listen to me," he said quietly. "We are now a war party, ready to fight. Everyone's medicine is prepared, so keep your horses quiet, and do not speak unless you see the enemy is about to ambush us. Loud noises disturb the medicine.

"You younger men ride hunting horses. Their speed will help you escape if we are attacked. Now, get mounted."

The party made its way across the stream, then through a small meadow until they reached the trees that grew along the banks of the Canadian River. Tall Elk remembered the stories of how it was from here the combined Cheyenne, Kiowa, and Comanche war party had struck the white hunters. It seemed he could hear the cries of the wounded, see warriors fall, and smell death in the air.

The lodges stood less than a mile away, easily seen as they jutted from the flat valley. Tall Elk felt it was an evil place.

Red Wolf stopped.

Tall Elk crowded forward, Porcupine at his side. In the distance, five white men had gathered—three in a wagon, two on horseback. One of the men in the wagon waved, and the vehicle rumbled off toward the village.

Red Wolf waited until the wagon was too far away to help the others, then ordered the assault.

* * *

Being in no hurry, Baldwin kept the detail at a walk. He tried to guess what he would find at the post. Was the place a shambles, the men drunken fools depending on God's good graces to keep them alive? Or was it fortified, the kind of place a soldier could use for resupply? He hoped for the latter.

"So, Bat, was this how the attack started?"

"No, sir," Masterson replied. "The Indians came across the valley from the Canadian. At least that's what I'm told. When the fight started, I was asleep in the Myers and Leonard corral."

"What woke you?"

"All the shooting, sir."

The patrol had ridden about half a mile when Baldwin heard Indian war cries. From his right, he saw two men fleeing a large party of Indians. Ahead of them, a wagon raced. As the wagon pulled into the corral gate, the Indians split ranks, trying to cut the riders off.

"Pull your pistols," Baldwin barked, "and follow me!"

He charged at the war party, not knowing what he was going to do.

Still out of range, he saw two members of the war party pull ahead of the others. One of the Indians rode beside the pair of terrified hunters. He lunged forward and drove his lance into one of the white men. The hapless hunter arched backward and tumbled from his horse.

The warrior then made a grab for the dead man's horse, missing the reins. He kicked his pony harder and reached again, only to miss a second time. Meanwhile, his partner had moved up and was trying to close on the remaining buffalo hunter.

"Fire!" Baldwin cried.

Almost as one, the pistols boomed.

Tall Elk heard guns in the distance, and looked back. "Soldiers!" he screamed.

Porcupine, who was preoccupied with capturing his first war trophy, ignored him. With a grunt he made another lunge for the horse's reins. He caught them and quickly checked the animal. Tall Elk broke off his attack and circled back to his friend. Porcupine grinned and started back to the war party, Tall Elk at his heels.

The war party had halted in its tracks. Tall Elk heard the soldiers shoot again. He saw some of the warriors turn to run, but Red Wolf's voice stopped them.

"What are you fleeing from?" he shouted. "There are but five of them. Shoot back!"

Every warrior with a weapon brought it to bear. The soldiers veered off from their charge and raced to the hunters' lodges. Red Wolf called for pursuit.

The war party had new prey.

Tall Elk rode among the older warriors in the front. He had no gun, but hoped he might hit a soldier with his tomahawk. But these soldiers must have had powerful medicine. Their horses flew across the ground as though pushed by a great wind. The warriors fired bullet after bullet at them, yet none fell. The longer he chased them, the lower his spirits fell.

Then he saw the whites ride through the corral gate, and the chase was over. He slowed his pony, and turned back toward the river. Across the valley, he saw many small white tipis, almost the same color as those of his people.

"Red Wolf," he called, "look at the little tipis."

Red Wolf spun his horse and looked where Tall Elk pointed.

"Quickly," he said, "we must leave. Those are the lodges of the soldiers."

The war party galloped back across the plain. Tall Elk heard a bugle. His heart thudded. How many soldiers were there? Would they be trapped and cut to pieces? Tears blurred his vision as he silently urged his pony faster.

He saw Porcupine's trophy jerk its head. The horse fell quickly behind.

Porcupine shouted. "My horse!"

"Leave it!" Tall Elk cried. "Do you want to die for a *horse?*"

Red Wolf turned toward a wide delta where another river met the Canadian. He led his men across the water and into the sand hills beyond.

Baldwin slid his horse to a stop. He was surrounded by what he guessed was about twenty men.

"I need you men to accompany me to my campsite before the Indians attack there."

"Are you crazy?" one of the hunters asked. "You see what they done to George?"

"Not me, brother," said another. "Man'd have to be a loon to ride out there. 'Sides, most of our horses are grazing. We figured we was safe with you soldier boys here." He spat tobacco juice into the dirt. "Guess we was wrong."

Baldwin seethed. "Goddam civilians!" he muttered, then scanned the men again. "Where's Dixon?" he barked.

The spitter spoke up again. "Out there. Reckon he thought it was safe, too."

"Shit!" He spat the word. "Shit! Shit! Shit!"

Baldwin struggled to recover his composure. He'd have given an arm for a drink.

"Very well, the detail will ride back with me, pistols at the ready." He wheeled his horse. "Open that goddam gate!"

The patrol rushed through the gate and turned south toward the mesquite flat. Baldwin heard no shots, saw no sign of a battle. Was it over? Were his troops wiped out like Fetterman's command?

His horse was jaded from its long run and lathering badly. Baldwin was thinking of slowing to keep from killing the animal when he saw a lone rider approach from the campsite.

"What the hell are you doing, McGinty?" he asked, reining to a halt.

"Just come up to see what all the shootin' was about," the scout said calmly.

"The camp's not under attack? You've not seen the Indians?"

"Injuns?"

"Christ, man, where have you been the last half-hour?" Baldwin dismounted. "My horse is ruined. Give me yours, then take this detail back to the post. Tell them to expect the rest of the men."

"Sure thing, Lieutenant," McGinty replied, sliding to the ground.

Baldwin took the horse and galloped to his camp. Once there, he found just his scouts.

"Leach," he called, "where's Henely?"

"He's chasin' them Injuns we saw. Hell, there was a right bunch of 'em. Ol' Lieutenant Henely took off outta here like the devil hisself was after him with a pitchfork."

"Damn," Baldwin swore. "Which way, and how long ago?"

Leach pointed at the Canadian. "They went to the Canadian 'bout ten minutes ago. There's some sand hills on t'other side. If I was a Injun, that's where I'd head."

"I'm taking the Delawares and following Henely. I want you to make sure this camp is struck and moved to the stockade at Adobe Walls. Understand?"

"Yes, sir, Lieutenant. Good hunting, sir."

Baldwin nodded his acknowledgment and rode to find Falleaf. He ordered the chief to gather his men and follow him. Moments later, the twenty-one-man unit raced after the soldiers.

They caught Henely's detachment just on the other side of the Canadian River where they'd been delayed trying to find a safe way across.

Baldwin split the column into two platoons, placing half of the Delawares with each. He led one, Henely the other. Experience told him the Indians would scatter as soon as possible to hide their trail, but he hoped to catch them before they separated.

The war party had ridden several miles before Bear Tooth made his way toward Tall Elk and Porcupine.

"Follow me," the older warrior ordered.

Tall Elk saw the other Dog Soldiers moving to their groups. Soon the war party was split into six groups again. As they continued to flee the soldiers, Tall Elk watched each group break up into smaller sections.

After sending Coyote and Moonface to the southeast, Bear Tooth turned to Tall Elk. "You and Porcupine ride southwest."

The pair split from their group and rode away. Soon they were alone and out of earshot of any other warriors.

* * *

Baldwin signaled for a halt and sat staring at the last trail left by the enemy. Six sets of hoofprints disappeared in as many directions. He removed his hat and wiped his forehead with a sleeve.

The soldiers had tracked the Indians for two and a half hours. By the time Baldwin gave up, he'd watched the trail diminish and finally vanish. Along the way, smaller groups of tracks had left the main group and led in every direction, but Baldwin wasn't going to waste time on these. A large group of men was hard enough to find among the breaks, washes, and low-lying hills. Two or three individuals would be almost impossible.

"What do you think, Frank?" Henely asked.

"The hell with it," Baldwin replied. "Horses are about done in, anyway. Let the Indian have this day. We'll have ours tomorrow."

Porcupine brought his horse to a trot. "Slow down, Tall Elk. We might need speed again later."

They crossed now-familiar country, watching closely for signs of the soldiers. Tall Elk shook so badly, he was afraid he might unseat himself.

"Can you believe it?" Porcupine complained bitterly. "I had it right in my hand, and that stupid horse ruined it all!"

"At least you got the kill."

Porcupine grinned. "Did you see that? Did you see how I slipped the lance into the hunter? He never made a sound, just fell off his horse. What a story that will be for my children."

"Yes, it will be. Now you'll be getting your adult name."

"And you, too."

Tall Elk made a sour face. "How, Porcupine? I haven't killed anyone. I don't have any coups. I've never even been in a real war party. What will I tell at the dances? How I almost got a white man in a wagon? How I almost killed a buffalo hunter?"

"Your time will come, Tall Elk. I bet that when you get your first trophy, you'll at least be able to hang on to it."

"It wasn't your fault the horse pulled free."

Porcupine smiled ruefully. "I was so excited, I forgot to wrap its reins around my hand."

"You were excited?" Tall Elk asked bleakly.

"Of course. The thunder of the ponies' hooves. My heart pounding like it would burst through my chest." He stopped and looked at his friend. "Why? Weren't you?"

"No!" Tall Elk cried. "I was terrified! I heard the sound of the soldiers and kept expecting bullets to crash through my body. I feared my horse would stumble, and I'd be captured. It wasn't fun."

Porcupine reined to a halt. "Let's stop here and make camp," he said. "Those soldiers will never find us."

The column arrived back at Adobe Walls in the middle of the afternoon, hot, tired, and thirsty. The remaining scouts and the post's inhabitants crowded around them, asking questions.

Baldwin slowly climbed from his horse and held up his hands for silence.

"Please, gentlemen. There isn't much to tell. We chased the Indians for about two hours, then lost the trail in the hills. You know how they are about scattering. Now if you don't mind, I'd like a cool drink and some shade."

He handed his reins to a private and walked toward the store. A row of pickets lined the top of the gate.

Neatly arranged, one to a stake, were a dozen heads. Empty-socketed eyes stared down at him while lipless mouths grinned. All were clearly Indian except one, and this appeared to be a black man.

"Them's the ones that didn't get away," a hunter said. "We figured maybe it'd serve as a warning to others."

Baldwin said nothing and continued his journey to the store. Once inside, he was amazed to see small shafts of sunlight pouring through a multitude of bullet holes in the walls. He blinked, trying to see in the dark building.

"My God," he said, slowly removing his hat. "It must have been hell inside here during the battle."

"Oh, it wasn't so bad, long as you kept your head down."

"Dixon? Is that you?"

"Yes, sir, Lieutenant Baldwin."

"Someone told me you were outside when the Indians attacked."

Dixon chuckled. "Both times. Only this time we was walking the battleground when we saw Huffman get his. Hell, we didn't have a gun between us, and the horses were too far away to reach.

"Then we saw you charge, and the Indians chase you. We heard the bugler and watched everybody ride off to the Canadian. By the time I could get to my horse, you were long gone, so I came on in to wait."

Baldwin found a bucket and drank several dippers full of cool spring water. He took one more and poured it over his head, enjoying the cold rush down his shirt. Refreshed, he replaced his hat.

"Well, Mr. Dixon, why don't you share your other adventure with me?"

Dixon led Baldwin out the front door of the store and pointed at the structure they'd just left.

"This here is the Myers and Leonard store. English-man named Fred Leonard ran it. Besides the store, there's a kitchen in the southwest corner where Old Man Keeler tried to poison his customers, and a stable big enough for about twenty head."

"This stockade, was it for defense?"

Dixon nodded. "More or less. Mostly it was used as a corral and for hide storage. Bat can tell you more about that. He was working for Fred at the time."

Baldwin gazed at the towers mounted on three corners of the stockade. "What of those?" he asked.

" 'Bout as useful as teats on a boar. Course, I did hear one fellow say the Indians enjoyed them."

They continued their journey to the end of the compound.

"That building over there," Dixon said, pointing to a twenty-foot-square picket structure, "is where Tom O'Keefe did his smithin'. That long, narrow sod house next to it was Hanrahan's saloon. That's where I was during the heavy fighting."

"You were in the saloon?"

"Not at first. It was hot as hell that night. We had a little rain the day before, but that just made it hotter. I parked my wagons out in front of Hanrahan's, reckoned I'd get me some shut-eye under one of them and an early start. 'Long about two in the morning, I heard a crack. Sounded like a rifle shot. Then I saw people runnin' from the saloon. When I got there, Hanrahan said the ridgepole cracked." Dixon paused and looked across the valley. "Y'know, we pulled on that pole like hell the next day. Seemed sound to me."

"So, do you think it was a shot you heard?"

Dixon shrugged. "I don't know. There's been lotsa talk since then about what it was and what it wasn't. But to make a long story short, we had repairs made in a couple of hours. By then it was close to daylight, and I decided to stay up and get an even earlier start.

"I remember Billy Ogg passing me on his way to gather the teams. Then I saw him running back my way. Behind him was nothing but Indians."

"Which way did they attack from?" Baldwin asked.

"From out of the sun," Dixon replied; then he pointed toward the Canadian. "They came across the valley from those trees. Well, you can believe I hauled my ass to the saloon. Did manage to get off a shot though."

"Hit anything?"

Dixon stared at Baldwin. "All I saw that morning was Indians, horses, and more Indians. If I did, I never knew it."

"I understand only three white men died in the fight."

"Yes, sir, that's true." He pointed at the Myers and Leonard compound. "One young fellow was shot through the lungs in Fred's store. Then two others, brothers, were trapped in a wagon out front. We buried them just on the other side of the store. In fact, we put George Huffman over there, too."

Dixon started toward the last structure at the post.

"This is the Rath store. Come noon, we were low on bullets, so Hanrahan and me hightailed it over here. Folks inside wouldn't let me leave. The only woman here was in this store, and the men were afraid the Indians would tear the place apart to get her."

"Did they?"

Dixon shook his head. "Far as I know, they never knew she was there."

Baldwin stopped and looked at the four buildings that made Adobe Walls. He tried to imagine the noise, the sheer terror of the trapped hunters and merchants.

Looking closer at the Rath store, he saw a structure on the top.

"Is that a lookout tower?" he asked.

"Yep, we put that up there the second day, I believe."

"Is that where you made that long shot from?"

"Nope, that was from the front window there. As I recall, it was the third day we'd been cooped up and picked at by the Indians. I saw ten, maybe fifteen riders on that bluff to the east."

Baldwin pointed to a low rise about five hundred yards away. "That one?"

"No, sir, the far one. It's almost a mile off."

Baldwin regarded Dixon with new respect. "What happened?"

"Not much really. I saw them up there, and I was feeling testy, so I popped off a round." Dixon chuckled. "I figure the only man more surprised than me was that Indian I hit."

After dinner, Baldwin strode through the store, calling people together.

"Gentlemen, I'd like to know your plans."

A hunter spoke up. "I don't know about the others, but I'm goin' with you."

"And you are?"

"Robinson, Tobe Robinson. It was my partner that got killed this morning. You cain't pay me enough to stay."

The others in the room murmured their agreement. Baldwin raised his hands, and they fell silent.

"I would like you men to reconsider. From what I've seen here, this post is well fortified. You've already seen that a handful of men can hold off hundreds of Indians. You have provisions for at least two months, and I can leave you as much ammunition as you desire."

He watched the faces of the men around him. Most looked skeptical, but he saw a few nod slowly.

"I want you to know how important this location is," he added quickly. "Your post sits right on the Canadian River, only three miles from where it joins White Deer Creek. That place where the rivers meet is the only decent ford for miles."

Robinson bit his lip. "I don't know, Lieutenant. Let me and the boys jaw it around tonight, and we'll give you an answer in the morning. Fair enough?"

Baldwin nodded. "Fair enough."

Tall Elk tore off a bite of jerky with his teeth. As he chewed, he stared at the campfire. "I wonder what your new name will be," he said.

Porcupine shrugged and tossed a twig into the flames. "I hope it's good. Something the girls will like." He frowned. "But you should be getting yours, too."

Tall Elk sighed. "Porcupine, you've killed an enemy—up close, no less. You have earned your name, even without the war party. Coyote did, too, and so will I."

"I still don't like it. We should be named together. We should enter the Dog Soldier Society at the same time."

Tall Elk smiled. "Actually, I've been thinking about joining the Bowstrings."

"What? Those old men? Isn't your father a Dog Soldier like mine? Have you told him you want to be a Bowstring?"

"I haven't decided yet. Many of our council members are Bowstrings—"

"But our greatest warriors have always been Dogs," Porcupine interrupted. "I think you've been in the sun too long. Go soak your head in the creek. Maybe then you'll stop this crazy talk."

"I don't know. . . ."

"And do you know who's a Bowstring? Moon Butt, that's who. So you see, you can't join. You're too skinny."

Tall Elk laughed. "And you're crazy. You should be one of the dog men. They need crazy men like you."

"Maybe I will," Porcupine said, staring into the night sky. "Maybe I will wear the dog rope and stake myself to the ground." He stood, raised his hands to the sky, and intoned, "Let all who see, know that I am here and will fight until dead or victorious." He looked at Tall Elk and grinned. "Pretty good, huh?"

"Go to sleep, mighty warrior. We have to find our people before you can get your rope."

"Bah, that's nothing. While the soldiers stumble around, we'll rejoin Red Wolf and Bear Tooth. Then we are back on the warpath."

THIRTEEN

Baldwin awoke feeling well rested. He wasn't sure if it was exhaustion or the stockade around him that made him sleep so deeply. Whatever the case, he was grateful for the rest—and in a good mood.

He opened his saddlebag and took out paper, pen, and ink. Using his journal as a makeshift desktop, he started a letter to Allie, carefully dating it August 20, 1874. He told her of the attack on the hunters and subsequent chase through the sand hills. He was careful to omit that he and only four others had attacked a large group of Indians. Some matters were best left unsaid until after the campaign.

Knowing Allie craved stories of action and bravery, he decided to wait until evening to finish the letter. There was no telling what might happen today.

He slid the unfinished missive between the pages of his journal, then headed across the corral to Clark's wagon for breakfast.

Bacon fried in a large iron skillet. He knew the Dutch oven held baking biscuits. Behind the coffeepot, on a hook, hung the black kettle—Clark's bean pot. Baldwin cautiously leaned over the cauldron. Through the boiling brown water, he saw the occasional bean. *Damn.*

"Good mawnin', Lieutenant," Clark said, as he came around the end of the wagon. "Is you eatin'?"

"Yes, sir, I believe I am, Mr. Clark." Baldwin stared at the pot. "But I think I'll just have some bacon and a biscuit."

"Coffee?"

"Of course."

Clark fished bacon from the grease and plopped it on Baldwin's plate. He opened the Dutch oven and took out a golden biscuit, then filled a cup with fresh coffee.

"I sho wish we had us some butter and preserves. Breakfast just ain't breakfast without eggs, butter, and preserves."

Baldwin smiled. "How true, but we do have breakfast beans."

Clark quickly glanced at Baldwin; then a slow smile creased his face. "Sho nuff, Lieutenant. You want a plateful?"

Baldwin turned and started for the store. "No, thank you, Mr. Clark."

"Enjoy the meal, sir!" the cook called.

"Thank you, sir," Baldwin replied.

A hush fell over the store as Baldwin stepped through the door. Hunters, soldiers, and scouts lined the walls and sat in any space available. Most had plates of army food. All stared at him; then some of the soldiers scrambled to their feet.

"Relax, gentlemen," Baldwin said with a smile. "We'll not stand on formality here." Baldwin noticed that none of the Delaware were present. "Where's Cottontail and the others?" he asked to no one in particular.

"Out front," a red-bearded hunter said. "We sorta let 'em know we'd had enough Injuns for now."

Baldwin let the comment pass, not wishing to start

trouble. He needed these men to stay and man Adobe Walls as a resupply camp for Miles's column.

He glanced around the room. "Have you decided whether to stay?"

The spitter from the day before left his trademark on the floor. "We're goin'. What with the fight here in June and yesterday, and Injun sign everywhere, it ain't worth it."

Baldwin glanced from face to face. "Is this how you all feel?"

Murmurs of assent filled the room. Baldwin knew better than to waste time arguing his point. These were selfish, small-minded men.

"All right, you can ride with us, but there are a couple of rules you should know." He looked at the spitter. "You will obey my orders at all times." Then to the hunter Robinson. "If we engage the enemy, you will fight with my men. If you fail to do so, I will shoot you myself."

Baldwin strode across the store. Holding his plate and cup in one hand, he opened the front door with the other, then turned back.

"One other thing," he said, staring at the red-bearded hunter, "if you lay a hand on one of my Delawares, I'll stake your sorry ass to the plains and leave you for the buzzards!"

Baldwin's column and the hunters left Adobe Walls and traveled all morning under clear skies. They rode east, following the Canadian, and keeping to the shade of the cottonwood trees as much as possible. When the land was too broken for the wagon to follow, the column was forced into the sunlight. The only water available lay in the almost dry riverbed, a dark red slurry.

"Pardon me, Lieutenant, gotta minute?"

Baldwin nodded, and one of the hunters rode up beside him.

"Name's Wilson, Lemuel Wilson. Most folks call me Lem."

Baldwin looked straight ahead. "What can I do for you, Mr. Wilson?"

"Well, sir, I been thinkin.' I don't rightly know what I aim to do, now that I cain't hunt. I don't really know nothin' else but tracking and such." Wilson paused and took a deep breath. "And anyway, if'n you don't mind, I'd like to join your outfit—as a scout, that is."

As Baldwin opened his mouth, Wilson hurriedly continued, "Now, I know you got your dander up about the way them Delawares was treated. I had no part of that. I don't mind them fellers none." Wilson grinned. "Hell, I don't hate all you Yankees just 'cause some of you tried to kill me."

The grin fell, replaced by a look of uncertainty.

"So, that's about it," he said hesitantly.

Baldwin coolly regarded the hunter. His first thought had been to refuse him, but there was something about the man. Maybe it was in the way he'd look him in the eye. It may have been his plain, open face. Whatever the man had, Baldwin found himself warming to him.

"All right, Mr. Wilson. You can have the job."

"Thanks, Lieutenant." Wilson paused, then said in a quieter voice, "Can I ask you a question?"

"Certainly."

"Well, it's about that feller—what's his name? Rabbit? Bunny?"

"Cottontail?"

Wilson smiled. "Yes, sir, that's him. Is he all there? I swear he's the damnedest Injun I ever saw."

Baldwin laughed. "Cottontail fancies himself a terror to both red and white men."

"Is he dangerous?"

"Only to himself. Now I have a question for you."

"Shoot."

"It's past noon, and I know most of the canteens have to be near empty. Do you know if there's any water around here fit to drink?"

Wilson pulled off his hat and scratched his head. "Well," he said, replacing the hat, "as I recall there's a little creek up here called the Guyena. Most of the time, water's good there. I can hunt it up, if you want."

"In a moment." Baldwin reined to a halt and called, "Mr. Dixon."

Dixon rode over to Baldwin and Wilson.

Baldwin said, "Mr. Wilson says he knows of a stream near here called Guyena Creek. You've hunted this country; know of it?"

Dixon turned to Wilson. "We're close to where Tommy and Dave got killed. Right, Lem?"

Wilson nodded.

Dixon looked at Baldwin. "We can find it."

"Good. Then I want you each to take another man and look for it. Which direction is it?"

Wilson pointed to the east. "She empties into the Canadian up there. Course, we might have to head upstream a mite for fresh water."

Baldwin nodded. "One team will ride due east, along the river; the other southeast. Fire one shot when you find the creek. Two when you find fresh water."

"Look, Porcupine—up there."

Porcupine gazed into the sky, where large black birds circled lazily. "Something's dead."

"Let's go see."

Porcupine stared at Tall Elk. "Why?"

"Why not? Maybe it's a *veho* hunter struck down by a buffalo. Maybe he's not dead yet. You know the buzzards. Not everything they eat has died completely. And if he's alive, we can count coup!" Tall Elk's voice rose with excitement. "He might have horses, guns, knives. Who knows what?"

"Might be a coyote," Porcupine muttered.

"I heard that! Aren't you the one who always wants to go on an adventure? Is this the same warrior who rode by my side through our village? Did I see you carry—?"

"Enough!" Porcupine barked. "If you must see this thing, then let's go."

A few minutes later, Tall Elk slumped in his saddle and stared dejectedly at the bloated corpse of a coyote. He sighed. "I will never count coup," he said morosely. "I'll never take a scalp, never capture horses, never get close to Crow Woman."

"Cheer up, Tall Elk. Soon we'll be back with Red Wolf. Then we'll fight the white men, and you'll get many scalps and ponies. Crow Woman will see you as a great warrior."

"You really think so?" Tall Elk asked with hope in his voice.

Porcupine laughed. "Of course! That's what women like: scalps and ponies."

Tall Elk straightened. "Then what are we waiting for?"

"Wait a minute, great warrior. I'm hungry. If I remember right, there's a stream near here. Let's kill a rabbit, maybe even a skunk, and eat."

Porcupine led the way to a small, clear stream splashing between narrow banks. At one side was a sandy washout. Tall Elk tied the horses to some nearby sagebrush and dropped their blankets on the sand. He built a small fire while Porcupine hunted for game. Porcupine returned with a small rabbit, which he quickly dressed and put on the fire.

Tall Elk waited impatiently for the meat to cook. He wasn't particularly hungry, but he knew Porcupine would not move on until after the meal. Silently, he urged the meat to cook faster.

"Quit staring at the fire, Tall Elk. It won't get any hotter."

Tall Elk grunted and sat back. In spite of his eagerness to get back to the rest of the scouts, he started to relax. The day was hot and dry; the stream cool, the water fresh. Had the water been deeper, he might have taken a swim.

"You're right, Porcupine. There really is no hurry. Maybe I'll take a nap after we eat. It'll be much easier to ride later."

Porcupine chuckled and rose.

"Where are you going?"

"To get some sticks by that stump," Porcupine said, with a wide grin. "The sooner we eat, the sooner you'll win Crow Woman."

Tall Elk watched Porcupine gather wood. He heard a sound, but before he could ask Porcupine if he'd heard anything, he saw the white man.

What happened next, Tall Elk would never be able to explain.

The image of the white man was seared into his mind. He sat a chestnut mare. He wore a brown hat, had yellow hair and mustache. Above, blue eyes widened in surprise; below, lips slightly open.

Porcupine stood, not six feet from the white man. The man's expression turned to one of terror, curiously mirrored in Porcupine's face.

Porcupine dropped his sticks and grabbed for his knife. The white man grabbed for his pistol.

Both weapons came free.

A bright yellow flower erupted from the pistol's barrel.

A bright red flower erupted from Porcupine's chest.

Porcupine's eyes bulged, mouth open in surprise. He flew backward and landed on the ground.

Tall Elk bolted.

He crashed through bushes, unaware of cuts and scratches. He never heard the sound of the pistol, but would never forget the angry zip and zing of the bullets as they cut through the underbrush. Soon more hornets joined, many more. More than one gun could spit out.

Tall Elk finally broke into clear land. Exhausted and weakened by grief, he dropped to his knees and waited for the soldiers to kill him.

Baldwin rode to the scene of the shooting at a full gallop. As he arrived, he saw Wilson standing over a fallen Indian. Dixon, Charley Morrow, and McGinty were still mounted, holding smoking pistols.

"He's dead, Lieutenant," Wilson said.

Baldwin dismounted and walked to the body.

He groaned. "My God, he's just a boy."

Wilson looked at Baldwin wide-eyed. "I had to do it, Lieutenant. He went for his knife. Jesus, we wasn't more'n six feet apart. I had to do it. It was either him or me. Jesus, I had to do it."

Baldwin laid a hand on Wilson's shoulder. "It's all right, Lem. Now put your gun away."

Dixon said, "He's not alone. Just as we got here, we heard another buck heading through the bushes."

"Probably another boy," Baldwin said quietly, then louder. "Oh, well. What's done is done. Let's get out of here."

"Hey, Lem, get you a scalp," a voice called.

Baldwin glanced up sharply, but couldn't identify the speaker.

"No one goes near that boy. We do not make war

on children." He remounted and turned his horse. "Sergeant Lamont!" he bellowed.

The sergeant, short and thin with a bright red handlebar mustache, rode forward. His bearing spoke discipline.

He saluted Baldwin. "Aye, Lieutenant," he said with a Scottish accent.

"Sergeant, I want you to take two men and guard this body for the next fifteen minutes."

"Aye, sir."

"I want you to shoot anyone who comes near it, understood?"

"Very good, sir. It'll be a pleasure to shoot the scavengin' dog," Lamont said, looking at the hunters from Adobe Walls. "They'll get no joy from comin' here, sir. I'll see to that."

Baldwin nodded, then turned his horse toward the stream. "I don't know if you can hear me," he said loudly. "I don't know if you speak my language. The United States Army does not wage war against children. My man had no desire to kill this boy. But what is done cannot be undone, so we will leave you everything you see. My men will be watching over your friend for a few minutes; then they will depart as well." He looked at the slain boy. "Take him home."

"Oh my God, Lieutenant," McGinty said slowly. "Look to the south."

Baldwin gazed in the indicated direction, and his heart almost stopped. A huge, white dust cloud boiled along the horizon. "What the hell is that? Another dust storm?"

"No, sir. If I had to guess, it might be Injuns comin' to see what the shootin' was all about."

Baldwin bit his lip. "Do you think it's the same ones we chased yesterday?"

"Could be."

Baldwin glanced back at the body, then returned his attention to the cloud. "Well, this is wonderful! Not only are they equal to us in strength, they have the added impetus that we've slain one of their children."

He scanned the riverbanks. "Damn it, we've no cover!"

Dixon pulled his revolver. "We ain't got the time for talk. I can already hear 'em. They'll break through that dirt any minute now."

Baldwin nodded. "Lem, mount up!" he shouted. "The rest of you, ready your weapons! When the Indians are close, we will charge. Maybe the surprise will buy us enough time to find cover."

Baldwin stared at the dust cloud, licking suddenly dry lips. His heart pounded; his breathing rapid and shallow. He was frightened, but very excited. He remembered the same feeling as he watched the Rebels charge his position at the Stones River Bridge, the sheer exhilaration of a warrior awaiting combat.

He saw movement along the cloud's edge. Dark shapes too far away and obscured to recognize. One broke free. Then another.

"Aw, shit!" Dixon swore. "They're buffalo!"

The stampeding bison turned at the river's edge and ran past the soldiers. Over the thunder of the hooves came the sound of grunts and snorts. The animals continued their flight unchecked until they disappeared from view, leaving Baldwin's column covered in choking dust.

Coughing, Baldwin pulled his neckerchief over his nose. "You're the expert, Dixon. Do you think the Indians did this?"

Dixon wiped dirt from his eyes, and grinned. "Hell, no, Lieutenant. We probably spooked them shooting at that Indian."

"Then why did they come *this* way?"

The scout shrugged. "Buffalo run, they run."

Finding Dixon's answer frustrating and useless, Baldwin fumed quietly until the dirt settled. He lowered his neckerchief, removed his hat, and slapped at the dust that covered him.

"Sergeant Lamont," he called, "gather your detail." He turned back to his scout. "Mr. Dixon, will you kindly lead us downstream?"

When he'd heard the white man's voice, Tall Elk crept back through the brush. Hidden in the bushes, he watched the men on the other side of the stream. The soldier who talked was tall and mounted on a large horse. His words seemed sad.

How strange, Tall Elk thought, *that a warrior would mourn the death of his enemy. He would make a very bad Cheyenne.*

He almost laughed aloud when he saw the soldiers' reaction to the buffalo. Porcupine was right. These *vehos* knew nothing about the Cheyenne, and even less about buffalo. The thought of his dead friend brought tears to Tall Elk's eyes. He choked off a sob, knowing any sound could get him killed.

Covered in the same dirt as the soldiers, Tall Elk watched them ride away, leaving three of their number behind. One was short and had a red mustache. He sat straight in the saddle, his eyes always on the move, constantly scrutinizing his surroundings. There would be no catching this one off guard. He was both a warrior and a chief.

His companions were another story. They slumped in their saddles. One whined like the camp dogs begging for a bite. Tall Elk smiled bitterly. *Easy prey.*

He had no idea how long the soldiers would remain, but he would wait, too. Porcupine deserved the proper songs and the proper burial. Tall Elk would not go home alone.

One of the soldiers slid off his horse and approached Porcupine's body. He bent and stared. Then he reached for the eagle claw necklace Porcupine's father had given him.

The chief said something, but was answered curtly by the man on the ground. Again the chief spoke, his words louder and harsher. Tall Elk didn't need to understand what was said to know what was happening.

The soldier grabbed for the necklace; the chief drew his pistol. He cocked the weapon and leveled it at the other man. He spoke in a soft voice.

The soldier's eyes widened, then narrowed. He spat out a single angry word, rose, and climbed back on his horse. He said the word again, but the chief just laughed. Waving the pistol at the soldier, he pointed downstream. Slowly, the trio left.

Tall Elk waited, thinking *veho* may be weaving a web to catch him. Finally, he decided it was safe.

He walked across the stream and retrieved Porcupine's knife and blanket. Tears rolled off his nose as he slid the knife into its sheath. He sniffed and took a deep, shuddering breath. Then he gently wrapped his friend in the blanket and carried him to the tethered horses.

Now, he gathered strength for the more difficult job. He lifted the body and draped it over Porcupine's horse, securing it with a spare horsehair rope he had.

He leaned against the horse and wept, allowing the pain and grief to flow unabated. He cried for the death of his friend, the death of a warrior, the death of a part of the People. He didn't care who heard him or what they might say. Tall Elk felt as though his heart had been ripped from his body.

He snuffled and wiped his eyes, then gathered his

own possessions and prepared to leave. As he worked, he found his grief replaced by a cold, deep anger. Not the crazy rage of the suicide boys who attacked the enemy naked and defenseless, but a calculating, seething desire for vengeance.

Mounted on his own pony, Tall Elk grabbed the reins of Porcupine's horse and led the animal away. There would come a time for repayment.

The column marched another six miles before Lamont and the detail caught up. Baldwin immediately called for a halt, and they made camp. Dinner was the usual—dinner beans. Baldwin ate little, spoke less.

He retired early and wrote his report and diary entry. Then he took out the letter to Allie. He read what he'd written earlier that day. The words were excited and joyous, nothing like his present mood. He dipped the pen in the ink bottle and jotted carelessly.

Had another fight today. Killed one Indian, lost no men.

Baldwin regarded the terse statement of fact. He should have written *slaughtered a child today.*

He shoved the letter back into his bag.

Porcupine was buried as a warrior.

Carefully washed and dressed in white buckskin leggings and war shirt, with new moccasins, beaded in the old way with porcupine quills. His hair was braided, wrapped in ermine, and tied with scarlet ribbons. They painted his face as that of a Dog Soldier, the warrior society he planned to join.

They wrapped Porcupine in a fresh, wet buffalo hide, tightly bound with rawhide thongs. The process was repeated with several more hides, then the body gently placed on a travois in preparation for the funeral.

Porcupine's father walked at the head of the procession leading his son's horse. His hair was unbraided. He wore only a breechclout, war shirt, and moccasins. His legs were slashed from the knees down in long vertical cuts. He carried Porcupine's medicine bag, quiver and arrows, and other personal possessions his son would need in the next life.

The horse was dressed in mourning as well, its mane and tail cut short and bright red spots painted all over its body.

Porcupine's mother came next, riding the horse that dragged the bier. A blanket covered her body, even her head, so only her eyes showed. She carried Porcupine's lance. Behind her were Porcupine's friends and the rest of the people.

A short distance from the camp, Tall Elk and some of the other young men had erected a scaffold. It was made of four strong poles long enough to keep scavengers at bay. Atop the frame sat a platform of intertwined branches tied with rawhide.

Tall Elk watched the funeral from the crest of a nearby hillock. The procession moved slowly to the burial site. Porcupine's friends lifted him from the travois and carried him to the scaffold, placing his feet toward the rising sun. There he was lashed into place.

Porcupine's father loosened one of the travois poles, and fastened his son's lance, quiver, and medicine bag to it. Then the pole was tied to one corner of the scaffold.

As he intoned a prayer for his son's safe passage to the next world, mourners began to drift back toward the campsite. Soon only Porcupine's parents remained.

His father finished praying, turned, and walked away, leading Porcupine's horse.

That the warrior had not slain the animal surprised

Tall Elk. While not unheard of, it was a very unusual act.

Porcupine's mother climbed from her horse and approached the scaffold. She dropped to her knees and cried, calling Porcupine's name over and over. She wailed and lamented, piteously asking why her son was dead. She drew her knife, and laying her hand on one of the scaffold supports, brought it down hard.

Her screech unnerved Tall Elk. He knew she had just severed the tip of one of her fingers, or perhaps an entire finger. Again the knife blade rose and fell. Another shriek cut its way across the prairie.

Tall Elk shuddered. The woman could have been his mother. It could have been her fingers lying in the grass. Why had he lived? Why had the soldiers not hunted him down? So many things made no sense anymore.

He nudged his horse into a walk and rode toward the scaffold. As he approached, Porcupine's mother covered her face, peeking at him through a fold in the blanket.

"I know your pain is great," he said gently. "I feel like I've lost a brother. I don't know what to do."

"You have done much, Tall Elk," she said in a flat monotone. "You brought him to his people."

A tear rolled down Tall Elk's cheek. "I've done nothing!" he cried. "I should have fought! I should have attacked the soldiers to avenge Por—your son's death."

Porcupine's mother rose, slowly and awkwardly, and faced him.

"Foolish child," she said bitterly, "would you have died for such a reason? Isn't it enough that one boy is dead, that you would throw away your life as well?"

"But he must be avenged!"

The woman stumbled forward, bloody hand outstretched. "Look, child warrior! Look at my hand. Is this the fate you wish your mother?"

Tall Elk backed his horse away, terrified by the woman's ferocity. He wheeled his mount and hurried toward the campsite.

"Run away!" the woman screamed behind him. "Run and hide in your tipi. Live to tell stories about my son." Her voice cracked with grief. "My son! My son!"

As Tall Elk galloped across the land, he heard the wail begin again. Its sound was like icy water pouring down his back. He kicked his pony harder and harder, urging it on to greater speed.

FOURTEEN

The ember glowed a fiery red as Tall Elk blew on it. He touched it to the tobacco and slowly drew on the pipe stem. Stifling a cough, he raised the pipe toward the sun that rode low on the horizon.

"Grandfather Buffalo, it was you who showed me the coming of the white soldiers. Now they have killed my friend."

Tall Elk lowered the pipe, smoked, and raised it again.

"Grandfather Buffalo, I have come to ask how I may help my people."

He lowered the pipe again.

Tall Elk sat at the edge of the highest bluff near the village. Below him, he saw tipis glowing red in the sunset light. As the sun sank, blackness crept across the land.

Directions played a vital part in the People's lives. The sun was born in the east and died in the west. Then the monsters appeared, free to prey on any caught in the open, until the moon rose and offered its protection. The demons could be avoided, and Grandfather Buffalo had told him that a fight was unavoidable, so the threat could not come from the east or west.

If that's true, he thought, *then where is the real enemy?*

The north! The idea struck him like a blow. *The north is where Old Man Winter lives. Each year he drives the sun to the south. Then he comes and makes everything white. He kills the earth until the sun is strong enough to bring back the summer.*

Tall Elk looked to the north. Suddenly, far away and near the horizon, a bright, white star shot into the sky. It lingered a moment, then fell to the earth.

White.

The color of winter.

The color of death.

The setting sun painted the sky in magnificent shades of red, pink, and orange. Long strands of gray and purple cloud rode low on the horizon, like locomotive smoke. Shadows of men on horseback stretched twenty feet long, like thin black centaurs crossing the plains.

As the temperature dropped, soldiers removed their hats to enjoy the bit of cool breeze from the southwest. Buzzing insects retired for the night, and chirruping crickets took their place. Far to the east a lone coyote sounded his high, keening wail.

Baldwin barely noticed as day sank into night. His attention was fixed on a series of small bright lights in the distance. Gauging from the wagon ruts the column had followed throughout the day, he guessed he was approaching Miles's supply train.

As he drew nearer, he saw the tall, conical Sibley tents. The eighteen-foot-wide tipilike structures, left over from the war, housed as many as twenty men. Scattered among the Sibleys were small two-man pup tents.

Sixty wagons encircling the tents and campfires served as both a defensive perimeter and a corral for the mules. Baldwin saw shapes gathered at cook pots and milling around the shelters and sentries standing guard between wagons.

At hailing distance, Baldwin signaled his column to halt.

"Hallo, the camp!" he called.

In the distance a voice answered, "Advance and be recognized."

Baldwin rode forward slowly. "I am Lieutenant Baldwin, chief of scouts for General Miles. I am accompanied by my scouts, a cavalry detachment, and civilians from Adobe Walls."

He stopped in front of a young Fifth Infantry private. The soldier looked Baldwin over closely, then lowered his rifle and saluted.

"Good evening, sir. If you'll give us a minute, we'll move a wagon and let you through." The private turned toward one of the fires. "Hey, Davy," he called. "Grab Harry and Smitty, and help me move a wagon."

Men ran forward and pushed the wagon out of the circle to make an opening for the column.

Baldwin turned in his saddle. "Mr. Henely, bring the men forward."

He turned back and walked his horse inside, toward the camp's center and largest fire. Bedrolls lay scattered around the blaze, the teamsters seeming to prefer sleeping in the open.

As he approached, a thin, bowlegged man walked toward him.

"Evenin', Lieutenant," he said. "Name's Callahan. I'm the wagon master."

Baldwin dismounted and offered his hand. "Good to meet you, Mr. Callahan. How far are we from the main column?" In the faint light, Callahan's features were obscured, except for his long handlebar mustache.

" 'Bout a day. Miles pushed hard to get here, but mules and foot soldiers can't keep up with horses. Last word we got was that he was waiting on you."

"We saw the signal rockets last night."

Callahan grunted. "Hell, I bet every redskin within a hunnert miles of here seen 'em."

As if to illustrate Callahan's complaint a bright white star burst into life to the south.

"Ah, shit! Here we go again," the wagon master said.

"Mr. Baldwin?"

"Yes?" Baldwin glanced up from his paperwork. "Oh, it's you. Robinson, right?"

"Yessir," Robinson answered, then nodded at his companion. "And this here's Ira Wing. We was wonderin' if you might be lookin' to take on some new men."

Baldwin put away the report he was preparing and rose to his feet. "You know the men I dismissed?" he asked.

Both men nodded.

"You know why I discharged them from service?"

"We can guess," Wing said in a rich baritone.

Baldwin regarded the hunter and saw the small smile, the twinkle in his eye. He decided he liked Wing. He turned his attention to Robinson.

"If I hire you, it is with the understanding that this is not your opportunity to get even for what happened to your friend. Our purpose here is not to destroy the Indians, but to drive them back to the reservation and make them stay."

Robinson frowned and narrowed his eyes. "But if they fight, we get to fight back. Right?"

"Yes . . ."

"That's good enough for me," the hunter said, nodding his head vigorously. "I don't figure no Injun what's got balls enough to ride up on a man the way they did George is gonna turn tail and run from soldiers."

Baldwin looked from man to man, and shook his head. "You've ridden with us these past few days, seen the kind of life we live, and you still want to join?"

"Yes, sir," the pair said in unison.

"Well"—Baldwin smiled—"it's against my better judgment to hire on men who are obviously crazy." He stuck out his right hand. "But welcome to the United States Army, gentlemen."

"Thank you, sir," Robinson said, shaking the hand.

Wing took his turn. "You won't have to worry about us, Lieutenant."

The performance started with the crack of a whip as the first wagon pulled out of the circle and headed south.

Each wagon played its part. Some rumbled, others groaned. Occasional accents came from the squeal of a wheel short on grease or the thud of one driving over a rock. Counterpoint was the jingle and clink of harnesses and doubletrees. Above it all rang the obligato shouts and curses of the drivers. It was a cacophonous symphony Baldwin was positive could be heard twenty miles away.

Baldwin's column walked alongside the wagon train for a short time; then, taking advantage of the cooler morning temperature, he ordered the unit into a lope. He waved to Callahan as they passed the lead wagon. They soon left the train far behind. His force now comprised just the scouts and Henely's detachment. The hunters, discharged scouts, and Mr. Clark remained behind.

Henely's troops were arranged in columns of two,

with the scouts riding single file on either side. Baldwin had sent three teams of scouts and trackers ahead, one with instructions to ride until they found Miles's column and then report back. Two more teams he deployed rearward to watch the column flanks and give warning of possible attack. Free of the cook's wagon, the scouts were able to range over more broken country at greater speed.

By midmorning, as the temperature climbed steadily upward, Baldwin slowed to a trot. By noon, the temperature was well over a hundred degrees. The column reached a small stand of cottonwood trees where Baldwin called a stop for a meal and to let the horses cool off.

The heat was unbearable. It seemed almost a living entity that gained strength as it sucked the life out of everything it touched. Flowers wilted; grass yellowed; water holes dried up or turned into alkaline sludge pits.

The column trudged over the open prairie, the only shade the shadows of man and horse. Hardest hit were the soldiers, whose uniforms included heavy woolen coats. Many had shed their coats, and white galluses showed plainly over dirty white or faded red long-handled underwear. Some doused themselves with water to mitigate the searing heat. Others just rode, heads bowed, seeming oblivious to their surroundings.

Sweat ran down Baldwin's face and dripped off the end of his nose. His lips were cracked and swollen. He'd rolled up his sleeves to the elbows. Salt-rimmed sweat rings had formed around his arms and along his belt line.

He was convinced they had descended into hell. He rode with his eyes closed, allowing the horse to follow the others.

"Is it just me or does it seem a tad warm?"

Baldwin opened one eye and gazed at Cottontail, now riding beside him.

"Your grasp of the obvious amazes me," he said thickly.

Cottontail, stripped to the waist, laughed, sweat slinging from his beard. "Cheer up, Lieutenant. The general's camp is in sight."

Baldwin looked across the land. "Where?"

"Look to the south and a little east. See them trees? If you look real hard, you can see tall white tents."

Baldwin blinked rapidly trying to clear his vision. He stared where Cottontail had indicated and saw a thin green line in the distance. Heat waves obscured any detail.

"I reckon I'll just have to take your word for it." He straightened and started to roll down his sleeves.

"I got even better news," Cottontail said, grinning. "There's a spring between us and them. Lots of cool water." Cottontail shifted in his saddle. "Yes, sir, way I see it, them pony soldiers has had a long time to rest up. Now we look like something that's been drug around by a bear and chewed on. Course, if we was to stop and clean up a mite . . ."

Baldwin chuckled. "Don't you know that'd chap ol' Compton's butt?" He licked his cracked lips and nodded. "Great idea, Chumumte. Why don't you take us to that spring?"

As the sun started to set, the column crossed the valley at a canter, the cavalry guidon snapping in the breeze. As they neared the camp, Baldwin heard the sentries announce them. Soldiers poured from the tents and cheered as they rode through the camp.

Baldwin called a halt at Miles's tent. He dismounted and smartly saluted his commander.

Miles returned the salute with a wave of his cigar. His eyes roamed the column's ranks, noting the sharp deportment, proper dress, and semiclean uniforms. He regarded them with raised eyebrows. A small smile tugged at his lips. "Lieutenant Baldwin, it's good to have you back. Why don't you dismiss your men while we talk."

Baldwin performed a precision about-face. "Mr. Henely, take command of the column. Find a suitable campsite, and dismiss the men."

"Yes, sir." Henely rode forward and held out his left hand. "Your reins, sir."

Baldwin handed them over.

"Baldwin's scouts!" Henely bellowed, straightening in the saddle. "Columns of two, forward at a walk. Ho-o-o!" He saluted. "Lieutenant." He looked at Miles. "General."

Henely dropped the salute, turned his mount, and followed his column.

Miles reentered his tent with Baldwin close behind. Once inside, the general started to chuckle.

"My God, that was priceless!" he said, laughing. "You come riding out of hell's own fire fresh as a daisy, snapping salutes, and spouting orders. Then Henely and his 'Baldwin's scouts.' " Miles cackled. "I bet Compton shit himself on that one."

The lieutenant smiled, but said nothing.

Miles picked up his cigar box, offering it to Baldwin. "Help yourself, son, then grab a chair."

Miles returned to his desk. "Were you successful?"

Baldwin lit the cigar and dropped the match in an ashtray. "More or less, sir. We saw many Indian scouts following us. Then we chased a pretty big war party, but lost their trail southwest of Adobe Walls. Finally, one of my white scouts jumped a couple of bucks near a place I called Chicken Creek. He killed one, but the other got away."

Miles sat back and stroked his mustache. "You realize that Indian was the first casualty I've heard about in this campaign. In fact, I'll give good odds that yours was the first kill in this whole damn war." He grinned. "You did good, very good."

He stood. "After you see to your men, write me a complete report. Of course, Henely will have to return to his company and normal duties."

Baldwin rose. "Yes, sir, I'd figured that. It's a shame, though. Austin's a good man, much better than many of his superiors."

"I'll keep that in mind, Frank. War, ambition, and talent made me a general. Nothing says the same can't happen to Henely—or you."

FIFTEEN

The trio rode several hours in silence until Bear Tooth signaled the others to stop. He dismounted and ran up a tall hill. Standing at its crest, he gazed down the other side for a while, then motioned Tall Elk and Moonface to join him.

The youths jumped from their horses and raced up the hill. The summit ended abruptly in a cliff. Tall Elk looked over the edge to see a river, a stand of trees, and the large white tipis of the soldiers. The tipis covered the area near the water. To one side was a long string of horses.

Men moved about the camp. Some chopped wood, while others cooked or tended to the horses. The rest just sat and talked. Except for the lack of women and children, Tall Elk could have been watching his own village.

"Look at all the soldiers," Moonface whispered.

Bear Tooth nodded. "Many more than I expected," he said grimly. "Tell me, Tall Elk, are these the soldiers who attacked you?"

"No. I don't think so. There weren't nearly so many, and other white men and Indians rode with them."

"Maybe there is more than one war party that seeks us," Bear Tooth said. "Moonface, ride back and tell the council what we have seen. Tell them Tall Elk and I will wait here until the soldiers move. Then we will return."

He gazed at the youth. "Be careful."

Moonface rose, his chest puffed out. "I won't fail you, Bear Tooth."

Moonface raced down the back side of the bluff. Soon only a thin dust trail betrayed his presence and that quickly faded.

Bear Tooth signaled for Tall Elk to follow. "We will hunt now, and cook some meat. Maybe gather some berries. Then we'll come back and see what the soldiers do next."

The blast put a violent end to Baldwin's slumber. He pitched from his bunk onto the dirt floor of his tent.

Rebels, he thought wildly.

He grabbed his pistol. Bootless and in his underwear, he bolted through the tent flaps, sleep-blurred eyes frantically searching for the enemy.

In the distance, an off-key bugle played To the Colors. Baldwin slowly lowered the gun.

"What the hell was that?" Cottontail asked, running up to him.

Baldwin took a deep breath, trying to slow his heart. "They're posting the colors," he replied.

"What?"

"The flag, Chumumte. Each morning they run the flag up the pole and salute it with the Parrot—" He caught the blank look on Cottontail's face. "The cannon. They'll do it again tonight when the flag comes down."

Disgust twisted Cottontail's features. "Good God Almighty," he said, "they got to scare a man half to death to raise a flag? No damn wonder we can't catch any Indians!" He spun on his heel and stomped off.

Baldwin returned to his tent to dress.

The mess line was in the middle of the camp. Baldwin took his place at the end and patiently waited his turn. Looking around, he saw how the camp had been clearly segregated.

He reached for a coffee cup and plate.

"Good mawnin', Lieutenant!"

Baldwin glanced at the smiling face of Nigger Clark. "Why, good morning to you, Mr. Clark."

"You eatin' beans?"

Baldwin held out the plate. "Wouldn't miss it for the world."

Clark grinned and filled Baldwin's plate. He nudged the young cook's helper next to him. "Boy, fetch the lieutenant a couple of them fresh biscuits from the Dutch oven." As the helper hurried away, he handed the plate back to Baldwin. "You enjoy the meal, suh."

"Thank you, Mr. Clark."

The helper came running back, juggling two hot biscuits, which he plopped in the middle of the beans. The officer nodded his thanks and moved down the line for coffee. Plate and cup filled, Baldwin walked back to where his men camped.

The scouts had started a small fire and set a pot on it. They took turns stirring it.

Baldwin sat beside Cottontail. "Whatcha cooking?"

"Jerky soup," Cottontail answered morosely.

"Why? Army food not good enough?"

Cottontail shrugged.

Baldwin looked at the others sitting around the fire. "What's going on?"

McFadden spoke up. "We were told to keep to ourselves, eat our own food."

"Bullshit! As long as you're drawing army pay, you're entitled to army chow."

"That's what I tried to tell 'em," McFadden complained. "Only they wasn't listenin'."

"Who was it? Officers or enlisted?"

"It was both," Dixon said bitterly. "That same bunch that rode over the day before we left Dodge."

"Tupper," Baldwin muttered. He stood and kicked the pot over, putting out the fire. "You men get in line for breakfast. Any enlisted man gives you grief, whip his ass. That's an order! Any officer accosts you, send him to me."

"You gonna whip his butt, Lieutenant?" McFadden asked.

"No, sir, that's the general's job."

The scouts hurried away. Baldwin shoveled beans into his mouth, wanting to get breakfast out of the way so he could get to reports. As he drained his coffee cup, he saw George Baird coming his way with two civilians. He set the plate on the ground.

"Morning, George."

"Frank. These are two new scouts for you."

"Morning, men." He held out his hand to the older man. "Frank Baldwin, chief of scouts."

"I'm Ben Clarke, and this here boy's Amos Chapman. He's interpreter at Camp Supply."

Baldwin shook Chapman's hand. "Amos. What languages do you speak?"

"Cheyenne, mostly," Chapman replied. "But I know a little Kiowa and Comanch, too."

"Good. That should come in handy later." Baldwin bent and picked up his plate and cup. "Well, welcome to the outfit, boys. You men had breakfast yet?"

* * *

When Miles announced a dinner in Baldwin's honor, none was more surprised than Baldwin himself. He'd been under the impression that all rations were cut to a minimum to extend the campaign as long as possible. But more than surprised, he was pleased that his efforts had been recognized, especially since the honor probably rankled the horse soldiers.

When Baldwin arrived, he saw the guests were arranged by rank. The higher the rank, the closer to Miles. The notable exception to this was the presence of Scout Marshall, seated to Miles's left. As he walked into the tent, he was led to the only chair available—at Miles's right hand. Next to him sat a red-faced and sullen Major Compton.

Baird stepped to the table and called the men to attention as Miles entered from his private quarters. The general waved the others to sit. Baird smiled at Baldwin before moving down the table to the lieutenants' section.

"Welcome to you all," Miles said. He turned to the steward. "Let's eat."

The meal was roast antelope, potatoes, and bread, washed down with coffee. Conversation was kept light and to a minimum. When cigars and brandy were offered, Baldwin accepted the first, but declined the second. Soon Miles's tent was filled with blue smoke.

"Gentlemen," the general said, rising and lifting his glass, "I give you First Lieutenant Frank Baldwin, Fifth United States Infantry."

The others joined the toast, the cavalry officers reluctantly.

Miles emptied his glass and signaled his steward to refill it. "Now, Frank, here, has the distinction of being the only man on this campaign to have met and killed the enemy. This is very good for us, and Mr. Marshall has promised to get the story told."

"Indeed I will, General Miles," Marshall said. He addressed the table at large. "I shall see to it that all of the United States knows of the exploits of Baldwin's scouts"—he glanced at Miles—"as performed under your command, of course."

"Thank you, Mr. Marshall." Miles faced Baldwin. "Frank, why don't you tell us about your encounter with the Indians."

For the next hour, Baldwin related the events of his patrol at Adobe Walls. When he talked about the killing at Chicken Creek, he was careful to leave out the boy's age or the argument over trophies.

"When you came across the Indians at Chicken Creek, did you find any others?" asked Major Biddle.

"No, sir. I think they were a part of the raiding party we'd chased the day before."

Tupper looked up at Baldwin, bleary-eyed. "So you don't know if there were others present?"

"No, sir, Captain. Other than the one who ran away, that is."

"And you didn't search him out?"

"No, sir, there was no advantage in risking my men to catch one Indian. My orders were to seek out and report on hostile forces, not wage war on—"

Baldwin paused. He had almost said "children." He drew a breath and continued, "I thought it prudent to continue my scout and report back to General Miles."

Tupper unsteadily gained his feet. Baldwin could see the man was almost reeling.

Is that what I look like when I'm drunk? he thought.

"Well, sir," Tupper said, raising his glass of brandy, "I salute you on your prudence." He drank half. "An' as long as we're salutin' Injun lovers and their red niggers, I propose a toast to a *real* soldier. To Gen'l George Armstrong Custer, the greatest sojer to sit a saddle!"

He emptied the glass, turned, and stumbled from the tent.

All eyes turned to Miles. His only indication of anger was red creeping up his neck.

"Major Compton, I believe that man is under your command," he said quietly.

Compton felt the blush burn his cheeks. "Yes, sir, Colonel, er, General Miles. He's one of my company commanders, and I can assure you—"

Miles interrupted, "What you can assure me, Major, is that his punishment is suitable for the embarrassment he has caused this command." He faced the scout. "My apologies, Mr. Marshall. It is neither proper nor common for the army to air its laundry in front of civilians. I trust this will not tarnish your view of the command."

Marshall waved his cigar. "Think nothing of it, sir. The army cannot be held accountable for the actions of one man. I am of the conviction that we will keep this matter in the family, so to speak."

"Thank you. Your graciousness is most appreciated." Miles faced the table. "Gentlemen, I must leave to write reports for Washington. Stay if you care to." He rose, and the others rose as well. "Good night."

After a chorus of "Good nights," the officers started to leave. As Baldwin stepped through the tent, he was met by Compton and Captain McLellan.

"Lieutenant," Compton said, "I'd like to apologize for Tupper. I really can't imagine what got into the man. Usually he's a very good officer."

"That's all right, Major," Baldwin said lightly. "I guess he can't respect someone like me: I didn't go to the academy, was a recruiting officer, and my scouts are . . ." He scratched his head. "Oh, yes, red and white niggers."

* * *

Tall Elk and Bear Tooth worked their way around the bluff, closer to the camp of the white men and Indians.

"Those are the men who attacked us at the stream," Tall Elk whispered.

Bear Tooth nodded, then moved on. They skirted the circle of wagons and headed for the horse herd.

Once in the clear, Bear Tooth looked anxiously around. "I don't know why I let you talk me into this," he said quietly.

"Because you knew I'd come alone."

Bear Tooth grabbed Tall Elk's arm. "Listen, we can still go back. *Veho* hasn't seen us yet."

"Nonsense. I'm going on."

"But what if we're killed? Who will tell the People what the soldiers are doing?"

Tall Elk frowned. "Go back, then. If I'm killed, then there's still one to watch the soldiers."

Bear Tooth thought a moment, then sighed and shook his head. "No, it is better that we stay together. We can fight better, and perhaps even escape. Besides, I don't want to try to explain this to Red Wolf."

"Good," Tall Elk said loudly. "Now, I want to look at the ones nearer the river."

"Shh!" Bear Tooth hissed. "They will hear us and come over here."

"No, they won't. I watched them all day. These men stomp around and shout. They will only be suspicious if we're *too* quiet."

"I don't know . . . but I still think you're crazy." Bear Tooth smiled ruefully. "Me, too, I guess."

As they approached the remuda, a sleek black stallion caught Tall Elk's eye.

"Look at that one, Bear Tooth. See how his coat shines in the moonlight. This is the one I want."

"What? Do you think you can just take him? He is

probably a soldier's war pony. Why else would they keep them separate from the rest? No one will let you walk away with another man's warhorse."

Tall Elk walked over to the horse and stroked its neck. He was prepared to slip off its halter when he saw a guard walking their way. The man shouted.

"Hello, white man," Tall Elk said. "I just came to steal this horse, and my friend wants your scalp. What do you think?"

The soldier repeated his previous statement and motioned for them to leave.

"Oh, you don't want me to have this one? Why? I walked all the way down here just for this horse. You have so many."

The guard slid the rifle from his shoulder and aimed it at the warriors. Tall Elk got the message.

"All right, we'll leave this one alone for now." He pointed at the herd. "Is it all right if we steal some of these?"

The soldier said nothing. He just waved them away with the rifle.

Tall Elk and Bear Tooth sauntered to the herd and looked it over.

"No wonder they don't want these," Bear Tooth said. "What kind of warrior would ride such a beast?"

They quickly searched the herd, each picking an animal. Leading the horses, they walked through the wagon camp, Tall Elk keeping a running monologue on the physical attributes of the men they passed. They were met with blank stares.

Once outside the first encampment, they veered to the left, and quickly disappeared into the gloom. Neither spoke until they returned to their camp.

"Did you see that?" Tall Elk crowed. "Not a shot; not a word in anger."

"I'll admit you were right," Bear Tooth said, "but we could have been killed."

"Yet we weren't. Those men killed my friend. When we get back to the others, we'll tell them the story of the theft of these horses. Then they'll know the white man is no match for the Cheyenne. Then they'll be willing to take the fight to the soldiers."

He suddenly grinned. "But first we go back. I want that stallion."

SIXTEEN

"Baldwin! You son of a bitch! I want that stallion!"

Baldwin rolled off his cot. Tupper stood outside the tent, hands on hips, a murderous look in his eyes.

"What can I do for you, Captain?" Baldwin asked.

"You goddamn know what you can do! Your thievin' redskins stole my horse. I want it back."

"How do you know it was *my* men?"

"Because the remuda sentry saw them. He said that he ran off two Indians near my horse. I'm warning you, Baldwin, I want that animal returned immediately."

Baldwin decided he'd had enough. "Captain Tupper, you and your men are more than welcome to search my camp. If you find the horse, you can do what you will with the thief. On the other hand, if you don't, I expect an apology to my men."

"Bullshit! I intend to find my horse if I have to horse-whip every red nigger here."

Baldwin felt the presence of his men behind him. He heard the distinctive click of a hammer being pulled back, followed by another, then more. He was trying to think of a way to ease the situation when Henely rode up at a gallop.

"Captain Tupper!" he called. "General Miles has ordered Officers' Call at nine o'clock. Word is he's holding a surprise inspection."

Tupper glared at Henely, then turned a poisonous eye toward Baldwin. "This isn't over, Lieutenant. I serve notice now that I will shoot any man I see astride that horse. Mark my words!"

As the captain stalked away, Henely dismounted and walked to Baldwin. "He's fit to be tied, Frank. That's two horses in as many weeks."

Baldwin grinned and shook his head. "I know. I know." He turned his head. "Cottontail!"

"No, sir, not one finger. I swear it, Lieutenant. Not that he didn't have it comin'."

"I believe him, Austin," Baldwin said, looking back at the lieutenant. "Are you sure it was Indians that sentry saw?"

"Yes, sir. I talked to him myself. He says there were two, dressed in buckskin. One older and one that looked like a kid."

"A kid? Look at these men, Austin. You think any of them could be mistaken for a child? And the only one who likes buckskin is—oh my God! Do you know what this means?"

Henely thought a moment; then his jaw dropped open. "Sweet Jesus, they were hostiles!"

Baldwin started to laugh. He was joined by the scouts, particularly the Delawares.

Henely saw nothing funny in the situation. "Really, Frank, I don't think that's at all a proper response. We have been *infiltrated*."

"And brazenly to boot!" Baldwin wiped tears away. "Done in by our own prejudices. They knew we think all Indians look alike, and played us." He scanned the hills around them. "Of course, the man who thought that up ought to be easy enough to spot."

"Really? Why?"

"He'll be the one with balls the size of six-pound shot."

"Bear Tooth!" Tall Elk called excitedly. "Bear Tooth, come look. The soldiers are leaving."

The elder warrior raised his head and looked at his companion. Then he slowly sat up, stretched, and yawned. He moved closer to the edge of the bluff, scratching his chest.

"I wondered what all the noise was," he said, then yawned again. "Those soldiers couldn't sneak up on a rock. And look at all those wagons! What do they need them for?" He sneered. "Real warriors don't sleep in tipis on the warpath."

"They're coming our way," Tall Elk said as he watched the soldiers splash through the river.

Bear Tooth nodded. "They'll probably find our camp, but that may be good."

"Why?"

"Because then they will see our tracks and the tracks of the horses we stole. We'll ride to the west first, leave a big trail. *Veho* might think that we're riding to warn the others and follow us. We'll lead him all over the plains until he gives up and goes home."

Tall Elk stood, still watching the men below. "What if he doesn't quit?"

"Then we will do what we can to slow him down."

As Tall Elk turned to leave, he saw a lone rider approaching from the south. He and Bear Tooth continued down the bluff to their camp. By the time they reached it, the rider had arrived.

"I came back as soon as I could," Moonface said. "I told Chief Stone Calf about the soldiers. He decided to move further southwest to get to the plains faster." He saw the four extra horses. "Where'd you get these?"

"We stole them," Bear Tooth said, mounting his horse.

"From who?"

Tall Elk climbed on his pony and grabbed the leads of his new horses. "From the soldiers, Moonface," he said.

"Oh." Moonface watched as Tall Elk and Bear Tooth slowly walked their mounts away. "I thought we were just supposed to watch the soldiers."

"We are," Bear Tooth called over his shoulder. "That's where we're going now."

"Oh." Moonface frowned. "Then where are the soldiers?"

Tall Elk turned in the saddle. "Coming this way."

Moonface glanced about nervously. "This way?" he asked, his voice cracking.

"If you wait much longer," Tall Elk continued, "you can ask them where they plan to camp tonight."

Baldwin watched as two Delaware trackers rode back to the column and fell in beside Falleaf. They spoke quietly for several seconds and one pointed to a bluff they'd rounded earlier. Falleaf then made his way to Baldwin.

"Scouts say they find fresh camp back at hill," Falleaf said.

"How old?"

The chief shrugged. "Maybe one day. Say they see tracks go south. White man's horses and Indian ponies. Two, maybe three riders."

"Let's go take a look," Baldwin said.

He turned his mount and, in the company of Falleaf and the original two trackers, rode back to the bluff. They found a recently abandoned campsite with ashes in a small fire pit. The trackers spread out and searched the brush, while Falleaf examined the area near the fire.

"Footprint," he said. "Moccasin. Over there another, smaller." He followed the prints a short distance up the hill. "Trail leads to the top."

Baldwin grunted. "So that's where they watched us from. Any closer and they might as well have come on into camp."

Falleaf chuckled. "They did." He moved to the edge of the campsite.

"Strange," he muttered, then turned to Baldwin. "Three riders leave, but only two walk on ground."

A shout came from the distance.

"Him found tracks coming into camp," Falleaf translated, then grinned. "Third rider." Then he listened as the scout continued. "Say found where six horses stay. Lotsa horseshit. Some new."

The other tracker called from his position.

"Other scout find Indian shit, real new." Falleaf grinned. "Him say other Indian shit stink."

Baldwin smiled. "Let's get back to the column. Send one of your men to see where that trail leads."

Falleaf shouted orders while remounting, and one of the trackers rode off westward. Baldwin started back with the remaining scouts.

The Delaware assigned to follow the three riders paralleled the column's course. Then he changed direction and angled back to the east, crossing the column's trail. By the time Baldwin was back with his men, the tracker had turned south again and was almost out of sight.

Cottontail pulled up next to Baldwin. "Well, whoever they are, they're sure bird-doggin' us."

"I never thought we'd catch anybody by surprise," Baldwin replied. "What bothers me is how easy it is to follow that trail. You see that tracker? He never had to stop or double back. Kind of makes a body wonder if we're being led along."

"I certainly wouldn't put it past no sneaky Injun to try."

"Mr. McFadden," Baldwin called, "please find the general and tell him that we're going to head southwest to Gageby Creek and from there to Sweetwater Creek."

"Yes, sir, Lieutenant." McFadden spurred his horse.

Baldwin turned his mount, signaling for the others to follow.

Bear Tooth pursed his lips as he watched the soldiers split into two groups. "Moonface, what did Stone Calf tell you?"

"That he was leading the tribe southwest."

"Then we'll follow these men. They are few and can move quickly. More importantly, they just took the same path as Stone Calf."

The three warriors returned to their horses and hurried away. After several miles, Bear Tooth stopped at the foot of one of three buttes.

"From these we will be able to see the whole valley," he said. "Moonface, climb this one. Signal when you see the soldiers. Then ride toward the next one."

As Moonface dismounted, Bear Tooth and Tall Elk galloped to the next butte. Bear Tooth took the extra horses and rode on.

Tall Elk climbed to the top of the rise. He saw the creek, the narrow valley it had carved, and the outcropping where Moonface waited. He sat cross-legged and played with the small mirror Bear Tooth had given him. He gazed at his reflection, wondering if someone like Crow Woman would find him attractive.

Not bad, he thought. Then he scowled, frowned, and

put the mirror down. *What's the use? I still look like a child.*

Tall Elk stared at the clouds awhile, watching their ever-changing shapes form one or another animal. He watched a line of ants as they marched along like a tiny patrol of red soldiers. He watched a hawk as it circled, swooped, climbed, circled, and swooped again in its search for prey. All these things he saw, and he was interested in none. He longed to be off this hill and back among his people.

A flash of light from the north.

Another flash, then another.

Tall Elk jumped to his feet, and frantically wiggled his mirror, hoping the sun would send his reply. A single silver wink answered. Feeling content, Tall Elk sauntered down the backside of the butte to await Moonface.

Moments later, Tall Elk saw a thin trail of dust heading his way. Soon Moonface appeared, a broad smile on his face.

"I saw them, Tall Elk," he called. "I saw them!"

"Good. Now, keep riding this same direction, and you'll find Bear Tooth. I'll catch up as soon as I see them."

Moonface nodded and rode away.

Tall Elk returned to his station. After several minutes, he wondered if Moonface had been seeing things. Then he spotted the first sign of dust. He waited only until he was sure of what he saw, then spun on his heel and signaled Bear Tooth. Two slow flashes replied. He quickly ran down the hill, mounted his pony, and rode. When he arrived at Bear Tooth's location, both the elder warrior and Moonface were waiting.

"The soldiers are less than a mile behind," Tall Elk said.

Bear Tooth nodded slowly. "You and Moonface find

some tall grass. Cut as much as you can carry, then bind it together with your spare ropes. When you've done that, return here."

Tall Elk grinned. They were going to leave the soldiers a gift.

Baldwin and his men moved slowly. He reined to a halt as his trackers stopped again to check the ground.

The heat had grown intolerable, rising in waves from the prairie. The constant wind blew grit into eyes already stinging from sweat.

Baldwin removed his sodden neckerchief and mopped his face. His lips were cracked and sore. He knew water would help, but hesitated to drink. Unlike the dirt, wind, and heat, water was in short supply.

His horse waggled its head and snorted, then stamped the ground as though eager to move on. Baldwin agreed. Anything was preferable to standing still.

"Well," he asked, "are there tracks or aren't there?"

Cottontail shrugged. "Oh, there's tracks. Old ones. Some of these been around so long, wind's mostly blowed them away. If we'd had any rain in the last month, there'd be nothing here."

"Damn!" Baldwin retied his neckerchief. "We'll keep marching upstream."

The scouts moved slowly, occasionally scanning the ground, but mostly watching the hills. They saw nothing as they passed the first hill, and were within a half mile of the second when Baldwin saw the flash. It was so small and quick, he was sure he would have missed it had he not been looking for it.

"Boys, let's mosey over to that last hill."

They turned from the river and drifted toward their target. When they neared the edge of the little valley, Dixon and Cottontail appeared from an arroyo.

"You see that, Lieutenant?" Dixon asked.

Baldwin nodded. "You find anything?"

"There's a fresh set of tracks between that first hill and the next one."

Baldwin paused a moment, feeling his excitement grow. "All right," he called, "we're going to cross this arroyo and ride over to the last hill. Once you're on the other side, draw your weapon, but keep to a trot. Last thing we need is someone's horse to keel over."

One by one, Baldwin's scouts rode down the arroyo and up and out onto the prairie. They formed a single column, moving quickly across the grass. As they rode, Baldwin shouted for two of the Delaware trackers to ride ahead and look for sign.

Near the hill, Baldwin spotted the Delaware who pointed due south as he approached. With a clear trail before him, he dispersed the scouts and followed. Within a half hour's time, the trail was noticeably fresher. Then he saw the smoke.

He called a halt and gazed at the dark smudges along the horizon.

"What's on fire?" he wondered aloud.

"It's the prairie," McFadden said. "It's an old Injun trick. Whenever he gets followed too close, he sets fire to the land. Not only does it make it damn near impossible to find him, he cheats our horses of feed."

"Think we can ride around it?" Baldwin asked McFadden.

"You can, but the longer this burns, the longer it's gonna take to pick up the trail again."

"Then we'll keep to our course."

The scouts again took up the chase. As they neared the prairie fire, they saw tall flames under thick smoke. Baldwin called another halt. The horses whinnied, snorted, and danced about.

"We're going to charge this blaze through there,"

he shouted, indicating an area with smaller flames. Then he pulled his neckerchief over his nose, and waved the scouts forward.

Bear Tooth, Tall Elk, and Moonface lay on a small rise anxiously watching the fire before them. They were upwind of the flames and smoke and enjoyed a clear view of the plains.

"Do you think it will stop the soldiers?" Moonface asked.

Bear Tooth shrugged. "If it doesn't go out before they get here. If they come at all."

Disappointed with Bear Tooth's answer, Tall Elk decided it was time to be more positive. "Of course, it'll stop them, Moonface. Would you ride through that? Do you think *veho* has the courage?"

Suddenly a rider broke through the flames at a full gallop. He wore a soldier's uniform and brandished a pistol. Immediately behind him, more men appeared. Once past the fire, they stopped, dismounted, and slapped at their bodies with their hats.

"Come, children," Bear Tooth said. "We must gather more grass."

Silently, the three slipped away and sprinted for their horses. They rode a mile before Bear Tooth reined to a stop.

"Quickly, cut some of the taller grass while I start a fire."

Tall Elk and Moonface jumped from their horses and pulled out their knives. They grabbed large handfuls of the knee-high grass and cut along the ground.

"Do we need our ropes again?" Moonface asked, sweat dripping from his round face.

"No, don't bother," Bear Tooth replied. "Just twist it together and bring it here."

Bear Tooth took each grass bundle and shoved one end into the small blaze.

"Take this torch," he ordered, "and run as far as you can setting the grass on fire."

The boys did as they were told and promptly returned to their horses. Bear Tooth was mounted and waiting.

Tall Elk watched the flames grow. "Do we wait to see if they turn back?"

"No," Bear Tooth answered, shaking his head. "Even if this fire stops them, they will return when it goes out. No matter what we do, we can't hide the path our people have taken, so now we have to warn Stone Calf that *veho* has found us."

Baldwin burst through the second wall of fire and into the open. He pulled off his hat and frantically beat his clothes and his horse's mane. The ground beneath him was scorched, and acrid smoke still rose from charred grass. He coughed and blinked rapidly to clear his watering eyes.

As the others came through, they gathered around Baldwin, repeating his actions. Cottontail was among the last. He rode up eyebrowless, singed beard smoking.

"If you think I'm going to do this again," he said, fixing a watery gaze on Baldwin, "you can go straight to hell!"

Baldwin chuckled, then coughed. "What happened to that great Indian stoicism you're supposed to be famous for?"

"Burnt off with my eyebrows." Cottontail gingerly rubbed the nude ridge above his eyes. "Damn! Now, folks'll think I'm a damn Comanch, for sure." He turned his horse and walked it toward the south. "All

I got to say," he called over his shoulder, "is that somebody owes me a drink. Man damn near sets hisself afire
deserves that much."

"I couldn't agree more," Baldwin replied quietly.
Then he turned south and joined the rest of his men.

Baldwin's trackers found the Indians' trail. He ordered the scouts into a trot. They rode through the
afternoon, trailing the Indians, who made no effort to
conceal their passage.

As the sun started its descent, Baldwin heard two signal shots in the distance. He ordered the scouts into a
lope until they reached the edge of an Indian encampment.

The site was huge. Hundreds of old campfires dotted
the landscape. To one side, over an acre of grass was
cropped to the soil and covered in horse droppings.
To the southwest, a massive swath cut through the prairie grass, trampled flat by thousands of feet.

The scouts quickly dispersed, searching the site for
anything useful. Baldwin walked his horse past long-
dead fires. He spotted an arrow in the grass, its shaft
broken just behind where the arrowhead should have
been. He found what looked like a child's doll, except
it had no head or right arm. He saw sticks that looked
as though they had been carved for canes, cast off bits
of clothing, utensils, and scraps of leather.

He felt sad, seeing his enemy as people for the first
time. As was true for most societies, the majority of the
population were not warriors, but women and children.
Of course, these were no ordinary women and children. He remembered the story of when the Texans
had tried to arrest the Comanche chiefs in San Anto-
nio. One of the soldiers had been killed by a twelve-
year-old's arrow. He also remembered tales of soldiers
attacked by squaws. He reminded himself that the Indians fought with no quarter.

"This here camp is old," Cottontail said. "Horse apples is all dried up, and we ain't seen anything other than cold ash."

Dixon appeared from the southwest.

"Those fellows we were following rode right into this camp. I went about a mile or so down that southwest trail, but no tracks came out either side."

"We chasin' them some more, Lieutenant?" Cottontail asked.

"Oh, hell no," Baldwin answered. "It doesn't matter whether they're five or fifty miles away, the men that set fire to the plains will find the rest of the tribe before we do. I'm not about to ride into *that* mess. We'll wait for the general to catch up, and let him decide what to do next."

Excitement permeated the air as Baldwin called his men together the morning of August 27, 1874.

"Gentlemen," he said, "we have our marching orders. We are to follow the trail we found near Sweetwater Creek. We will ride with minimal rations and as much ammunition as you feel comfortable with. If you see the enemy, come find me."

"What if the Injuns see us first?" Robinson asked.

McFadden called out, "You start fightin' 'em, and we'll catch up."

Several scouts chuckled, others grinned. They all knew the odds they faced.

Robinson snorted. "Any Injun chasin' me is gonna die."

"How, Tobe?" a voice asked.

"Broken neck," Masterson chimed in, "from slipping in the shit trail he leaves behind."

Robinson turned red and frowned, but as the others

laughed and slapped his back, he shrugged and offered a sheepish grin. "What can I say?"

Baldwin rose and stretched. "I hate to break up this tea party," he said, "but we've got work to do. Let's get mounted."

The scouts rode at a trot, quickly reaching the Indian campsite. They moved past the discarded items and swung onto the path the Cheyenne had left. Baldwin's confidence rose as three miles went by without any change in the trail.

His heart sank as he saw the wide path before him split. He knew it wouldn't be far before it separated into many small trails and disappeared. He chewed his lip and stared across the plains. Where would they go?

The Indians had several options. Their current course would lead them back to the Llano Estacado, the great Staked Plains of Texas and Indian Territory. Along the way, there were numerous canyons and breaks to hide in. One set of canyons he'd heard about were supposed to be thousands of feet deep. Once they were in there, he had no hope of finding them.

He halted the unit and gestured at Falleaf and McFadden.

"We have to locate the Indians before they reach the Staked Plains," he said. "I want you to divide the scouts into two-man teams, one Delaware and one white. You know who gets along and who doesn't. I'll take Cottontail with me.

"One team is to ride back to General Miles and tell him to meet us at Sweetwater Creek. The others are to pick one of these trails and follow it until they lose it or reach the Sweetwater. Unless I'm mistaken, the Indians will regroup somewhere, and I'll bet it's going to be near water."

After the teams were established, the men fanned out. Soon they began to disappear as one after another chose what he thought to be the best trail and followed it.

Baldwin and Cottontail rode slowly, closely examining the ground. They saw the prints of several horses and two long drag marks in the dirt.

"We'll take this one," Baldwin said. "They'll have a hard time hiding the travois tracks."

The trail led to the west along the creek, plainly visible.

The path remained clear until it reached dense grass, where it disappeared. Unsurprised, the scouts continued in the same direction. Within moments, they found a patch of sandy soil devoid of tracks.

"Damn!" Baldwin muttered. "Chumumte, ride ahead about a quarter of a mile, and see if you can pick up the trail again. I'll start circling here and see if they changed direction. If we don't find anything, we'll cross the creek and do the same on that side."

Baldwin turned his horse and started a wide, sweeping circle. He studied the grass intently for any sign of passage. Soon he was blinking sweat from his eyes. His vision blurred and he constantly had to wipe his face. After half an hour, he concluded the Indians didn't ride in the direction he was searching. He looked upstream and motioned Cottontail to cross over.

Baldwin forded the creek, and both men continued their search. He was studying what looked like trampled grass when he heard a whistle. In the distance, Cottontail waved his arms. Baldwin spurred his horse and hurried to the scout.

"I found them travois tracks again. Looks like they walked the creek a while, then come ashore here."

They followed the stream until the trail took a sharp turn to the right. The pair changed direction and continued their pursuit, quickly losing sight of Sweetwater Creek.

Within a mile, the land became more broken. Arroyos cut the path; the travois tracks disappeared and reappeared on the other side, suggesting that the entire apparatus had been lifted and carried across.

After dropping into a shallow valley, the trail led them up the side of a tall mesa.

Cresting the hill, Baldwin rode out on the wide, flat surface.

"Goddammit!" he shouted. "Son of a bitch!"

Not a hundred feet away lay an abandoned travois, a large rock tied between the poles.

Baldwin spied the general at the head of the column, as always, leading his mounted forces. The wagons and infantry were still several miles behind.

Baldwin slowly gained his feet and waited for his commander's arrival.

"Good evening, General," he said, saluting.

"Baldwin," Miles replied and returned the salute. He gazed around the campsite. "I hope you have some good news for me."

"Yes, sir, I believe so." He briefly reported the episode with the vanishing trails. "After I dispersed my men," he continued, "we followed several sets of tracks. They all eventually turned back to the south."

"Where are they going?" Miles muttered, rubbing the stubble on his chin.

"I think they're headed for the Red River. If you'll look at the map, General, you'll see that once there, they have two good locations to choose from: either west into a huge canyon or south again onto the Staked Plains."

"Neither choice bodes well for us," Miles said grimly.

"No, sir, on the plains, only they know where the water is, not to mention that we can be seen from miles away. The canyon is even worse. Not only will it shield them from our sight, but it affords them a perfect opportunity for ambush. Most of that area is uncharted. They can hide anywhere and strike in their own sweet time."

Miles grunted, and pulled a cigar from his uniform coat pocket. He bit off the cigar's end and spat it into the dirt. "In that case," he said, "our only choice is interception somewhere between the Red River and the plains, correct?" Baldwin nodded. "Can you do it?"

"Yes, sir, with a little luck. I figure he's no more than a day or two out."

"Good," Miles replied, lighting the cigar. "You do that, Baldwin. Find me my elusive red enemy."

SEVENTEEN

Steam hissed and billowed in a dense white cloud, filling the sweat lodge. Tall Elk, nude like the others, sat at the back. Sweat ran down his sides, and he watched it drip from his nose. His father sat next to him and his grandfather near the doorway.

"As the steam purifies your body with sweat," Gray Eagle said, "you must pray to cleanse your mind and spirit."

"Yes, Grandfather. But what shall I pray for?"

"The things that are proper: wisdom, strength, generosity."

Tall Elk pondered Gray Eagle's words. Wisdom came with age, so he prayed that the Great Spirit would keep his elk medicine strong so he could live a long time. He also prayed for Porcupine, hoping he was enjoying his new life. He prayed that, when the time came, he would have the strength to die as a proper Cheyenne warrior and bring no shame on his family. He asked for a generous heart—especially for those of the People he didn't like.

Even as he wished for these things, he wondered what he could do to show who he was, the man he had become. What deed could he perform that encompassed all the manly virtues of the Cheyenne? He raised his head as the thought struck him.

Of course, he thought. *It's so obvious.*

As the sun dipped low in the west, the Cheyenne gathered in front of Many Rivers's lodge. The Bow-string Society members carried bow lances, tall bows with a spear point on one end. The Wolves were there, too, the main chiefs displaying straight lances with eagle feathers. The Elks stood to one side, faces painted and carrying elk hoof rattles. The women dressed in white buckskin dresses and moccasins that exhibited their skills at bead work.

The People formed a great circle around Many Rivers, Gray Eagle, and Tall Elk. The three men wore their best clothes. Many Rivers carried his saw-toothed coup stick to signify his membership in the Dog Soldiers.

Tall Elk's hands were clammy. What name would Little Bird give him? As Many Rivers's oldest sister, she had the right to choose Tall Elk's new name.

The crowd grew quiet, and a shaman stepped forward. He offered smoke to the cardinal directions and asked that the spirits watch over the proceedings. He asked the Great Spirit to guide Little Bird so that she chose a name proper for a Cheyenne warrior.

Bear Tooth stepped into the circle, dressed in the full regalia of the Dog Soldiers. He carried a tall, crooked coup stick adorned with so many scalps it looked like a horse's mane.

"We are here to learn what Tall Elk's new name will be," Bear Tooth said. "But before that, I will tell you what he did to become a man."

As Bear Tooth recounted the story of stealing the soldiers' horses, Tall Elk glanced at those gathered around him. They stared at him, and he felt the weight of their expectations.

Normally, he'd have received his new name after participating in his first war party. But there had been none recently, so the People knew he had done something extraordinary, and waited to hear what.

He caught Crow Woman staring at him. When she noticed his look, she smiled slightly and lowered her eyelids. Tall Elk sucked in a long shuddering breath and stared at the ground.

"Not only did he steal these animals from under *veho's* nose," Bear Tooth continued, "but he later performed an act worthy of any chief."

Tall Elk stole a quick glance toward Crow Woman. She returned the look, unwavering. Tall Elk felt his knees weaken and feared he might collapse in front of everyone. He focused his attention on Bear Tooth.

"Recently, we have suffered the death of a young man," the older warrior said. "The mother's grief is great. She has cut her hair, gashed her legs, and severed her fingers. Tall Elk understood and felt her sadness, for this young man was his closest friend.

"He took the soldier's black stallion, one of the finest horses I have ever seen, and asked me to give it to the boy's mother. He told no one what he did, as was proper. He did not talk to the mother, asked for nothing in return. He gave up his best horse to soothe a grieving mother. No more could any man do, and it is for this that I say he has earned his new name. He has become a man."

The looks of admiration from the People bothered Tall Elk. He felt as though he was somehow made to appear superior to others. This was contrary to everything he'd been taught. Proper Cheyenne behavior precluded calling attention to oneself, especially if it made others look inferior.

Little Bird stepped forward. She gave Tall Elk a kind look and encouraging smile.

"Behold this young man," she said. "He is embarrassed that he is the center of attention. I say, hold your head high, Tall Elk. You have shown the traits of a man: cunning in tricking the white man, courage by walking into his camp, generosity by giving away your trophy."

Little Bird paced the circle slowly.

"Many names crossed my mind as I thought of you," she continued. "I thought of my father and his father, and the names they carried. I thought of other men who acted as bravely as you, men who will forever be remembered as great Cheyenne leaders. But the name I have chosen for you is new because you have done things no one has ever done before." She stopped and pointed at Tall Elk. "You will now be called Two Horses, so that all will remember the warrior who walked among the soldiers and took their animals."

The Cheyenne left shortly after daybreak. Immediately, they split into bands, then kindred groups, and finally, individual families.

The family units went in no specific direction, but generally moved to the southwest. By the end of the day, their paths changed, and they continued to a prearranged meeting place. Once together, the tribe selected a campsite and stopped. They prepared meals and erected tipis with minimal unpacking. After a good night's sleep, they struck and loaded the tipis, and the tribe moved on, only to again divide into family units.

While the Cheyenne trekked toward the Llano, a small party of men stayed behind to protect the families from attack. This band consisted mostly of young unmarried men, Two Horses among them, with a few seasoned warriors as leaders.

Now, he sat atop his hunting horse and scanned the horizon for any sign the soldiers were approaching.

"Tall Elk—I'm sorry, I mean, Two Horses."

"Don't worry, Moonface, I'm still trying to get used to it myself."

"I . . . I just wanted to say that what you did last night was a great thing. I'm sure that his mother was very pleased with the horse."

"It will not bring her son back," Two Horses said.

"True," Moonface replied. "But it was a gesture of respect and generosity. My father says that those are very important qualities for a man to have. He thinks that one day you might sit on the council."

Two Horses laughed. "Let me get used to being a man first."

Moonface stared across the prairie. "Do you think the soldiers will really come?"

"Yes, I do. The agent has told the council that we must come to the reservation or the soldiers will force us."

"Do you think they will?"

"They can try."

Two Horses waited through the day, but the soldiers did not come. He rode back to camp as the sun set, weary of sitting and doing nothing. He saw that the council had gathered again and walked his horse to the edge of the circle.

Stone Calf stood in the center. He rubbed his face and sighed. "It is not enough that we lead the whites astray. The travois trick is a good one, but for only the one time. What we must do is get to the Llano Estacado. The soldiers have never been able to find us there."

In the ensuing silence, Stone Calf returned to his seat. All eyes looked to White Owl, the oldest and most respected member of the council. It was said White Owl owned nothing, having given away his possessions to help the People. Wizened and frail as an autumn leaf, he rose slowly and regarded his fellow council members.

"Stone Calf speaks a great truth," he said in a tumbleweed-dry voice. "We must get our women and children to safety, but the warm days are nearly at an end. We have no meat stored for the cold times. Life on the plains in winter is harsh."

He shuffled to the center of the circle.

"I am old and do not wish to sleep on the open plains. The cold makes my knees hurt. Still we are faced with a formidable enemy and cannot fight him without the loss of many warriors. So I say we turn west, toward Palo Duro Canyon. Its walls will protect us and we will have the company of our Comanche and Kiowa friends."

After White Owl spoke, Two Horses turned his mount and started for his tipi. Whatever else might be said, the meeting was essentially over. Passing Moonface's father's lodge, he noticed the portly youth sitting on the ground eating a plum.

"You might as well start packing."

"Why?" Moonface asked, mouth stained with plum juice.

"Because we're going to the canyon tomorrow."

Moonface leaned forward. "What? I thought Stone Calf was leading us onto the Llano Estacado. Who said so?"

"White Owl," Two Horses said.

"Oh." Moonface grinned wryly. "Well, that's that."

Two Horses nodded. "I suppose. Of course, you could always go argue with White Owl."

Moonface sat back and took another bite of his

plum. "I don't think so. I'd just as soon face one of your *veho* soldiers."

Two Horses jumped as the big gun roared. He hated the sound of the thing and wondered what purpose it served.

"I wish they'd stop doing that," Moonface complained. "It scares the horses."

Two Horses nodded and rose. "The only good thing about it is that we know where they are every morning." He walked back to his pony, Moonface in tow.

Once mounted, Two Horses started toward his tribe's latest campground.

"Will they catch us?" Moonface asked.

"I don't know," Two Horses replied. "Today they are closer than they were yesterday. The small scouting party moves as swiftly as you or I, but the war party is slowed by the wagons and the walking warriors."

"Then you think we'll get away?"

Two Horses sighed. "I don't know. Sometimes I wish they would catch us."

"Why, Two Horses," Moonface asked, "do you want to fight? Is that it? They have the giant gun, you know. I've heard stories about that. The old ones say it can shoot holes right through a horse! Is that what you want? To face that gun?"

Two Horses regarded his companion. The past days' riding had shaven some of the softness from him. His face had started to take on the chiseled look of his father, but his chronic whining and complaining seemed to worsen as he matured.

"You know, Moonface, sometimes I think you listen to too many stories."

"What?" Moonface replied, shocked at the other's insulting remark. "How do you think we learn? From the old ones, that's how? They talk, we listen. That is what it means to be a child. Of course, now that you're a man, I don't guess you have to lis—"

"Quiet, Moonface!" Two Horses barked. He reined to a halt, and leaned forward. "Yes, I want to fight. I want to kill white soldiers because they kill our people. They are making us run and look afraid, and it brings shame to the Cheyenne. I want to kill these men to get even for Porcupine!"

Moonface's mouth dropped open and his eyes grew wide. He pointed at Two Horses. "You said his name!" he said in a horrified whisper. "He has not been dead a year, and you said his name."

"Porcupine, Porcupine, Porcupine! There, I said it again. A thousand curses upon me from the spirits! Grow up, Moonface. Porcupine's death was a great loss for our people. He was smart and strong and brave. He would have been one of our greatest warriors and chiefs, not like—"

Two Horses bit off the remark, but too late. He watched as Moonface's expression grew passive and aloof.

"Me?" the youth asked. "Moon Butt? The one too fat to ride his horse, who talks all the time, who should wear a dress?"

"No, that's not what I . . ." Two Horses let the lie die unuttered.

Moonface wheeled his horse and kicked it into a full gallop. As Two Horses helplessly watched, the boy who might have been his friend rode away, disappearing behind a cloud of dust. Two Horses sighed and shook his head, then once again returned his attention to the north.

"Where are you, *veho*?"

* * *

Baldwin looked across the vast, empty land, and cursed himself again for his brashness. He had all but promised Miles that he'd deliver the fleeing Indians in two days. Millions of acres to search with less than thirty men and a constantly disappearing trail. What was he thinking?

"Chumumte!" he bellowed. "You found me those goddamn Indians yet?"

Cottontail rode over, frowning. "My, oh, my, aren't we grouchy today? What's the matter, you and the old lady split the blanket?" He caught the murderous look on Baldwin's face. "What I mean to say, sir, is that we have not located nobody. I got the boys lookin' everywhere, but these here folks disappear like a dust devil."

"Baldwin!" a distant voice called.

Baldwin looked up as Falleaf rushed toward him.

"We find good trail!" he announced, then spoke rapidly in Delaware to Cottontail.

"Cap'n Falleaf says that Young Marten found a trail leadin' directly south."

"What's so special about that?" Baldwin snapped.

"If you'd give the man a minute, Lieutenant," Cottontail snapped back, "he just might tell me."

Baldwin took a deep breath and forced himself calm. "My apologies, Captain Falleaf. Please tell us what you know."

Falleaf spoke slower, never taking his eyes off Baldwin.

Great, the lieutenant thought, *now I've gone and made the old man mad.*

Cottontail spoke. "All right, Cap'n, I'll tell him." He faced Baldwin. "First off, Cap'n Falleaf says you shouldn't go promisin' the moon, 'cause most of the time you cain't deliver it."

"He said that?" Baldwin asked warily.

"Not in those words, but he knows what you told the general."

"Shit! How the hell does— Never mind. What else?"

"He says the feller that made that trail was movin' at full gallop. He wasn't turning, riding through rocks, or nothin', just making a beeline."

"Must have been something important for him to ride so recklessly," Baldwin mused.

Cottontail nodded. "Gets better, too. Young Marten backtracked the trail and saw it started just south of where we camped last night. He said there were two horses at first. They stopped; then one galloped off. The other rode a bit, then hid his tracks."

Baldwin smiled wearily. "I reckon this will be the best offer we get. Let's get that Young Marten back on the trail and follow him."

Two Horses charged across the plains until he saw the first of the rear guard. He frantically searched for Bear Tooth, finally locating the warrior near a stand of trees.

"Have you seen Moonface?"

Bear Tooth shook his head. "No, but I heard talk that he rushed in here like a winter storm, then rode out again. Why?"

"Because he is bringing the soldiers here!"

Bear Tooth's eyebrows raised.

"No, not on purpose," Two Horses said quickly. "In some ways, it's worse. We had an argument, and he rode away. He left a trail so clear, *anyone* could follow it. The soldier wolves found it and are riding this way."

Bear Tooth frowned. "That fool!" he said bitterly, then glanced at Two Horses. "Are they close?"

"Not really. They are riding at a trot and haven't reached last night's campsite yet."

Bear Tooth hurried to his horse and mounted. "You find Red Wolf," he said. "Tell him what you told me, then warn as many people as you can."

Two Horses quickly found his old leader and gave him the news. Red Wolf immediately ordered the rear guard to return to the tribe. As they approached the slow-moving mass of Cheyenne, Two Horses wondered if they were in time.

The tribe's ranks thinned as word spread. Valued possessions were cast aside for the sake of speed. Old people and children fell as they tried to keep up with the others. Panicked hands grabbed them and dragged them along. Soon Two Horses and a handful of other warriors found themselves alone on the prairie, the trails of fleeing Cheyenne being quickly blown away by the wind.

At Red Wolf's signal, the small party rode back to the north, back toward *veho*.

The scouts slowed as they approached the new camp-site. Once inside the site, they quickly split up and searched the area. Scattered among dead embers, they found more personal items. Baldwin saw buffalo hides, iron and brass pots, and bundles of cloth.

"It looks like we've got 'em on the run," he said to Cottontail.

"Maybe on the run, but not runnin' yet. Most of this stuff you see is what they like but can live without." He pointed at the hides. "They can shoot more buffalo. They can get hides for clothes, and bellies for pots."

He gazed around him. "But this here camp is fresh, a day old at the most, not like the others."

Young Marten rode up and spoke quickly to Cotton-tail. He pointed to the south, then pushed his hands out in front of him, fingers splayed.

"He says the trail he followed leads to a great big one farther on, but then it splits up like before. He says there's lots of stuff there, too."

"Very well, we'll do what we did the other day."

"Yes, sir, Lieutenant."

As Cottontail turned to leave, Baldwin saw Dixon sitting on his horse staring to the south.

Baldwin looked as well, but saw nothing other than a bluff. Still, something about Dixon's attitude bothered him. "Wait, Chumumte," he said.

"Hunh?" Cottontail reined in, then followed Baldwin's gaze and shuddered. "That boy gives me the willies."

The pair rode over to where Dixon waited.

"What is it, Mr. Dixon, feelin' Injun again?"

Dixon smiled and rubbed the nape of his neck. "As a matter of fact, I am," he said. "Not that it matters."

"Why?"

"If you take a gander at that cliff, you'll see."

Baldwin looked where Dixon indicated. He saw an Indian ride atop the bluff, then another and another, until about a dozen men lined the crest. One rode forward and raised a lance high over his head.

"What's he want, Cottontail?" Baldwin asked.

"Hell if I know, Lieutenant! I'm Delaware, remember?"

The Indian on the hill plunged the lance into the earth. It stood rigid, feathers along its shaft waving in the breeze.

"I've seen this before, Lieutenant," Dixon said. "It's like he's staking his ground, telling us to go no further unless we want to fight."

Baldwin stared at the lance and the Indian. "If we charge, will they fight?"

"That's what scares me," he replied. "Most Indians I've dealt with will fight only when the odds are on their side. Now, that tells me that those boys are real desperate and willing to die to slow us down, or there's a whole passel of 'em we cain't see."

"Cottontail?"

"Who the hell am I to argue with your medicine man? I don't know what it is about him and Injuns, but if he says leave, I'm ready."

As the three discussed what they saw, the other scouts had gathered around them. Baldwin turned to McFadden.

"You're a veteran of Indian campaigns. Do you know what those men on the hill are telling us?"

"Oh, I could guess, but whyn't you ask Amos? After all, those *are* Cheyenne up there."

"Mr. Chapman!" Baldwin called.

"Yes, sir?" Chapman rode forward.

"Scout McFadden tells me those Indians are Cheyenne."

"Yes, sir, I can tell by the shape of the war bonnets. I probably know most of them."

Baldwin pursed his lips. "So then you can tell us what they're doing?"

"Oh, sure. The fellow with the lance is a dog man. What you can't see is that he's got one end of a sash tied to that spear and the other hanging over his chest like a bandolier. He's telling us that he will stand where he is and fight until he's dead—or we are."

"Hmm. So is he looking to fight?"

Chapman shook his head. "I don't think so, Lieutenant. I think he wants to buy time for the rest of his people to get away. Likely as not, if we turn and ride off, he'll do the same."

"You sayin' he's a coward?" Robinson asked.

"Hell, no, Tobe. You ride up that hill, and he'll show what he's made of. He's just saying that now ain't the time or the place to settle up. When he's ready, you'll know it."

As the *veho* wolves rode away, Bear Tooth pulled Red Wolf's lance from the ground, freeing the war chief of his dog man pledge.

"I'm glad we didn't have to fight on this hill," Bear Tooth said wryly.

Red Wolf grinned. "So am I." He turned. "Tell me, Two Horses, are those the men who attacked you?"

Two Horses nodded. "I remember the tall one with the soldier clothes, and I recognized another who was not at the stream."

"Really?"

"Yes, he's a white man married to one of my cousins. They call him Amos."

"I know him," Bear Tooth said. "He is the one who always tells us what the whites say. I like that young man. It will be a sad day when I take his hair."

EIGHTEEN

To the Colors sounded through the cannon's fading roar. Baldwin couldn't believe Miles still saluted the flag each morning and night, but command decisions were not for him to question. He had more than enough of his own concerns.

Officers' Call sounded, and Baldwin rushed to Miles's tent. He was among the last to join the others waiting outside the general's quarters.

Baird stepped from the tent and called attention. Miles followed.

"At ease, gentlemen," the general said. "For those of you who do not know, Lieutenant Baldwin and his scouts are within striking distance of the Indians we've been chasing." He smiled. "Not bad for only eighteen days into the campaign. By the way, our Indians have been positively identified as Cheyennes." He raised his hands as murmurs ran through the crowd. "I know what you men are thinking. It's been said that it was the Cheyennes who killed the German family and took those little girls. Now, I don't know if those Cheyennes are our Cheyennes, but be careful when we get into their camp. I don't want to see *any* women or children shot—but God help the man that shoots a white child."

He paused to allow his warning to sink in.

"As to today's business, Baldwin is again to take the lead with his scouts. Since he saw hostiles yesterday, I'm detailing Lieutenant Henely to accompany him with a troop of cavalry. We are very close to engaging this enemy, so I want all soldiers in top condition. Good day, gentlemen."

Baird again called the men to attention as Miles left. Then he addressed the officers.

"General Miles has called for a formal inspection of all troops before we strike camp. The exception being Baldwin's scouts and Henely's detachment, who are to proceed immediately. Dismissed."

As the group commanders scattered to prepare their units, Baldwin saw some envious or even openly hostile looks. He ignored them and sought out Henely.

"Well, Austin, we're together again."

"I'm glad, Frank. It's been hell dragging through the day with nothing but sweat to show. At least you've been near the action."

Baldwin laughed. "If you call chasing phantoms across the plains action, you're welcome to it."

The two shook hands and reported to their respective commands. Baldwin gathered his men around him.

"Boys, we're going to push the Cheyenne hard. Austin Henely's riding with us again in case we run into more of Amos's friends."

"We fightin' today?" a voice asked.

Baldwin shook his head. "General Miles wants us to get as close as possible without warning them. I believe he intends an early morning strike, but he hasn't told me his plans. So eat some breakfast, and we'll move out."

* * *

"They're spooked for sure," Cottontail said grimly. "There's whole travois left behind. I reckon they're only carrying what they need, and no two of anything at that." He looked at Baldwin. "We'll catch 'em by tomorrow."

Baldwin regarded the scattered Indian possessions and wondered if they panicked or just dropped their bundles and walked away. When he caught them, would they fight or meekly surrender to Miles's authority? So many questions, but no answers among the litter.

"How about the trail, Chumumte?"

"Split up, just like always."

Baldwin removed his hat, and squinted at the sun. The sky was endlessly clear and blue, the morning chill not quite burned off. He scratched his head, sighed, and replaced the hat.

"All right, Chumumte, you know the drill. Tell McFadden and Falleaf."

The teams of scouts and trackers scattered across the prairie like quail. Baldwin rejoined his interpreter; the pair picked a clear trail and followed it.

"I wonder how the old people and children handle this runnin' every day," Cottontail said. "Hell, I'm still a young man on a good horse, and it's about to kill me."

"People do whatever they must to survive."

Conversation fell into companionable silence as the pair continued to follow the Cheyenne tracks. By early afternoon, they sweated under the unrelenting sun, lips cracking with thirst. Baldwin emptied his first canteen and was looking for a suitable waterhole, when he found the body.

The woman was tiny, gray, and frail. She'd been left where she fell, a small bundle wrapped in a blanket.

"That's a damn shame," Cottontail said, climbing

off his horse. "It's sad when a old lady like this don't get her proper respect."

"Why do you think they just left her here?" Baldwin asked, still staring at the body.

"Who knows?" Cottontail answered with a shrug. "Could be she wandered off. Could be the rest were too sick or weak to carry her. Hell, could be they just didn't care." He walked around gathering stones.

"What are you doing?"

"What's it look like, Lieutenant? I'm gonna cover her up. We cain't give her a proper burial, but maybe we can keep the animals away long enough so's her spirit can make its journey."

Baldwin slid off his horse and gathered stones. "You're right, Chumumte. Our fight is not with this old woman."

Thirty minutes later, the job was complete, and Cottontail muttered a brief Delaware prayer. The men remounted their horses and continued the pursuit.

Within the hour, the trail made a decided turn to the south. Not surprised, Baldwin followed. Topping a small rise, he saw some of his men in the distance. Many were afoot and wandered around what looked like a marketplace.

As he approached, Baldwin saw that the market was actually piles of discarded goods. Travois poles littered the site, and opened parfleches lay everywhere. Buffalo hides had been stacked to one side, beside pots and pans. Several of the scouts helped themselves to blankets, moccasins, trade knives, anything that caught their interest.

Cottontail tapped Baldwin on the shoulder. "Look there," he said, pointing to a butchered buffalo. "They took nothin' but meat." He gazed around the campsite. "They're really runnin' now, and we're close."

"How many Indians do you think there are?"

"Cain't really tell. Judging from the trails we seen, two, maybe three thousand."

Baldwin sat back and rubbed his face. "That many?"

Cottontail nodded. "Could be more, could be less. What's real important is how many menfolk they got. But no matter how you cut it, there's a whole heap of Injuns out there runnin' for their lives."

Baldwin sat a moment, reflecting on his choices. Mind made up, he summoned Henely.

"Austin," he said. "Cottontail thinks we may be in pursuit of a band of hostiles more than twenty times our size. I don't intend to tangle with them. We're going to split into two forces. You will take your detachment, ride one hour to the south, then sweep west. I'll head west, then south. If we see no clear indication of the enemy, we'll return here and follow trails again. Understood?"

Henely nodded, saluted, and left.

Baldwin turned to his interpreter. "Chumumte, round up the boys."

Two Horses sat on top of the bluff and stared. The land to the north was empty. He saw no soldiers, no water, no sign of life. Even the wind had stopped blowing, and he felt as though he stood close to a huge fire.

Water was getting harder to find, but Stone Calf planned to move west along the river. When all had drunk their fill, and the gourds and buckets were full, they'd make the final push to the canyon.

"Two more days and this will be behind us."

Bear Tooth, who lay near him, dozing, grunted. "Not soon enough for me. First thing I'm going to do is wash my body and my hair and put on fresh paint. Then I'm going to take my woman and disappear for a few days inside my lodge."

Two Horses laughed. "What? No food?"

"When you have a wife, you'll understand that there are some things more important than food—for a while, anyway."

Bear Tooth slowly rose and looked over Two Horses's shoulder.

In the distance, near the site of their latest camp, he saw a glint of sunlight on metal.

He pushed Two Horses toward their ponies. "Come— the soldiers are closer than we thought."

The council hastily convened as word of what Bear Tooth saw spread. Many warriors refused to attend, retiring instead to their tipis to make medicine and prepare for war. Two Horses wanted to get ready as well, but Gray Eagle stopped him.

"Think," the old man said. "Do you believe the chiefs will make war without allowing you time to prepare? Do you think they will let you go without leaders? The others are too eager to fight. You wait, and listen to the council."

Unconvinced, Two Horses made his way to the meeting. The pipe had already been smoked and Stone Calf was speaking.

"We cannot lose heart now. The canyon is too far away for us to reach before the soldiers catch us. Even if we get there before they do, it protects us only as long as *veho* doesn't know the way in. What happens if he follows us?"

Stone Calf paused and shifted restlessly.

"Our women and children need protection," he continued, "so we can't mount a war party and attack. We need a trick. I say turn south, make a big trail. We will lead the soldiers through the breaks, where the water is bad. We will lead the whites onto the plains, where only we know where the water is. There we will leave them to die! Afterward, the People can go to the canyon in peace, free from *veho* and his armies."

NINETEEN

Baldwin absently chewed on an unlit cigar and stared at the map. It showed all the land from Dodge City to Fort Concho, but his interest was in a small area west of Camp Supply.

Earlier that day, after he and Henely had separated, he'd ridden west, then south. He ran across a wide trail, which divided over and over until only a single set of tracks remained. Clearly, the Cheyenne were moving south again. But where?

Baldwin believed they were headed for the plains.

"You know what bothers me, General?" he asked.

Miles looked up from his reports. "What, Frank?"

"All this time, these Cheyenne have been leading us along, scattering when they could. Now that we're close, they suddenly band together and ride due west toward a canyon almost a hundred miles away."

"The cavalry officers are convinced the Indians are running scared."

"Frightened, yes, but not panicked. No one but Henely and myself have been following these people. What I've seen is an orderly retreat with time taken for provisioning and to discard all but essential items." He tapped the map. "By heading to the canyon, they risk being trapped if we somehow get ahead of them. No, sir, I think they're going back to the south and the plains." He turned toward Miles. "I'd like to send a couple of my men downstream and see where the Cheyenne are going."

Miles paused long enough to set his pen down and regard his chief of scouts. Baldwin's hunches hadn't failed him yet. Miles nodded. "All right."

"Are you sure?" Baldwin asked.

Both Dixon and Chapman nodded.

"Yes, sir," Chapman answered. "We got about six miles downstream when the trail turned south."

Baldwin's grin was lost in the darkness. "I knew it! They're making for the Staked Plains. Thanks, men. Now, I've got a general to see."

Baldwin hurried across the camp. He stopped at Miles's tent.

"George?" he called softly. "George Baird?"

The tent flap swung open, and the bleary-eyed adjutant looked out. His hair was flattened on one side and stuck straight out on the other.

"Christ, Frank! You know what time it is?"

"Nope."

Baird stared at the ground. "Well, shit, neither do I." He looked at Baldwin again. "What do you want?"

"My scouts are back. I need to see the general's map."

"Of course you do, Frank." Baird stepped back. "Why do something stupid like wait 'til daylight?"

Baldwin grinned. "War is hell, George," he said, and entered the tent.

He heard the scratch of a match, then saw the brief flare as Baird lit a lamp. The adjutant wore red long-handled underwear and socks. In one corner, Jack lifted a sleepy head. He glanced from Baird to Baldwin, yawned, and laid his head back down.

"There, Frank, light," Baird said.

"Thanks, George," Baldwin replied as he crossed to the map table.

"Yeah, whatever."

Baldwin traced a line from the Salt Fork to the Staked Plains. He carefully measured the distance, then nodded.

"Jesus, Frank," Baird exclaimed, looking at his watch, "it's four in the morning! Goddamn Reveille's not for another hour."

Baldwin walked over and grabbed Baird's arm. "Shut up, and come here." He led the adjutant back to the map table. "Look," he said, pointing at the Salt Fork. "We're here. The Indians have gone six miles along the river, then back to the south here."

Baird followed Baldwin's directions, then continued the path from the river to the plains. "Oh, I get it. They take off out of here south by southwest, then up on the Cap Rock, and out on the plains."

"That's right, George. Out on that massive prairie where they'll scatter."

Baird was fully awake now. He drew a deep breath and blew it out. "Brace yourself, son. I'm going to wake up the old man."

Two Horses woke instantly when he heard the horse charge through the camp. He quickly hurried over to the rider who had dismounted near Stone Calf.

More warriors gathered around the chief and wolf, each trying to hear what was being said. Two Horses only caught the word "soldiers" during the hushed conversation. Finally, Stone Calf nodded and the rider left.

"The soldiers are closer than we thought. Wake everyone, we must leave now."

The warriors ran through the campsite, shouting for people to wake and pack. Startled faces peered from tipi doorways. Children cried at the sudden, loud activity going on around them.

As soon as the camp was torn down and stowed away, the Cheyenne resumed their trek to the plains.

Two Horses was preparing to join his family when Bear Tooth caught up with him.

"We are forming a rear guard. Red Wolf wants you with us."

Though the honor was great, Two Horses worried about his family. "But what of my father and mother?"

Bear Tooth grabbed Two Horses's arm. "Listen closely, but say nothing to anyone. The wolves found the soldiers only three hours' ride away. You can best help your family by keeping *veho* as far from them as possible."

Baldwin was mounted and ready to ride. His scouts were dressed and armed to the teeth. Miles stepped from his tent, Jack at his side.

"You have a plan, Lieutenant?"

"Yes, sir," Baldwin replied. "I'm going to ride southwest until I intersect the Indians' trail, then proceed along that trail until I find them."

Miles nodded. "Good enough for me. We'll give you a two-mile head start. Good hunting, Frank."

Baldwin saluted. "Thank you, General."

The scouts rushed from camp. Baldwin kept a quick pace to take full advantage of the cool temperature. Within an hour, the sun was out, and they'd found the trail leading from the river. Another hour, they slowed the pace as it grew hotter. Then they rode through the latest Cheyenne campsite.

Baldwin called a halt among the scattered remains, allowing the horses to rest a moment. He mopped at his neck with a sodden neckerchief.

"You know, Chumumte, it'll be September in a couple of days. Back home in Michigan, the air will already be cooling off. Before you know it, it'll smell like autumn, with cold foggy days and gentle rains."

Cottontail took a swig from his canteen, letting the water drip off his beard. "I sure could do with some of that cool right now."

"Yes, sir," Baldwin replied, nodding. "Me, too." He took a deep breath and nudged his mount forward. "Come on, boys. Let's get back to it before Miles catches up."

When they came to the broken country of the Salt Fork, Baldwin slowed the advance even more, as much for the heat as the terrain. They finally climbed out onto a tableland about four miles wide. Along its southern edge loomed the escarpments and weatherbeaten mesas of the Cap Rock.

The morning sun warmed Two Horses's back, driving away the shivers he'd suffered before dawn. He licked his lips and wondered why his mouth was so dry when his palms almost dripped sweat. Bear Tooth lay near him, apparently asleep.

"Do you think we'll really fight today?"

Bear Tooth opened an eye and shrugged. "Perhaps. If not today, then another. I would prefer another."

"How . . . how do you think it will happen?"

"I don't know, Two Horses. Hopefully, they will ride up here, and we will ambush and kill a bunch of them, and the rest will leave."

Two Horses licked his lips again. "Are you scared?"

Bear Tooth yawned mightily and shook off his drowsiness. "I haven't had enough sleep to be frightened."

"Oh."

Two Horses returned to watching the valley before him. He knew their position was good. They had both surprise and the high ground on their side. He didn't know what the soldiers had, but hoped their medicine would prove weak.

He stiffened at the first glint of sunlight on metal. Then flinched as another came. Soon he saw a thin trail of dust, and at its head a tall man in a blue uniform.

The scouts rode as two units a hundred yards apart. With Falleaf in the lead, the Delaware trackers, ahead and away, moved quickly across the plain. Baldwin thought of ordering them back, but decided against it. They were still close enough to cover, should trouble arise.

He studied the rough land before them, spotting a cleft between two buttes he remembered from Miles's map. He signaled McFadden to join him.

"See that cut up there?" he said, pointing.

McFadden nodded.

"Well, there's a trail on the other side that leads to the Red River. Catch up to Falleaf, and tell him to make for there."

McFadden kicked his horse into a gallop and sped away. Baldwin saw him slow at Falleaf's side and point out the route. The Delaware changed course, and Baldwin ordered his men to follow suit.

He was still trying to guess where the Indians might head next when the hillside before him erupted in gunfire.

* * *

Two Horses watched *veho's* Indians leap from their mounts as the warriors opened fire. He saw two men, one white and one red, still on horseback and apart from the others. He jumped up and ran toward them, gathering men with him. The last warrior in was Moonface, who brandished a lance larger than he was tall.

The warriors fanned out to form a line between the trapped men and their comrades. In a sudden flanking movement, their quarry spun their mounts and rode down the line—right at Moonface.

"Do something!" Two Horses yelled. "They'll get away!"

Moonface launched his spear at the Indian, but his aim was off. Rather than piercing his enemy, it struck him a glancing blow on the head, knocking him from his horse.

The white man jumped to ground and pulled his pistol. Firing at any movement he saw, he stood over his downed companion.

Two Horses and most of the others hid behind rocks and short juniper trees, but Moonface made a mad dash for the Indian's horse. He grabbed the reins and scampered back to the relative safety of the rocks.

Seconds later, the downed Indian was on his feet, shaking his head. A small stream of blood ran down one side of his face. He hung on to the white man's arm, and the pair quickly joined the main body of soldiers.

Disappointed, Two Horses wove his way among the rocks, back to his position. He was careful not to expose himself to the gunfire now coming from the valley. Along the way, he ran across Moonface.

"Look what I have," the round-faced boy crowed. "This means that soon I will get my new name and be a man! No more 'Moonface'."

Two Horses looked at Moonface's prize. The horse was scrawny and looked sick. Its bridle and halter were cheaply made and had been repaired often.

I would have expected the soldiers to treat their own Indians better, he thought.

"You're jealous, aren't you, Two Horses? The battle has just begun, and I have already counted coup. And don't think I'm going to share it, either."

Two Horses sighed. "Believe me, Moonface, the last thing I want is your pony."

Baldwin reined in and dismounted. He drew his pistol and ran toward his trackers. All of the Delawares, except Falleaf, were on foot. The old chief rode his horse back and forth in front of his men. He talked to them, occasionally shouting at the Cheyenne hidden on the slopes above.

Baldwin grabbed Cottontail. "What in the hell is he doing?"

Cottontail grinned. "He's showin' our men and the Cheyenne that he's bulletproof."

A close ricochet made Baldwin and Cottontail duck their heads. Slowly they raised up and watched Falleaf. Bullets kicked up dirt all around the chief. One round took off his hat.

"Now he's sayin' that it ain't magic that makes him bulletproof, it's the Injun's bad aim."

A bugle sounded in the distance.

"Someone else has arrived," Baldwin said. "Soon we'll all be here, and the fun will really begin."

* * *

Bear Tooth slapped Two Horses on the shoulder. "Look, here comes Red Wolf and the rest of the warriors. Now we'll see who fights and who runs away."

Two Horses watched as more than four hundred warriors streamed down from the plains. At the sound of the bugle, he looked into the valley, to see a large charging force of soldiers approach the first group, then veer away to the left.

"What are they doing?" he asked Bear Tooth. "How are they going to help their friends from over there?"

Bear Tooth shrugged.

Two Horses's question was answered by a second bugle, announcing more soldiers, who rode into the valley and stopped near the white wolves. This second body of men was as big as the first. A knot formed in his stomach.

He raised the rifle he'd been given, pointed it downhill, and pulled the trigger. He'd only shot it a few times, and the sudden lurch was uncomfortable. He had a vague idea of how to aim the thing, but he'd been given only a handful of bullets and told not to waste them.

"Double the waste since I can't hit anything," he muttered.

"What?" Bear Tooth asked.

Two Horses shook his head and drew another bead. A bullet struck the boulder he was using for cover, ricocheting away and pelting him with bits of rock. He flung himself down and lay flat, breathing hard. His heart beat like a hummingbird's. He took a deep breath, swallowed, and slowly started back up.

Two more rounds shattered against the boulder— right where his head had been earlier. He sprawled on the earth again, showered by more debris.

"Try not to stay in one place too long," Bear Tooth called. "Their rifles can shoot a long way."

Two Horses nodded and offered the older warrior a weak smile. "Thank you," he said. He thought, *Why didn't you tell me that earlier?*

Two Horses crawled around the stone and leaned out. Below he could see soldiers running about. Men shouted, their voices faint in the distance. He wondered what they were planning.

Baldwin stole from rock to rock, gazing intently uphill. He'd never suspected the Cheyenne would wait to ambush them. They'd avoided a fight all along. The only thing he could think of was that he must have come too close to the main group and these warriors were fighting to allow their families to escape.

He watched First Battalion ride in. Compton broke away from the unit and remained in the rear with his adjutant and several enlisted men who would be used as messengers. The company commanders controlled their individual units in battle. When the battalion first veered away, Baldwin thought Compton meant to abandon the scouts to the Indians. When Biddle arrived and took position next to Baldwin, the lieutenant understood what Miles had in mind.

Pope and his artillery rode in next. Baldwin saw Miles in the lead. While the lieutenant arranged his pieces, the general rode up and down the line.

Baldwin rose to a crouch and prepared to dash to the next position. He took a deep breath and hurried across the short open area. The gunfire from the bluffs seemed to triple, bullets zinged and caromed, spraying him with dirt and bits of stone. He leaped the last six feet, almost landing in Cottontail's lap.

"What the hell was *that?*" he cried, raising himself to a sitting position.

"You been lookin' the wrong way. While all our purty soldiers been comin' in, so has theirs."

"My God, how many, Chumumte?"

Cottontail scratched his chin, brow furrowed in thought. "There was a Bible word my pappy used for just such an occasion." He grinned. "Multitude."

Baldwin wiped sweat from his eyes. He saw movement behind Miles.

"Here comes the infantry, Chumumte." He shook his head slowly. "Look at them run. Poor bastards; bet they're dying in this heat."

Strains of music came from the valley.

"What's that?" Cottontail asked. "I've heard it before."

"Officers' Call. Miles is meeting with the commanders."

"You're in charge of us. Shouldn't you be there?"

"Kiss my ass! I'm not about to get my tail shot off for one of Miles's—" Baldwin paused, then grinned. "Hey, that's not a bad idea."

"What?" Cottontail asked, suddenly wary.

"The meeting. We need to be represented, so you'll go as liaison."

"Lee who?"

"Go-between. You go down and tell Miles we're all right. Then he tells you what he wants us to do next, and you come tell me."

Cottontail frowned, narrowed his eyes, and regarded Baldwin closely. "Why don't you go, and save a step?"

Baldwin shrugged and held out his hands, palms up. "I *want* to go . . ."

"Uh-huh?"

". . . But I can't."

"Why?"

"Because I have to be here."

"Oh," Cottontail said slowly, "I get it. Send the dumb Indian."

He rose and started walking down the hill. Bullets flew around him. "That's been the story of my people and you white folk," he said as a round kicked dirt on his moccasins. "If somethin' dirty has to be done, send the Indian. If it's dangerous, send the Indian."

"For God's sake, Chumumte, get down before you get shot!"

Cottontail stopped, turned, and pointed an accusing finger at Baldwin. "I hope I do! It'd serve you right."

He spun back around and continued his journey, muttering under his breath.

"Look at all those soldiers," Moonface said, wide-eyed. "Why don't they shoot more? I have never seen so many soldiers who did not shoot. What are they doing down there?"

"Don't worry, Moonface," Two Horses said, looking down in the valley. "When *veho* makes up his mind, he'll let us know."

"You really think so?"

"Of course. After all—"

Below, the big gun flashed a great light, and a white ring of smoke surrounded its barrel. Even as he heard the gun's roar, Two Horses's world disappeared in a cloud of dirt and stone.

TWENTY

As soon as the cannon fired, Baldwin was on his feet. He rushed up the hill, calling his men to join him. He quickly divided them into two teams, ordering each team to fire at the Indians while the other advanced.

To his right he saw Sixth Cavalry, I Company, commander Adna Chaffee raise his pistol over his head and wave it in a circular motion.

"Forward!" Chaffee cried. "If any man is killed, I will make him a corporal!"

The troops rose and charged as a mass, screaming and firing into the rocks overhead.

Baldwin heard a distinctive *pop-pop-pop* in the distance and hit the ground. Bullets from the Gatling guns peppered the hillside, ricocheting in every direction. He glanced uphill and watched a line of sparks, debris, and shattered rounds crawl across the crest of the bluff.

Again the ten-pounder fired. Its shell exploded high and far to Baldwin's right.

Two Horses slowly opened one eye and stared at the blue sky. He heard nothing but a high-pitched ringing far away. He felt no pain and seemed strangely disconnected from everything.

Am I dead?

He tried to open the other eye, but it was stuck Reaching up, he felt something wet and sticky covering the side of his face. He lowered his hand and saw blood on his fingers.

The noise of battle returned in a deafening chorus of shots, shouts, and screams. He sat up slowly, dirt falling from him, and gazed around.

The boulder he had used for cover was gone. He wiped at the blood blanketing his eye and managed to get it open. Relief washed over him as a blurry image of the ground presented itself. He blinked rapidly, and his vision cleared.

Two Horses looked around and saw two figures lying a few feet away; neither moved under a thick coating of rocks and dirt.

"Moonface," he called. His mouth and throat were so dry his voice was a papery whisper. He worked up some saliva and swallowed. "Moonface!" he called again in a loud croak.

One of the figures stirred, and a head slowly raised and turned toward Two Horses.

"Two Horses?" Moonface said, wide-eyed. "Are you a ghost?"

"No."

"But your face!"

Two Horses gingerly felt the side of his head, wincing when he pressed on a gash covered in dirt. "I've got a cut. Are you all right?"

The hillside suddenly came alive with so many bullets that Two Horses was sure every white man in the valley was shooting at him. He curled up in a ball, hands atop his head. The sound of the bullets moved away and he cautiously raised his head. Along the top of the bluff, other warriors came out of hiding as the firing passed them.

He crawled to the edge of the cliff and looked down. Below, a soldier crouched behind a boulder watching others climb up. Two Horses raised his rifle and aimed at the man's head. As the front sight of the rifle slid across the target, he placed his finger on the trigger.

He lowered his rifle. He recognized the soldier as the chief who had protected Porcupine's body.

"Today, you live, *veho,*" he muttered.

"Two Horses!"

He turned and saw a warrior waving at him.

"Come on. We are moving back to the next ridge."

Almost as one, four hundred Cheyenne warriors melted away.

Baldwin didn't know how he made it to the top. He was drained of energy, but there he was, pistol out and cocked. Cottontail appeared at his side.

"They're gone," Baldwin said.

"Yessir," Cottontail said. " 'Pears to be."

Other scouts peeked over the summit before joining Baldwin. The only shooting to be heard came from the troops charging new positions.

"There's a blood trail over here," Masterson called. "But it's small."

One of the trackers came from the other side of the ridge, talking excitedly in Lenape.

Cottontail translated, "He says the Injuns is climbin' the next hill over."

Baldwin groaned. "There's more?"

Two Horses lay behind a large rock and gazed back at his last position. Soldiers appeared in a long, ragged line along the hilltop. Several warriors shot at them and laughed as the white men jumped for cover. Two Horses held his fire to save the few bullets he still had.

He felt a hand on his shoulder and turned.

Bear Tooth's eyes widened when he saw the blood on Two Horses's face. "Are you hurt?" he asked.

"No. When they fired the big gun, some flying rocks cut my head."

"We've been fortunate," Bear Tooth said. "They shot it at the Comanche guide, but his medicine wasn't as strong as yours."

Two Horses looked back across the valley. "I wish they'd go away."

"The chiefs think they will. Almost everyone is across the river, and starting to set up camp."

Two Horses turned and stared at the older warrior. "And what will happen if they're found?"

"The council decided *veho* can't fight without his strange new guns, and that he will not pursue us past here."

Two Horses looked back at the opposite ridge and said nothing. The chiefs had underestimated the white soldiers, he was sure of it. These were men who had pursued them relentlessly across the prairie, and when they'd finally come so close, he couldn't imagine them just quitting.

He saw a horse crest the hill to be quickly followed by four more pulling a small wagon and the giant gun. More horses appeared, and the other two strange weapons rolled onto the summit.

"I wonder if the chiefs thought about this," he said dryly.

Baldwin heard the Parrot fire and looked to his right. The gun's barrel pointed away from him, and as his gaze followed its line of trajectory, the top of a cliff over

Compton's force exploded. Indians scuttled to the back edge and dropped out of sight as two more rounds landed, cloaking the top of the bluff in a cloud of smoke, dust, and debris.

No sooner had the explosions' echoes faded, than Baldwin heard a bugle sound Charge. He stood to see almost all of First Battalion run down the hill and up the next ridge. They disappeared around the base of the bluff. He heard the constant staccato of pistol and rifle shots.

"Give 'em hell, boys!" Cottontail shouted. "Yee-e-e-haw!"

Up and down the line, soldiers stood, cheering. Baldwin looked across the valley; the Cheyenne were on their feet as well. Both sides had taken a short break from the battle to watch the outcome of this one small piece of war.

Suddenly a lone figure crossed the top of the bluff. He wore no feathers, no hat; he had a long staff in his hands.

Was it a spear or a guidon? Baldwin's heart pounded as he waited.

The figure dipped the object and a guidon unfurled. He swung the pole back and forth. Baldwin could almost hear the small flag pop as it flew through the air.

A wave swept down the ridge. Men rose and cheered; hats flew in the air.

"Well, Cottontail, that's one for us," Baldwin said with a smile.

He dived back behind the boulder as bullets peppered the ground where he'd been standing. Cottontail landed next to him and chuckled.

"I don't reckon them boys is all that pleased."

Another bugle sounded, and both men cautiously looked back down the hill. From the center, a force of

Fifth Infantry soldiers stormed the ridge, their shouts of joys changed to war cries.

"Those are my boys," Baldwin said proudly. "Now, you'll see *real* soldiers in action."

The infantry scrambled down into the valley, then started up the slopes. One unit fired while another advanced. The men threw themselves flat on the ground as Pope opened up with his cannon and Gatling guns.

"The only place safe is *behind* them guns," Cottontail observed sourly.

"He's trying to keep the Indians pinned down on the hill."

"Hmph. You ask me, he's doing a right good job of keepin' everybody pinned down."

As soon as the artillery ceased, the Second Battalion made its move. Each company moved as a separate unit.

"We got to go, Mr. Baldwin. They're leavin' us behind!"

Baldwin waved his scouts forward. Unlike conventional soldiers, these men stayed in units of two or three, darting among the rocks and sparse vegetation, running a zigzag course down the hill. Firing from the enemy was sporadic and seemed halfhearted.

Cottontail shouted and went down. Baldwin ran back and leaned over the fallen interpreter.

"Chumumte," he shouted, "are you shot? Where? As he talked, he grabbed at Cottontail's arms and legs, frantically searching for bullet holes or the shaft of an arrow. "Talk to me. Are you all right? Can you hear my voice? Speak to me!"

"Jesus, Lieutenant, if'n you'd—"

"Are you hurt? Where?"

"—shut the hell up a min—"

"Don't you worry, we'll take good care of you."

"—it, I'd tell you—"

"C'mon, Chumumte, talk to me."

Cottontail grabbed Baldwin's shirt with both hands. He pulled the lieutenant close to his face.

"I'm all right, Frank!" he said through clenched teeth.

Cottontail released the shirt and Baldwin sat back.

"You're not hurt?"

"Hell, no!" Cottontail answered, sitting up. "I tripped over a root or some such back there."

"Well, goddammit, Chumumte, you scared the shit outta me!"

"Me?" Cottontail shouted back, placing his hands on his chest. "The way you was jabberin' and carryin' on and blubberin', I was startin' to believe I *did* get shot and was just too stupid to know it."

Both men gained their feet; they scowled at each other.

"Yeah, well, don't do it again."

"Don't you worry none about that, brother. Even if'n I *do* get shot, I ain't about to tell *you* about it. I'll just bleed real quiet."

"Just like a good Indian should, right? Suffer unto thyself only."

Cottontail's chin jutted out. "You bet your sweet ass! Now, are we gonna jaw all day or climb this goddamn, son-of-a-bitch hill?"

Baldwin spun on his heel and started back toward the crest.

"Oh, we're gonna climb it, all right," he called. "And I'm not looking back to check up on you, Rabbit Butt!"

Cottontail's eyes widened, and he hurried after his commander. "Hey, Lieutenant, you ain't got no reason for name callin.' "

When Baldwin didn't answer, Cottontail suddenly feared his secret might get out.

"Now, we had a deal, Lieutenant Baldwin. Remember?"

No reply.

"Baldwin!" Cottontail shouted. "Frank? No hard feelin's, right?"

Two Horses fired every bullet he had at the soldiers running across the valley toward him. Rounds ricocheted off rocks and thudded into tree trunks. Some knocked off bark or scattered dirt into the air. For all his firing, no enemy fell.

How could this be? It was as though *veho* had some special medicine that made him bulletproof.

Now he lowered his rifle and peered down the hillside and across the valley. The ground swarmed with soldiers.

He stood and ran along the ridge, asking each warrior he met for ammunition, but no one could spare any. Just as he was about to give up, he saw Bear Tooth helping a wounded warrior down the back side of the hill. He hurried to Bear Tooth's side.

"Help me get Red Hat away from here," Bear Tooth said.

Two Horses reached for the warrior's arm and he was horrified to see nothing below the elbow. A leather thong had been tied around the biceps to slow the bleeding.

Two Horses gasped. "What happened?"

"I don't know," Bear Tooth replied. "I found him this way."

The warrior groaned as Two Horses slowly raised his arm, then cried out. Two Horses did his best not to touch or look at the stump.

"Here, let us take him," a gentle voice said.

Two Horses saw two women approach, then realized

they were men in dresses. *Hemaneh* were tribal healers. They did not wish to lay with women and could not lay with men. They served as powerful medicine men, made even stronger by their enforced celibacy.

The older of the two took the arm Two Horses was holding while his companion relieved Bear Tooth.

"We have very strong medicine," the elder *hemaneh* said. "It is our job to care for the sick and injured. You men have fighting to do." He paused and appraised Two Horses. He reached, gently grasped Two Horses's chin, and turned his head from side to side. "You're just a boy," he said. "It is a sad time for the Cheyenne when the children must go to war."

Chanting softly, the *hemaneh* half carried the warrior down the hill and out of sight.

Two Horses turned to Bear Tooth. "Do you think he'll live?"

Bear Tooth shrugged. "Perhaps it is better if he doesn't. How can a one-armed man provide for his family? What can he do for the People?"

Two Horses knew the Cheyenne man earned his place in the tribe by hunting and protecting the people. Once crippled, he would be forced to rely on the pity and charity of his neighbors.

"You're right," he said, gazing at his bloodied hands. "He'd be better off dead."

Two Horses scrambled down the bank of the Red River. His feet sank in the dry riverbed as he stared across half a mile of red sand. A tall cliff rose on the other side of the river and a long narrow canyon opened to one side. Two Horses longed for a horse, but Bear Tooth had told him the animals were already on the plains, waiting.

Other warriors appeared on the bank, then passed him, offering encouraging words. Two Horses started to run. His feet churned, but the sand resisted every effort he made at speed. Parched and panting, he could feel the sun suck moisture out of him with each breath.

Soon his head drooped until all he saw was the riverbed and his feet. The ringing in his ears drowned out all sound except for his labored breathing. Nothing existed but his need to cross the river. His thigh muscles burned from the strain of dragging one foot, then the other out of the sand. Each foot was a buffalo, his rifle a tree trunk. His heart pounded. His vision blurred. He stumbled and fell.

Baldwin made his way to the valley floor and joined his men. He plopped down next to Cottontail, leaned back against a large rock, and used his hat to fan himself.

The sun had moved past its zenith, but it seemed hotter. He uncorked his canteen and drank deeply. He didn't care that he'd empty the vessel sooner, or that there was no fresh water to be had. All he wanted was to flush dirt out of his mouth.

"Lieutenant, we have a small problem," Masterson said, leaning over the rock.

"I'm getting too old to do this," Baldwin grumbled as he rose to his feet.

Masterson smiled. "Aren't we all?"

The pair moved a few yards uphill and crouched behind a dwarf cedar tree.

"Take a look about fifty yards ahead, near the base of a large bush," Masterson said.

At first Baldwin saw nothing except grass, rocks, and the bush Masterson mentioned. Then he spotted boots sticking past the edge of the brush.

"Who's that?" he asked.

"Lem Wilson."

"How'd he get way up there?"

Masterson shrugged. "I guess he didn't stop when the rest of us did. It gets worse."

"How? Is there someone ahead of him?"

"About half a dozen of them."

"Indians?" Baldwin asked quietly.

"Yes, sir."

"Shit!" He glanced at Masterson. "They know?"

"Oh, yes. Actually, they know that we know that they know. Way I figure it, they're deciding if it's worth trying to get to him before we can come to the rescue."

"Go back and round up the others," Baldwin said, pulling his pistol. "As soon as you hear me shoot, come like hell."

He watched Masterson gather the scouts together. Satisfied with the numbers he saw, he stood, fired off three fast shots, and charged up the hill. Almost immediately, gunfire erupted behind him, along with the yells of the scouts. Baldwin ran past Wilson, straight up the hill, and crested the ridge alone. A feathered head disappeared down the other side.

Baldwin stopped and fought for breath. The others waited just below the summit, giving their commanding officer some room. Baldwin started back down the hill.

Wilson offered him a sheepish grin. "Sorry, Lieutenant, I—"

"Not a word, Lem. Not one word."

Two Horses was on his hands and knees in the red sand. His muscles were so fatigued, his arms shook. He panted and willed himself to rise.

Two pairs of moccasins swam into view.

"Ho, ho," said a familiar voice. "What do we have here?"

"Looks like someone lost his blanket," said another voice Two Horses recognized.

He glanced up, to see the two warriors who had captured him when he tried to sneak up on Stone Calf.

How long ago was that? he thought. *A lifetime?*

He tried to speak, but his mouth was too dry and his tongue too swollen.

"Shall we leave it?" the first asked.

"I don't know," the second replied. "If we do, someone will get cold."

"True."

Strong hands reached under Two Horses's arms and lifted him up. The warriors all but carried him to the cliff, then up its narrow pathway to the top. They unceremoniously dropped him by Bear Tooth. He landed facedown in the dirt.

"I think you lost your blanket in the river," the first said.

Two Horses heard his mentor sigh.

"Thank you," Bear Tooth said. "I'll try not to lose it again."

After the warriors left, Bear Tooth gently turned Two Horses over. He poured water on his face and held his head while feeding him small sips of water.

"Do you understand what has happened?"

"No," Two Horses managed to croak.

"You've tried to save your water, drinking only a bit here and there. Your body needs much water in this heat. Too little is as bad as none at all, but you should already know this."

Bear Tooth shrugged. "No matter. You know it now. And I believe you will not soon forget this lesson."

Two Horses shrugged weakly. With Bear Tooth's help, he managed to sit up. His mouth was still dry and his tongue sore. He held the water bladder with both hands and drank a little deeper.

Warriors had gathered along the edge of the cliff. Each carried a rifle, and piles of bullets lay everywhere. Clearly, they were ready for a lengthy fight.

"Is this where we stand?" Two Horses asked, his voice hoarse, but stronger.

"If necessary." Bear Tooth helped Two Horses to his feet. "Come with me, and I'll explain."

They made their way to the rim.

"Look below, and tell me what you see."

Two Horses saw the riverbed, the breaks beyond, and soldiers gathering in the distance. He told Bear Tooth what he'd observed.

Bear Tooth nodded. "Over your left shoulder is the beginning of Palo Duro Canyon. To the right is a small canyon with shorter walls, but *veho* doesn't know this. To him, one canyon is the same as the other."

"I see," Two Horses said. "We are in the middle of two pathways. The soldiers cannot know where our people are, so they must pick a path."

"And we guard both. We have the higher ground and can shoot them easily as they pass."

Two Horses watched the soldiers across the river. "What will the whites do?"

"If the soldier chiefs are smart," Bear Tooth replied, "they'll attack us. If they can drive us away, they will have a clear view of everything around here."

Two Horses stared at Bear Tooth. "Will we allow that?"

Bear Tooth smiled. "Eventually."

Bone-weary, Baldwin walked into the meeting. His feet hurt; his back hurt. His leaden legs shook with each step. Since his was the farthest unit out, he was the last to arrive. Miles stopped talking as he approached.

"Nice of you to join us, Mr. Baldwin," Miles said acidly.

Baldwin brought his feet together and offered a sloppy salute. "Thank you, General."

Miles opened his mouth as though to speak, then closed it again. He turned to the west.

"Gentlemen," he said, "we are faced with a classic military situation. The enemy commands the high ground on yonder bluff. Canyons lie to either side of his position, offering potential escape to the hostiles. We, in turn, are offered a choice of paths: one right, one wrong." He faced the group again. "I don't like the odds; therefore, I want the bluff taken."

Miles retrieved a cigar from his coat pocket.

"Closer examination of the objective has shown us there is only one way to the top," he continued. "A narrow path has been cut through the rock." He looked at his officers. "And, gentlemen, I mean narrow. One, maybe two men abreast is all that will fit."

Miles paused long enough to light the cigar.

"I will not order any unit to march on that position, but volunteers are welcome. Whoever attempts the climb will be fully supported by the combined firepower of all the remaining forces."

Silence spread through the gathered officers. Many averted their gazes. Disgusted no one offered to go, Baldwin rose.

"I'll go," Tupper said.

Baldwin stared at the captain, openmouthed.

Miles grinned. "Very good, Tupper. Gentlemen, we have a *soldier* among us."

Compton turned to Tupper. "Why you?" he asked.

Tupper drew himself fully erect. "Why not?" He

looked Baldwin in the eye. "Besides, those sons of bitches stole my horse, and I want it back!"

"Damn, I hate this waitin' around!"

"Relax, Chumumte," Baldwin replied. "We'll start as soon as Miles gives the signal."

"How's that come about?"

"When Tupper lets Miles know he's ready, we'll get the word."

Baldwin looked over at the cavalry troops preparing to charge the bluff. They carried only weapons, ammunition, and water.

Tupper's men looked tired and careworn. They fidgeted, licked their lips, and played with their rifles. Some removed their hats, running their fingers through their hair again and again. Very few spoke, and those who did were loud and brassy, seemingly brimming with confidence.

Assembly sounded in the distance and the soldiers slowly rose to their feet.

"All right, Chumumte, it's time to go."

" 'Bout damn time, too!" Cottontail said.

Miles's column marched slowly across the Red River toward the bluff. No one spoke; only labored breathing and the clink of equipment marked the passage. Baldwin's boots constantly sank and slipped in the loose sand. He dared not take a drink, though he was desperately thirsty. Four hundred yards from the base of the cliff, Miles called a halt.

No firing came from the bluff, and Baldwin wondered if the Indians had deserted their position. Then a lone warrior walked to the cliff's edge. Silhouetted against the afternoon sky, he raised a rifle high above his head. A song Baldwin did not recognize drifted across the quarter-mile stretch of riverbed.

A signal rocket left a sooty trail through the air. Immediately, the Parrot roared. The shell exploded against the cliff's face, well below the Indian. He turned and disappeared. Again the cannon fired. This time the round landed directly on top of the bluff. Dirt and debris exploded high into the air, falling back into a white cloud of smoke.

Red Wolf ran among the warriors and told them it was time to leave. Three warriors, each leading four horses, rode up. Bear Tooth helped Two Horses onto one.

As they started to leave, Two Horses saw the two warriors who had rescued him from the riverbed. They stood at the place where the trail emerged from below. He walked his horse over.

"Well, if it isn't the lost blanket," the first said. "Feeling better?"

Two Horses nodded. "Thank you."

The first laughed. "Think nothing of it, Blanket. It's nothing more than what we would do for any warrior. Besides, we like Bear Tooth and knew he'd be unhappy without his blanket."

The warriors uncoiled their dog ropes. Each attached one end to a lance, wrapped the other over his chest, and drove the lance deep into the soil.

"You intend to stay?" Two Horses asked.

The first shrugged. "Someone has to. If we don't, the soldiers will shoot you before you can get away."

"But if we hurry, all can escape. If you stay, you will die!"

The warriors glanced at each other, then looked at Two Horses.

"That is possible," the first conceded. "Then again,

we may not. If our medicine is strong, and if the spirits favor us . . ."

An explosion shook the hilltop. Two Horses's mount reared in fright as it was quickly covered in smoke and falling dirt.

Two Horses coughed. "The whites are using the giant gun. How can you fight such a thing?"

The first grinned. "They cannot bring it up here," he replied calmly. "You must go. We are the rear guard now. Your place is back with the People to protect them later."

Bear Tooth rode up. "Come, young warrior, we must hurry!"

A tear slid down Two Horses's cheek. He made no move to leave. How could he abandon the men who had saved him?

Bear Tooth glanced at the rear guard. "These men have made their decision. I would trade places with either of them, but it is not my time to stand." He fixed his gaze on Two Horses. "And it's not yours. We leave to fight another time."

As Two Horses rode off, he turned in the saddle. "We will not forget you. I will sing your praises to my grandchildren."

The first warrior waved. "You do that, little brother," he said quietly.

Miles's bugler sounded Charge, and Tupper's company scurried across the sand. Now the column fired at the hilltop, each man shooting slowly and deliberately. With the enemy hidden, targets were the rocks and chaparral along the rim.

Baldwin didn't bother to shoot, since all he carried was his pistol, but his scouts, the hunters in particular, seemed to be greatly amused. They called targets for each other and either cheered or hooted depending on whether it was hit.

"You'd think they was at a turkey shoot," Cottontail shouted above the noise.

Baldwin grinned.

A signal mirror flashed from the base of the bluff. "Cease fire" resounded from command to command.

Charge played in the distance. Tupper's men were now ascending the cliff through the narrow alleyway in the rock. To a man, the column stood and cheered, waving hats in the air.

"Give 'em hell, boys!"

The calling echoed off the cliff face and washed back across the river. Soon the men quieted, waiting.

A shot! Two! A pause and more shots. Then silence.

Baldwin held his breath.

He jumped as a flurry of shots rang out. Then silence again.

A solitary figure approached the cliff's edge. He stood a moment, then waved a hat. The column erupted in cheers, growing even louder as more troops lined the cliff. Miles charged out in front on his stallion. Jack ran beside him, barking excitedly. Miles circled his sword above his head three times, then pointed to the bluff.

Compton and Biddle rode to the head of their commands.

"First Battalion!"

"Second Battalion!"

The company commanders followed suit, calling out their units in order.

Miles stood in his stirrups and bellowed, "Charge!"

Seven hundred soldiers screamed in unison and rushed across the riverbed. After the first hundred yards, the cries became less enthusiastic. After the next hundred yards, they were nonexistent. Near the bluff, the troops on top waved toward the left. Shouts of "We saw them!" and "Head for the canyon!" inspired a new wave of war cries. The men scrambled up the bank and into the broken lands beyond.

By the time they crested the first ridge, the soldiers were more subdued. Few still attempted the heroic charge; most just struggled up the hill. Some reached the summit and stopped, hands on knees, sucking wind.

Baldwin reached the top, his chest heaving to get air into his lungs. Before him lay a shallow valley, then another hill. In the distance, he saw the walls of a canyon. Somewhere between, the Indians had started fires. Thick columns of black smoke climbed upward.

Cottontail stopped next to Baldwin. "How much . . . of a lead . . . you reckon . . . they got?" he gasped.

Baldwin shook his head. "Don't know."

"Shit! Wish I had . . . my horse!"

Baldwin nodded. "I want you to help me round up our men. We're not doing this madness. These Cheyenne have been one step ahead of us the whole time. What makes anyone think they aren't now?"

TWENTY-ONE

The pony's footsteps jarred Two Horses. He still hadn't recovered from his collapse in the riverbed—and felt even worse about the sacrifice of the two warriors who had rescued him. What had he done to deserve that? Who had he rescued? Certainly not Porcupine.

The thought of his dead friend brought back a strong sense of loss and unhappiness, made worse by his weakened condition. He angrily wiped his eyes as a hot tear slid down his cheek.

"It's not unmanly to weep for a dead comrade," Bear Tooth said softly.

Two Horses sniffed. "And for a friend?" he asked hollowly.

"They were all friends." Bear Tooth watched Red Wolf and several men turn toward a distant butte. "Come along, little warrior, we still have one more thing to do."

Two Horses followed Bear Tooth, not caring where they went as long as it was away from *veho* and his guns.

The party rode behind the mesa and dismounted. Red Wolf gathered his men together.

"We must watch for the soldiers," he said. "If they climb out of the canyon, we will have to fight them as well as we can. We must at least slow them enough to let our families escape."

Two Horses gazed at the dozen men around him. Many hours of fighting in the heat had taken their toll. He thought they wouldn't present much of a challenge for the soldiers. He was amazed at his own calm, for here he faced almost certain death, yet he felt no fear. Rather, he was irritated at having to wait.

"Let's go back," he said flatly.

Red Wolf's eyes widened. "What?"

"I say we take the fight to the whites." Two Horses gazed at his companions. "We can lie along the rim and shoot at those who try to climb out. Surely this is better than waiting for them to attack us here."

Bear Tooth grinned. "I think he's right. We have been running from the soldiers all day, but now that our families are on the plains, let's turn it back on them. It is something they would never expect."

Murmurs of agreement came from the group. Faces hardened into ferocious smiles—as a bear will do just before he stops fleeing and turns to attack.

At Red Wolf's nod, they remounted their horses, and rode back toward the soldiers.

Two Horses looked down into the canyon. The soldiers sat or lay in small groups, weapons carelessly tossed aside. Their chiefs rode among them, but the men seemed to pay little attention.

Red Wolf walked to where Two Horses and Bear Tooth lay. "I don't think they'll attack tonight," he said. "Do you?"

Two Horses was surprised the question was directed to him. "Uh—no, Red Wolf, I don't."

"Then you don't mind if we join the rest of the tribe?"

Two Horses felt the flush. He grinned sheepishly.

Red Wolf laughed and clapped the young warrior on

the shoulder. "Your idea was good. I am glad we came here and saw what the soldiers were doing. Now we can go back to our people with light hearts." He rose. "Come with me," he called. *"Veho* sleeps in this canyon tonight. Soon we will sleep in a canyon of our own."

The warriors rode swiftly across the grass. Two Horses felt relaxed for the first time in many days.

Baldwin surveyed the craggy walls and broken rim of the canyon. The canyon walls were colored in layers of red, pink, and yellow sandstone separated by bands of white gypsum.

His assignment was to follow the Cheyennes' trail and see if he could find them.

He divided his command into three groups and sent them looking.

His group concentrated its search along the canyon's north wall, riding toward the Salt Fork and the bluff where they'd found the two dead Indians. The Cheyenne had managed to get their people and their horses up to the plains quickly. Baldwin was determined to find out how they'd done it.

Cottontail, accompanied by two Deleware trackers, rode in from the south wall.

"We found a way up, Lieutenant," Cottontail said.

As they neared the escarpment, Baldwin saw a half dozen Delawares sitting on the ground. Three more trackers stood along the edge of the Cap Rock, waving. He waved back, then reined to a halt. Cottontail pulled up beside him and pointed to a path that led into the brush.

"That there trail wanders along about a hundred yards before turning into the cliff. Then it switches back and forth, movin' uphill through trees and cactus. Gets pretty narrow in spots, so it's best we walk the horses."

"You think the Indians made this?"

"Nah. Most likely it was deer or elk. Injuns just found it."

The scouts walked single file through stands of stunted trees and chinaberry bushes. They skirted large patches of prickly pear and yucca. The path continued uphill, gradually growing steeper as it wound through more shrubbery and trees before finally cresting on the edge of the Llano Estacado.

Baldwin stepped onto the plain breathing heavily, face bathed in sweat. After the last several days of chasing Cheyenne through broken country, the wide, flat expanse of land seemed endless. Tall grass waved in a southwesterly wind. The breeze felt good, almost chilling him as his skin dried. He pulled off his hat and shook his damp hair.

The scouts congregated in small groups, talking and smoking until the rest of their number arrived. Baldwin swung into the saddle; the rest of his men also mounted up.

"Well, boys," he said, "welcome to the great Staked Plains."

A saddle-weary and frustrated Baldwin rode into camp that evening. The day had been spent scouring the area near the Cap Rock. The scouts followed every trail they could find, but the tall grass and obvious care the Cheyenne had taken to hide their tracks made finding them almost impossible. They rode into box canyons, down arroyos, over hills, and through thickets.

Occasionally a set of tracks was found, and the men grew excited until the trail petered out. After twenty miles of searching, the only thing Baldwin knew for sure was that the Indians were not regrouping. The thought of all those families scattered across the plains heading to a secret destination was disheartening.

Baldwin slid off his horse with a groan. He placed his hands on the small of his back and arched, feeling the vertebrae crack and pop like knuckles.

"You know, Chumumte," he said, loosening his saddle's cinch, "I'm ready for a good hot bath and a soft bed."

Cottontail nodded as he pulled his saddle off his mount. "And a woman. Nothin' works the kinks out of a man's back like a willin' woman."

Baldwin laughed and pulled a currycomb from his saddlebag. "Miles isn't going to let us rest until we find the Indians," he said, running the comb down the horse's side. "I don't relish the thought of being out here in the winter."

"Perish the thought, Lieutenant," Cottontail said with a shiver. "You really think he'll keep us out here all winter?"

"General Miles has only one goal," Baldwin said, absently rubbing his horse's neck, "and that is to win this campaign. He intends to get his star even if it means leading us into the bowels of hell."

The People had climbed the canyon walls and run to where their horses waited. Then they rode the rest of the day and all night before doubling back toward the edge of the plains. Their goal was a box canyon hidden in the broken lands of the escarpment.

Sheer walls dropped straight into the earth, offering no invitation for descent. The trail through the mouth ended abruptly at the back wall, but closer inspection revealed a path between boulders that opened into a wide flat basin with a stream flowing through it.

As each family reached the valley, they quickly located relatives and erected tipis. The wounded were taken to the lodges of the medicine men and *hemaneh,* where they could receive proper attention.

When enough of the Council of Forty-four had arrived, a meeting was called. The council decided to have a dance that night to celebrate the escape from the soldiers. Hunters rode out of the valley to kill fresh game for the feast. Men and women dug through parfleches, searching for just the right attire for the evening.

When the sun rode low in the sky and shadows filled the canyon, cooking fires popped and sizzled with roasting meat. The sound was accented by joyous talk and laughter, and the air crackled with excitement.

In his tipi, Two Horses checked his paint one last time and laid the mirror down. Since he had not earned a feather, much less a bonnet as had the chiefs and elder warriors, he decided on simple dress. His smoked buckskin leggings were clean, if not new. Horsehair fringe ran along the yellow leather legs. He wore a matching shirt with the fringe along the sleeves. Neither garment was beaded to excess.

In keeping with the understated dignity of his clothing, Two Horses had freshly greased and combed his hair. He made sure the part down the middle was straight. His mother had tightly plaited his chest-length braids, and tied the ends with strips of scarlet cloth.

Outside, the drums started and the first song began. It was an old story about a successful Cheyenne raid on the Pawnee. He'd heard that new songs had been written about the battle near the canyon and the dash across the prairie.

Two Horses stepped into the warm night. Tonight he would talk to Crow Woman. He'd made up his mind to tell her how pretty she was, and what a fine family she came from. He refused to think about her reaction.

The tribe had formed two great semicircles around a large fire, women on one side, men on the other. Crow Woman stood near the end of the women's side. She wore a white buckskin dress that glowed in the firelight; she had flowers in her hair.

Two Horses's breathing faltered. Sound faded away as he stared at the vision before him. How could he hope she would even consider him as a husband?

Bull Buffalo's hand clapped his shoulder.

"Isn't she a sight?" the older warrior asked. "One day I will marry her, as I did her sister. She will give me many sons."

Bull Buffalo moved away, greeting others. Two Horses wondered if the warrior knew of his feelings and had offered a challenge or warning. Suddenly angry, he waited until the next song started and joined the men around the fire.

Who does he think he is? Two Horses thought furiously. *He's not married to her yet!*

As he danced his way around the blaze, he occasionally glanced in Crow Woman's direction. She stood with friends, talking and laughing. He timed his moves so he'd be near her when the song ended.

Early the next morning, Two Horses sat cross-legged on a blanket, hands in his lap. He'd walked far enough away from the camp to think. He was in a foul mood, full of self-recrimination.

"And why is it," Bear Tooth asked gently, "that you sit out here alone?"

Two Horses grunted.

Bear Tooth sat next to the warrior. "Ah," he said. "An answer."

Two Horses drew a deep breath and let it out slowly. "I am a wretched failure," he said quietly.

"Failure? How, my young friend? You fought well against the—"

"The dance, Bear Tooth. I failed there."

"The *dance?*" Bear Tooth slowly shook his head. "I saw you. You danced well enough."

Two Horses stared at Bear Tooth.

"Why don't you tell me about it."

Two Horses plucked a blade of grass and rolled it between his fingers. "Crow Woman was there, too. Before I left the lodge, I knew what she'd look like. I knew she'd be beautiful. Does that make sense?"

Bear Tooth smiled gently. "All too well."

"Oh," Two Horses replied. "Good." He frowned a moment, then closed his eyes. "I can see her now. She wore a new white buckskin dress with fancy stitching and beads of every color, and flowers in her hair." He opened an eye, looked at Bear Tooth. "I got close enough to smell the flowers."

"Did you tell her that you thought she looked nice?"

"I was going to." Two Horses hung his head. "I couldn't. Every time I spoke, it was about the coming buffalo hunt, the fight with the soldiers, the trek to the plains, anything but what I wanted to say. And all the time my heart beat harder and harder until I just knew she could hear it."

"Maybe it was because there were others around," Bear Tooth offered. "The whole tribe was there."

Two Horses laughed, a short mirthless bark. He looked at the older warrior. "I told myself that," he said. "I decided that if I was afraid to tell her there, then I would get her alone and—and just say it. So I walked her home. I kept a proper distance so people wouldn't talk, but I wanted to be much closer. I wanted to touch her hand, caress her cheek. I wanted so much!"

"Why didn't you tell *her* these things?"

"Why?" Two Horses cried. "What if she said that she didn't feel the same? What if she said she was waiting for a *man*? What if I asked and she said no?"

Bear Tooth sighed and contemplated the clouds for a few minutes. Then he placed his hand on Two Horses's shoulder.

"Listen to me," he said. "I understand how you feel. And you are right. You may tell her all that you told me, and she may reject you. But if you never say a thing, you will never know. If she says no, then the pain is sharp like a flint knife. It cuts quickly, but you go on. Uncertainty is like a porcupine quill, it stabs and stays to fester. Speak to her from your heart. Either way you will be better off."

Two Horses chewed on his lower lip and stared across the Llano Estacado. He heard the distant cry of an eagle, the bird who flies alone. Like him. Yet the eagle knew its place in the world, what it must do, how it must live. At that moment, Two Horses saw his path.

TWENTY-TWO

Breakfast over, Baldwin and his men saddled up for another scout. The past three days had been spent scouring the countryside for the Cheyenne who seemed to have vanished. After resting in camp the previous day, Baldwin was prepared for a long ride. He walked his horse over to Miles's tent, tying up to one of the guide ropes.

Sunlight streamed into the general's tent through open flaps. "Good morning, Lieutenant."

Baldwin drew himself to attention. "Good morning, sir. I want to let you know I intend to stay out in the field tonight."

Miles lit a cigar and shook out the match. "Why?"

"Well, sir, several reasons. First, we've exhausted this area. My men have searched in every canyon and arroyo within twenty miles. So if we're to find the Indians, we need to look further away—if they stayed on the plains."

"If, Lieutenant?" Miles asked, eyebrows raised.

"Yes, sir," Baldwin replied, warming to the main reason for his extended scout. "I'm not convinced the hostiles have moved completely away. The Llano covers a huge area. Imagine how many more canyons like this one there must be along its edge. No matter where we ride, the enemy could be less than a mile away and we'd never find him.

"Every trail we've followed leads due west. We ride out twenty or so miles, then turn back and search. Today, I plan to follow one of those trails until nightfall. If I'm right, it will either combine with others and lead us to the main force, or double back and lead us to a canyon we've missed."

Miles took the cigar out of his mouth and rolled it back and forth between his fingers and thumb.

"All right," he said at length. "You do that."

Baldwin saluted and retrieved his horse. Joining his men, he led them back to the now-familiar trail up to the Llano. Once on the plain, they spread out and picked trails.

The scouts moved swiftly across the prairie until they reached the area they had searched the day before. Baldwin signaled for a halt.

"Boys, let's hold up here a bit so the horses can cool off. Once you've watered and staked your mounts, gather around."

Baldwin quickly explained his theory that the Cheyenne had ridden back toward the Cap Rock and were hidden somewhere along the edge of the Llano.

"What I want to do is divide us up into three units. The Cheyenne aren't looking for a fight, but they might attack a smaller force. We will ride five miles apart and search the country between this trail and the Cap Rock."

The first unit, led by Falleaf, rode to the south. The remaining men continued west, until Baldwin took his group and turned south as well, waving farewell to the third section led by McFadden.

Baldwin had his men form a line abreast, and they moved slowly across the prairie. As he stared out over the seemingly endless expanse of land, he wished he had one of the observation balloons that had been used early in the war. From what he'd heard, a man could see for fifty miles in every direction from a height of five hundred feet.

He sighed and leaned over his saddle horn, prepared for a long ride. Wishful thinking had never gotten him anything before. What he needed now was tracks.

Two Horses sat quietly beside Bear Tooth, chewing a piece of roasted buffalo meat and contemplating the fire.

"You have little to say tonight," Bear Tooth said, scooping turnip mush from a tortoiseshell bowl.

"I have to know what *veho* is doing, if he is near us. I want to form a scouting party like the one we had before."

"And who would you choose to ride with you?"

"Any who wish to go. Of course, I want you there, but that can't be. You have been a good teacher and a better friend, but it is time for me to see if I can lead."

"And my presence would be a distraction to the others."

"And a temptation to me to depend on your help rather than think a matter through."

"Then that is how it will be," Bear Tooth said. "No matter how I feel."

Two Horses's heart skipped a beat. "Don't you think I can do this?"

Bear Tooth laughed. "Of course I do. But when you're in charge and start to believe you need only to rely on yourself, remember this moment of self-doubt. When you are unsure, you must think *before* you act. The true chief acts deliberately."

Two Horses began recruiting members for his scouting party, starting with the warriors of the original group that had followed Red Wolf. Many refused, but Coyote seemed eager to join.

"I still have my scalp," he said proudly. "I want more."

"But we are just going to watch the soldiers," Two Horses cautioned.

Coyote grinned. "That's how it started last time, remember?"

As Two Horses passed Moonface's tipi, a voice whispered, "Psst. Two Horses."

Moonface appeared from behind the lodge, Sparrow in tow. "Sparrow has never been on a scouting party."

Two Horses looked at Moonface's friend. The slight youth seemed nervous, eyes wide and darting back and forth. He licked his lips constantly.

"Are you two sure?"

"Yes, we are," Moonface said defiantly. "Is there any reason we shouldn't go? Bear Tooth said any were welcome."

Two Horses wanted to bite off his own foolish, wagging tongue. "You may go," he said tersely. "But I don't want any complaints."

"Don't worry, Two Horses," Moonface said. "We'll be the best warriors you have."

Two Horses grunted, then moved to recruit a couple of older, seasoned warriors who did not seem bothered by his youth and inexperience.

"Blanket!"

Two Horses turned at the name. Bull Buffalo was striding toward him.

"The men who named me that were friends of mine!" Two Horses shouted. "They died for me. No one else is to call me that! Understand?"

Bull Buffalo stopped short, a shocked look on his face, but he quickly recovered his composure.

"Very good, little warrior. You almost had me worried. Too bad Crow Woman isn't around to see you so brave." He shrugged. "Alas, she is digging potatoes with her mother, so this is pretty much wasted."

"I don't care who's here," Two Horses said through clenched teeth. "I will fight you or anyone else who calls me by that name. No one will dishonor those warriors."

Bull Buffalo regarded the young man before him and decided Two Horses meant every word. "All right, Two Horses," he said, "but that's not why I'm here. I'm going with you."

"Why?"

"I'm bored. Besides," he continued with a smirk, "someone needs to tell Crow Woman how well her little warrior leads."

Two Horses rode across the valley toward his scouting party. *His* scouting party. He liked the way it sounded.

The scouting party consisted of twelve warriors and thirteen boys who had some experience. Two Horses noticed that Moonface wore a war shirt and leggings, was carefully devoid of paint, and carried only two weapons. Apparently he'd been coaching Sparrow, for the youth was dressed the same.

"Before we start," Two Horses said, "I want you to understand that this is *not* a war party."

Several members of the group chuckled, and Two Horses blushed as he realized he had repeated Red Wolf's opening remarks almost word for word. He cleared his throat.

"What I mean to say is, that we only want to see what *veho* is doing. Finding him will be easy. When we followed him before, each night he played on a brass flute and fired his big gun, so we knew where he slept. Each morning, he would play a new song and fire the gun again, and we knew he was still there."

The scouting party broke into laughter. When the jokes and comments stopped, Two Horses continued.

"We are not afraid of the soldiers' war party, but he has wolves just like us. These were the men who chased us across the land and showed the soldiers where to find us. If we are found again, it will be these wolves that track us. So we must be careful. We'll ride from our canyon and up to the Llano Estacado at a new place. If we find the *veho* wolves, we will hide. If they find us, we will fight."

Baldwin awoke shivering. He sat up and drew his blanket around his shoulders, staring into the gray morning sky. The air was cold, and heavy with the feel of moisture. He grunted and struggled to his feet, then walked to the fire.

Those who had awakened earlier sat huddled together, hands wrapped around steaming cups of coffee. Small bluish flames flickered from the almost smokeless buffalo-chip fire. Though adequate for cooking, the chips' heat could not be felt three feet away.

"Mornin', boys," Baldwin said in a thick voice, as he poured himself a cup of coffee.

The men nodded and mumbled in return.

"Who's cooking?" Baldwin asked.

"Me," Cottontail answered. Dressed in his buckskin shirt, red long-handles, and boots, he had an iron skillet in one hand and a slab of bacon tucked under his arm. He walked to the fire. "I would've been here sooner, but I had to do my mornin' business." He rubbed the pan on his stomach. "Damn white man's food gonna kill me yet."

He placed the skillet directly on the fire and set about cutting thick slices of bacon.

By the time breakfast was over, weak sunlight filtered through the clouds. As they climbed into their saddles, a steady southwesterly wind blew the gray clouds north, leaving behind a clear, azure sky.

By noon, Baldwin was within two hours of camp. Stopped at the edge of the Llano Estacado, he peered over the rim and into the lands of the escarpment and the breaks below. They had searched all morning, riding through some deep arroyos wide enough for entire armies to move off the plains and others that barely allowed riders to pass single file.

He took off his hat and fanned himself. The noonday sun beat down on him. He was hot, thirsty, tired—and very frustrated. Two days and seventy miles of searching had netted him nothing.

Maybe after the resupply train arrived, Miles would order the column onto the plains. Then there would be an extended hunt with decent support. Wherever the Cheyenne were, they couldn't hide forever.

"I'm beat, boys," Baldwin announced. "I say the hell with it. We'll ride back to camp, rest up, and try again another day. Anyone disagree?"

He looked at his men. What he saw were mostly tired smiles on drawn and sweaty faces. Even the normally tireless Delaware seemed exhausted.

"All right, let's head home."

Two Horses carefully peered over the rim of the arroyo that concealed his scouting party. Less than a hundred yards away, the white wolves waited at the Cap Rock. He motioned to the others who lined the arroyo and watched the soldiers.

"The tall one with the blue shirt and mustache," he said, "is the chief of the *veho* wolves. Look at his feet.

He is the only one among them who wears such boots. That's why I call him Tall Boots."

"Who are the Indians who ride with him?" Bull Buffalo asked. "I have never seen them before."

Two Horses shrugged. "I don't know. They aren't Tonkawa or Paiute, or any that we fight."

"Well, they aren't Sioux or Shoshone either," Bull Buffalo said. "I met them once when I traveled to the lands of our northern cousins." He frowned. "Not that it matters. If they're *veho's* friends, they're our enemies."

They watched as Tall Boots abruptly spun his horse and rode across the plains toward the canyon where the soldiers stayed. Two Horses waited until they were out of sight, then led his men from the arroyo.

"What now?" Bull Buffalo asked.

Two Horses regarded the older warrior closely, but he saw no challenge to his leadership. From the beginning, Bull Buffalo had offered no resistance, no argument. The dreaded fight that he'd anticipated had never happened. Perhaps he'd misjudged Bull Buffalo. The other man had put personal differences aside as he took on his role of warrior, unlike Two Horses, who now felt ashamed of his thoughts.

"I think we should ride to the canyon as before. We can hide along the rim and watch the soldiers."

"What if one should wander our way?" Bull Buffalo asked.

Two Horses grinned. "The canyon is a dangerous place. There are bears and cougars and—"

"Wolves!" Bull Buffalo shouted.

Baldwin stepped into Miles's tent, freshly scrubbed, hair combed back, and wearing a clean uniform blouse. He came to attention and saluted.

Miles returned the salute, then waved to a chair. He handed him a dispatch from that morning. Baldwin read it, a frown creasing his face.

"How did they get behind us?" he asked.

"My question exactly, Lieutenant. Did you ever see any sign that the Indians had doubled back on any of their trails?"

"No, sir. Of course, it wouldn't be impossible."

"Yes, a few perhaps," Miles conceded with a dismissive gesture. "But two hundred? Surely there would have been a distinctive trail."

Baldwin nodded. "I agree, sir, and my men would have seen it. I think headquarters is guessing."

"Good, Frank." Miles smiled. "Now the real question is what to do. I believe these Indians pose a real threat to Lyman. Perhaps we are too late as it is. Shall I retreat the command? Shall I send a detachment back and search for the wagons? You can see my quandary. Every option seems to leave me in a weakened state."

Baldwin thought a moment. "Send back a small group of scouts, maybe three or four. We know the land and such a party could sneak past the Indians if necessary."

Miles nodded. "I agree, Frank. In fact, that is what I was thinking all along, but I wanted a fresher mind to weigh the options. Do you have any men in mind?"

"Yes, sir, myself and three others."

"I don't want you to go."

"But I'm the only choice, General," Baldwin insisted. "You need a military presence to clearly ascertain the situation at Lyman's location, if one exists. You also need someone who can speak to headquarters in their own language when it comes to describing what is going on here. No civilian can do that."

"Damn it, Baldwin . . ." Miles started. Then he stared at the lieutenant. "I still don't like it, but I suppose you're right. You have three men you can trust?"

"Yes, sir." Baldwin smiled. "They've already volunteered."

Miles laughed. "Do they know it yet?"

"They will as soon as I tell them, sir."

Baldwin left Miles's tent in a lighthearted mood. Rather than face the prospect of more days searching the plains, he was to find the supply train, then ride to Camp Supply and finally to Fort Leavenworth. Along with a copy of the regular dispatches, he carried a personal message from Miles pleading for more supplies, transportation, and troops.

He walked to the scouts, who sat around a fire drinking coffee.

"Wilson, Wing, and Schmalsle," he said. "I need a word with you."

The trio followed Baldwin away from the others.

"Gentlemen," Baldwin began quietly, "we are going on a little ride. We will follow the wagons and locate Captain Lyman. Then we'll continue to Supply and finally to Leavenworth. The general's adjutant is making copies of the dispatches each of us will carry. I'll get the horses. You men clean your weapons and get your grips ready."

Baldwin walked to the remuda, securing four stout-looking horses. He had a mule caught from the main herd, and tied the five animals outside his tent.

Baldwin started to clean his guns. He left the pistol loaded as a guard against attack, and quickly field-stripped the rifle. The borrowed Spencer carbine was old and worn, but surprisingly clean and well cared for. Each section required little or no cleaning and moments later, when he ran a patch down the barrel, he saw no sign of powder buildup. Satisfied, he added gun oil to a clean patch and swabbed the barrel.

Cottontail walked up. "What's this I hear that you're leavin'?"

"I'm not leaving, Chumumte. The general needs me to deliver some dispatches to headquarters."

Cottontail grunted. "Why ain't I goin'?"

Baldwin set the barrel assembly down. "I need you here," he said. "Someone has to be able to understand what Miles needs and to tell Falleaf."

Cottontail looked at Baldwin a moment, then turned and left without comment.

High on the canyon rim, Two Horses watched the soldiers below. Something was different.

"What's wrong?" Moonface asked, noticing the frown on Two Horses's face.

"There are wagons missing. Remember from before? Bear Tooth complained that the whites had too many wagons."

Moonface stared into the canyon. "Where did they go?"

Two Horses shrugged. "I don't know. That *veho* Coyote killed carried food, bullets, even clothes in his wagon. Maybe the soldiers do the same. If they are low on food, they may have gone to get more."

"Then we should follow the wagons," Bull Buffalo said. "If we burn their food, the soldiers might go home." He grinned. "Besides, we might get a scalp or two."

Two Horses nodded. "You're right. It doesn't take all of us to watch soldiers sleep. We will leave a few men here, and the rest will follow the wagons. Let's get some rest. We'll leave tonight."

Baldwin walked the big gray past the campfires, waving to the well-wishers. He was followed by Wing, Wilson, Schmalsle, and a small troop of friends. At the edge of the camp, he stopped and let his eyes adjust to the gloom.

The sun had set shortly after seven, and with no moon, the darkness seemed absolute. Baldwin knew otherwise. Once the men were clear of the campfires, the stars would light their path.

"You boys about ready?" he asked quietly. He looked down as he felt a hand on his leg. Cottontail stood next to him, face hidden in shadow.

"You watch your ass," the interpreter said. "I ain't about to break in no new soldierboy."

Baldwin smiled. "Yes, Mother, I'll be careful. See you soon, Chumumte."

He nudged his horse forward, and the four scouts rode into the night, accompanied by a hushed chorus of farewells and "good lucks."

In moments, they were engulfed by the dark. As the lights of camp faded, their eyes adjusted to the dim illumination from the stars. Soon they could make out the landscape.

Baldwin led the scouts back to the river and across its sandy bed. Once on the other side, they easily located the tracks of Lyman's wagon train.

"The trail seems clear enough," Baldwin said. "Let's ride in pairs, one set on each side."

Wilson joined Baldwin. Wing and Schmalsle went to the other side of the wagon tracks, and the four men rode into the darkness.

* * *

Two Horses and the Cheyenne wolves trotted across the dry bed of the Red River and up its bank. They moved easily through the night, eyes long accustomed to the dim starlight. Once past the broken land near the river, they began a concerted effort to find the trail left by *veho's* wagons. It was quickly spotted.

The wolves hurried along the trail. As they rounded a bend, Two Horses caught sight of four riders in the distance clearly silhouetted cresting a ridge. They moved slowly, comfortably, unaware of the Cheyenne behind them.

Moonface rode forward, his face alight with excitement. "Let's go get them," he said. "Just like before! Remember, Two Horses? Just like when Coyote got his scalp!"

Two Horses nodded. "We'll take them, but first I want to see where they lead us. Scalps are nice, but wagons, guns, *and* scalps are much better."

Two Horses and the Cheyenne wolves quietly pursued the four soldiers, following as closely as they dared without risking being heard. The last thing Two Horses wanted was for the whites to bolt. The trail would be too easy to lose in the dark, especially if the soldiers made an effort to hide signs of their passage.

Moonface seemed bored by the pace. He'd ride forward impatiently, then wheel his horse and ride back. He held muttered conversations with Sparrow, then moved ahead again.

"Keep off the trail, Bear Killer," Bull Buffalo said angrily. "You're covering *veho's* prints."

"What does it matter?" Moonface hissed back. "We are following the wagon tracks."

"And if they leave the trail? How long would we ride before we discovered that?"

"What are we waiting for?" Moonface cried loudly.

"Quiet!" Two Horses said. "Are you trying to warn them?"

Moonface lowered his voice. "Of what? We ride behind four men walking their horses. They don't know we're here. I say we take them. We can follow the wagons later."

Two Horses was about to reply but paused when he heard others murmuring in agreement. Apparently, Moonface wasn't the only warrior anxious for a kill.

"All right," Two Horses said, "we'll attack when they go into camp. Maybe we won't have to kill them all right away. Moonface, ride ahead and find the soldiers. Stay close to them. The rest of us will follow."

"Alone?"

Two Horses heard the fear and uncertainty in Moonface's voice. He smiled to himself. Moonface had wanted war and trophies. Now let him guide the rest in. Let him assume the burden of leadership.

"Of course," Two Horses said smoothly. "One warrior can almost ride among them and not be heard. After all, you said they didn't even know we were here. We need to know when they stop so we can prepare an attack."

"But—but what if they attack *me*?"

"How? They won't know you're there. You're a wolf. Go on. Hunt our prey!"

The other members of the scouting party joined Two Horses, calling on Moonface to find the soldiers and lead the wolves in.

Moonface glanced from face to face. Features hidden in shadow, the warriors looked almost like ghosts. He licked his lips and nodded vigorously. "All right," he said. "I'll do it! You'll see. I'll find the soldiers' camp. I'll take you right to them!"

Baldwin stopped as Wilson reined to a halt. The scout sat still, head cocked to one side. Then he moved forward.

"You fellers ride on," Wilson said. "I'm going to hang around here a bit."

"You hear something?" Baldwin asked.

"Cain't rightly say. I reckon it's more of a feelin', like somebody's trailing us."

"Either of you feel it?" Baldwin asked Wing and Schmalsle.

"I felt it ever since we left camp," Wing replied with a nervous chuckle, "but I figured it was just nerves."

"I feel nothing," Schmalsle said. "Including *mein* butt from sitting in zis saddle."

The men laughed quietly, the tension broken.

"It probably ain't nothing at all," Wilson said, "but you all ride on ahead, and I'll see."

Baldwin breathed deeply and nodded. "All right, we'll move on, but if you see anything, anything at all, you holler or run or start shooting. Understood?"

Wilson grinned. "Don't you worry, Lieutenant, there ain't a bit of hero in me."

As Baldwin and the rest moved on, Wilson rode behind a large bush. He shifted in the saddle, longing to be back on the trail. He didn't mind being alone, but being alone in Indian country was another matter. The night seemed darker. Images were hard to see in the faint starlight. Worse still, his hearing sharpened and magnified every sound, so he peered into the gloom, trying to put shape to noise.

He finally decided no one was following them. Chiding himself for being foolish, he spurred his horse and rounded the bush. He reined in sharply as he almost collided with another rider.

"What the hell?" he yelled.

The other rider froze. Wilson took in the painted horse, the bare knees, the buckskin shirt with fringed sleeves. He saw the tomahawk in one hand.

"Sweet Jesus!" he exclaimed.

He blindly groped for his pistol. Pulling the weapon free, he cocked the hammer.

The Indian stared at him wide-eyed—then at the pistol. He let out a blood-curdling shriek and reared his horse.

Wilson's roan, whether spooked by the scream or the horse, pitched violently to the side. He shouted and grabbed the pommel with both hands, almost losing his gun.

The Indian's mount dropped back to all fours. Still screaming, he wheeled the animal and galloped up the trail, his screech fading in the distance like a train whistle.

Wilson finally got the mare under control and hurried after Baldwin and the others. Less than a quarter mile away, he caught them, and reined in sharply.

"You all right, Lem?" Baldwin asked anxiously.

Wilson gasped for breath, his heart pounding. His pistol, still clutched in his right hand, rattled against his saddle as he shook.

"Damn Injun was following us," he said in a shaky voice. "Didn't even see the bastard—just about run him over when I was leaving. Good God, I don't know who scared who the most!" He leaned over his saddle. "I feel sick."

"Back up, boys," Wing warned. "He's gonna puke."

Wilson heaved and retched, dumping his stomach's

contents on the ground beside the roan. He coughed a couple of times, then spat.

"God, I just hate that," he said, sliding his pistol back in its holster and reaching for his canteen. He pulled the cork, took a deep drink, and spat it out. "Sorry, Lieutenant, but I got a nervous gut. Sometimes it just lets go."

"Don't worry about it. I've seen men lose their suppers before. It's pretty common in war. You see any other Indians?"

"No, sir," Wilson replied. He took another drink and swallowed. "My whole attention was on that one buck. He looked to be nine feet tall. Scared the bejesus outta me." He chuckled and restoppered the canteen. "Course it musta shook him pretty good, too. He screamed to high heaven and lit out."

"We'll have to assume he's not alone," Baldwin said. "Probably rode as advance scout." He turned the gray. "Let's ride for the hills and see if we can lose 'em. Last thing I want to do is get in a pissin' match with a war party."

Two Horses reined in sharply when he heard the horse approaching. A rider appeared from the gloom and slid to a stop close to the wolves. Moonface's eyes were so wide they shone in the dark.

"Soldier!" he gasped, then continued speaking between short, hard breaths. "Soldiers . . . ambush . . . me . . . waiting . . . knew I . . . was coming."

"Are they behind you?" Bull Buffalo asked sharply.

Moonface shook his head, still panting.

Two Horses moved closer to the youth. "Moonface, take a few breaths and calm down. Then tell us what happened."

Moonface breathed deeply, gradually slowing until,

with one shuddering breath, he began, "I was following the soldiers like you said. Then I was attacked from behind a bush."

"How many?" Bull Buffalo asked.

"I don't know," Moonface replied warily. "Too many to fight. One was right beside me, almost ran his horse into me. Before I could do anything, he had his gun out."

"What did you do?" a voice called.

Moonface glanced at the men around him, realizing that every word he said would be remembered. He shrugged, then puffed his chest out. "I gave him my war cry. His horse tried to run away, and he could not shoot. Rather than try to fight them all, I returned here to warn you."

Two Horses was sure there was some truth in Moonface's story. He wasn't interested in what the boy did, but he had to know how many enemy they faced. What if another group of riders had joined the four?

"Moonface," Two Horses said, "I want you to think carefully. Do you remember how many soldiers attacked you? Were there more than the four we've been following?"

"They were all around me. It was dark, and I couldn't see any faces, but I think it was just the men we've been after."

"It's amazing you weren't shot," Bull Buffalo said. "The spirits must have been keeping a close watch over you."

Moonface looked toward the source of the voice, but Bull Buffalo's face was hidden in shadow. "I suppose," Moonface said, not sure if the other was making fun of him. "I did a lot of medicine before we left."

"That's not important," Two Horses said impatiently. "Since we do not know how many soldiers we face, we will have to wait until daylight to attack. Let's start back down the trail. Bull Buffalo, you're probably the best tracker here, so I want you in front." He paused and looked at Moonface. "Unless, of course, *you* want back up there."

Moonface shook his head. "Oh, no, I'll wait back here. Bull Buffalo is much better at following a trail than I am."

TWENTY-THREE

Baldwin picked his way carefully down a hill. He was exhausted. Moving off the wagon trail was dangerous enough during the day, but at night, it was doubly so. Obstacles and pitfalls easily seen in daylight were hidden by shadow and darkness.

They crossed a small meadow, and the tracks of Lyman's wagon train reappeared. Baldwin turned and rode beside them.

"You reckon we lost them Injuns?" Wing asked.

"I don't know, Ira," Baldwin replied. "Even if we shook them off for now, come daylight, they'll find us easy enough. All I hope is that we find Lyman before then."

They followed the ruts for another hour before Baldwin led them back into the foothills. He tried to find passages between stands of bushes or trees and rode over rocks when possible, though he knew the horses' shoes would leave marks. He chose grass over dirt and doubled back on his trail, anything he thought would help them avoid contact with the Indians behind them.

The moon finally appeared well after midnight, but its thin crescent offered little light. Baldwin cursed his luck and the unhappy chain of events that seemed to be stacking the odds against them.

They followed the wagon tracks again, the temperature dropping steadily as dawn approached. Shivering, Baldwin watched the sky turn a deep royal blue. Then it lightened to the east, the indigo painted over by yellows and pinks. He glanced around him in the growing light, making out the haggard faces of his companions.

Finally, the sun peeked over the horizon, sending bright shafts of golden light across the plains. Baldwin scanned the countryside, but saw no sign of Lyman. He turned in the saddle and looked back down the trail.

No Indians. That he couldn't see the enemy brought no relief to the chief of scouts. He didn't believe for a minute they'd quit and gone home.

"Don't this country look familiar, Lieutenant?" Wing asked.

Baldwin turned back toward the front, then gazed around him. "Now that you mention it," he answered.

"Well, I sure as hell remember it," Wilson said. "How about you, Will?"

"*Ja,*" Schmalsle replied. "Ve stopped here one day to eat. If I remember, zere *ist ein* creek by those hills, *ja?*"

Baldwin nodded and turned his horse toward the cliffs. Within minutes, he came across a small stream. The clear sparkling water looked cool and inviting.

The scouts rode quietly along the creek. Baldwin checked to the rear several times, but there was no dust cloud, no sudden reflection of light, no indication of Indians at all. As they neared the bluffs, he noticed that the water ran from the mouth of a canyon.

He led his men into the canyon. As they rode, the walls rose beside them until they towered forty feet overhead. The passageway grew darker—and cold.

Wing chuckled, the sound ringing off the stone walls.

"If it ain't burnin' up, it's freezin'. Leastways, it'll be cool come noon."

Schmalsle turned in his saddle and looked back along the trail. "Zis is not a very large place. Ve can only ride one by one."

Baldwin nodded. "That's what I'm counting on. I don't think those Indians want to ride in here single file, especially if they think there are four armed and desperate men waiting. Would you?"

They reached the head of the creek where the water bubbled into a natural depression and pooled before starting its long trek downriver. The canyon floor widened enough to allow the horses to be brought together. The eastern wall dipped here and gradually sloped uphill, as though washed away by a great flood.

Baldwin eyed the top of the ridge. "Say, Lem, do you think you can climb that?"

When he received no answer, Baldwin looked at the scout. Wilson sat relaxed in his saddle, sound asleep.

"Wilson!" Baldwin barked.

The scout jumped. "What? What? Injuns?"

"Jesus, man! How can you sleep?"

Wilson rubbed his face. "Sorry, Lieutenant. I'm so goddamn beat, I reckon I must've just drifted off." He grinned ruefully. "Never even knowed it was happening. Now, sir, what did you need?"

Baldwin pointed at the shorter canyon wall. "Can you climb that?"

"I reckon," he said, gazing at the bluff.

"Good. Then you climb that ridge while we strip the horses and start breakfast. Soon as one of us eats, you'll be relieved." Baldwin looked closely at Wilson. "Can you stay awake?" he asked sharply.

Wilson pulled out his plug of tobacco and bit off a chew. "With this I can," he replied evenly. "If I have to, I'll just spit in my hand and rub it in my eyes. Nothing stings like tobacco spit."

Nothing more had happened since Moonface met the men on the trail. How many were there? Moonface insisted he was surrounded, but if there were so many, why didn't they attack? Unless he told more of what had happened, and Two Horses doubted that, they would have to wait until they could locate the men.

He wondered who these men might be. He hoped Tall Boots was among them and that he would put up a good fight before he was captured or killed. The white wolf was known and feared by the Cheyenne. What a great honor it would be for Two Horses to come home wearing those boots!

Bull Buffalo appeared in front of the wolves, riding toward them at a trot. "The white men's tracks lead to a stream near here," he said. "They follow the water's path toward some cliffs."

Close to the cliffs, the tracks petered out in the short grass and hard-packed earth. Bull Buffalo crossed to a rift in the walls, and climbed to the top of the bluffs. When Two Horses reached him, the older warrior was sitting motionless.

"What is it, Bull Buffalo?" Two Horses whispered. "Do you see them?"

The other shook his head.

"Then you can hear them?"

"No," Bull Buffalo murmured, "but they are very close."

Confused, Two Horses looked to the other members of the party. They just shrugged.

"What then?" Two Horses asked loudly, frustrated. "Do you *smell* them?"

Bull Buffalo slowly turned toward Two Horses, a

smile on his lips. "What I smell is the best thing the white man ever gave the People." His eyes widened. "Coffee."

The aroma of coffee and frying bacon made Wilson's stomach growl. Occasionally, he leaned over the edge of the ridge and looked down, hoping to see someone eating. Disappointed, he returned to his guard duty.

He stared out across the rocky terrain, seeing nothing but stone, sparse grass, and random stands of bushes. The only thing he'd seen with feathers so far was a buzzard, which suited him just fine. In fact, the only thing he wanted was some breakfast and shut-eye.

His eyes grew heavy, and he shook his head to stay awake. Once he dozed off, and awoke frightened. He spat in his hands, and rubbed the spit in his eyes.

"Goddamn!" he muttered. "Shit, if I'd knowed it was going—" He stopped rapidly blinking his eyes, trying to clear his blurred vision. He'd heard something, but couldn't place the noise. Through watering eyes, he scanned the land around him. Movement caught his eye.

Wilson stared at a clump of bushes less than a hundred yards away. He thought he was only seeing shadows caused by the wind, when an Indian rode into plain view.

"Jesus!" he whispered, the stinging forgotten. He lay on the ground.

The Indian, on a chestnut stallion, moved silently through the brush. He seemed intent on seeing something over Wilson's head because he never looked at the ground. He walked his horse one way, then abruptly turned and rode back the way he'd come, disappearing into the bushes.

"Oh, shit! Oh, shit! Oh, shit!" Wilson muttered as

he frantically slid to the edge of the ridge. He leaned over. "Hey!" he whispered.

No one paid attention to him.

"He-e-e-e-y!" he said in a loud, hoarse whisper.

Again he wasn't heard.

On the verge of panic, he picked up a small stone and tossed it over the edge. It struck next to Baldwin, who looked up sharply.

"They are coming!" he called softly.

Baldwin, Wing, and Schmalsle dropped to the ground beside Wilson. The three breathed hard from charging up the steep embankment with their rifles.

"Are you sure?" Baldwin asked Wilson.

Wilson looked wounded. "Hell, Lieutenant, I *know* what a Injun looks like."

"Where was he?"

"Just over yonder," Wilson said, pointing to the bushes where he'd first seen the Indian. "He come outta that brush, then went back in again."

"You think he seen you?" Wing asked.

"Hell, I don't know. I was about to shit myself, so I wasn't payin' no mind as to what he was looking at." He paused. "Course, he seemed to be lookin' over my head. Kinda peculiar, huh?"

Schmalsle frowned. "Not if he was looking for smoke."

"Damn, Will," Wilson said, "I coulda gone all day without you saying that."

Baldwin grunted. "Well, I still don't see anything. What are the chances they don't know we're here?"

" 'Bout the same as pissing into the wind and staying dry," said Wing.

Wilson grinned. "Or a whore gettin' to heaven."

"Or *ein* snowball in ze hell," Schmalsle offered.

Baldwin sighed. "If I live through this, remind me to make you boys morale officers."

Wing grabbed Baldwin's arm. "Something's happening."

Less than a hundred yards away, about two dozen warriors broke through the underbrush, riding at a trot. They were well-armed, but they rode casually. Baldwin realized they might have a chance.

He raised his rifle. "Boys, pick a target," he whispered. "I got the gent in the lead."

"I vill take ze one to ze left, on dat bay."

Wing nodded. "Then I got the one on the black to his right."

Baldwin sighted his Spencer. "Ready . . . aim . . ."

The word "fire" was lost as the three weapons discharged at the same time. The heavy boom of Wing's Sharps set Baldwin's right ear ringing.

Three Indians went down. The remainder scattered and disappeared.

"Let's get back to camp!" Baldwin ordered. "Once those boys get over the shock, we're in for a hell of a dance."

One by one, the four scouts dropped off the edge of the canyon wall and scampered down its side.

When he heard no more firing, Two Horses cautiously stuck his head up. With the first shot, he'd jumped off his mount and lain down. Now, after the initial panic, the hilltop was silent. He waited another minute, then rose to his feet. Others around him stood, but three lay still, motionless as only the dead can.

"What happened?" he asked.

Bull Buffalo shook his head. "I don't know. I was too busy running away."

"I saw," Sparrow said. "There were men by the canyon. I saw the smoke from their rifles. Then they jumped over the edge."

"How many, Sparrow?" Bull Buffalo asked.

The young man shrugged. "Three, maybe four."

"What should we do, Bull Buffalo?" Two Horses asked.

"Move along the edge of the canyon. There are many places to hide, and we can shoot down at the *vehos*. Maybe we can kill their horses."

As the wolves spread out and prepared to advance, Moonface hung back.

"What about the dead men?"

Two Horses regarded the bodies lying in the grass. "We'll return for them," he said curtly.

He moved swiftly, but carefully, toward the canyon rim. As soon as he found a position, he cautiously leaned over the edge. First he saw a mule, then four horses. He stretched a bit farther and saw the campfire, but no men.

A shot rang out.

"I saw them!" someone called.

"Where?" a dozen voices asked.

"Near the wall, just north of their fire." The warrior stood and pointed. "See? They're—"

A rifle boomed hollowly from inside the canyon, and the warrior toppled over the edge.

Two Horses caught movement below, and opened fire. He didn't really care if he hit anyone, he just wanted to keep them from shooting. Others joined him.

Baldwin flattened himself against the canyon wall as the warrior plummeted to the ground and almost rolled into the fire.

"Well, he won't be gettin' no breakfast," Wing commented.

Wilson laughed. "And no coffee, neither!"

The canyon filled with the flat cracks of rifle shots, and the scouts found themselves in a leaden hailstorm. They hugged the rocks as bullets sprayed across the ground.

When the shooting slackened, Baldwin tracked where he saw smoke. Then he started peppering those locations with his Spencer. His men followed his lead, and the opposing fire slowed considerably. The Indians seemed content to wait and snipe.

"How much longer you reckon they'll stay?" Wilson asked.

Baldwin shrugged, then ducked as a round ricocheted off a rock near his head. "What do you think?" he called back. "They have the high ground and more men. The only thing that's saved us so far is that they don't dare charge through the canyon." He fished out his pocket watch and opened the face. "Christ," he moaned, snapping the cover shut. "It's not even six yet. This day's barely started."

"Vell, ve can't wait here too much longer," Schmalsle said. "How long they vill keep missing us?"

As if to emphasize his point, a bullet carried his hat away. He jerked his head back, smacking it into the rock wall.

"*Scheisse!*" he swore. "Dat hurt like a summun na bitch!"

Baldwin leaned out to see if he could spot the Indians above him. The firing increased dramatically, and he ducked back.

Then the focus shifted away from the scouts and toward the horses. Rounds pinged off rocks and plowed the ground all around the animals. As the bullets got closer, the horses pulled on their tethers, eyes wide with fright.

"My God, they're trying to shoot the horses!" Baldwin yelled. "We're goners for sure if they kill our mounts."

Wing winced as a bullet punched a hole in the dirt at his pinto's feet. "It's a good thing they're piss-poor shots."

"We can mount up and try to ride out," Wilson suggested.

"Ha!" Schmalsle barked. *"Und* get picked off one at a time."

A round cut the lead holding the mule. The frightened animal started toward the canyon mouth moving faster as bullets kicked up dirt all around it. Then it screamed as it was hit in the neck. Two more rounds caught it on the right hip; then a bullet shattered the right hind leg. In shock the mule staggered on, more bullets slamming into its body, each round making a loud smack. As the forelegs buckled, it fell forward and onto its right side. The firing slackened again.

"Shit!" Baldwin said. "That settles it. We're leaving."

"But where?" Wilson asked. "Will's right about this canyon: it's a death trap."

"That's why we're going up this side. It's steep, but we managed, and the horses will, too." Baldwin slid the magazine from the Spencer's buttstock and fished .50-caliber rounds from his Dyer pouch. "Lem, give your rifle to Wing. When we start shooting, you and Schmalsle make for your horses and saddles. You've got fourteen shots." He slapped the magazine back in place. "Ready?"

The two scouts nodded, grim-faced.

"How about you, Ira? Ready to make some noise?"

"Oh, hell, yeah," Wing said with a grimace.

"All right. One . . . two . . ." On "three" he leaned out and started firing. Wing matched his move.

Baldwin fired at every movement he saw and into every position he recalled seeing gunsmoke. He paid no attention to his scouts, but concentrated on keeping the Indians' heads down. Emptying the magazine, he leaned back against the wall.

Wilson and Schmalsle were on his right, both men breathless, their horses beside them.

"You boys all right?" he asked.

The men nodded.

"Nary a scratch," Wilson said.

"Then saddle up."

With their mounts saddled, Wilson and Schmalsle were prepared to offer covering fire. Baldwin and Wing raced into the center of the canyon floor. Fire from the Indians was sporadic and badly aimed.

Baldwin heard a round buzz by his ear. He scrambled to the gray and pulled its tether free with a mighty jerk. Heart pounding, he half dragged the terrified animal to the opposite side.

The animals saddled, Baldwin ordered the scouts to fully load all their weapons. They ignored the customary practice of leaving one chamber of the pistol unloaded to prevent accidental discharge. Every round would be needed. They slipped their rifles into their saddle scabbards.

"We'll go up in pairs," Baldwin said, with more calm than he felt. "Keep your pistols handy. Once on top, mount up, and we'll make for open country. The only way I see we're going to live through this is to outdistance the Indians." He paused. "One other thing, if anyone is hit and can't keep up, he's to be left behind." He glanced from man to man. "That includes me."

* * *

Four warriors had been killed, and still the white men hid in the canyon. So far, the Cheyenne wolves had managed to kill only a mule. Now the horses were out of sight, hidden against the wall.

Two Horses motioned the warriors away from the canyon rim. Something needed to be planned. They had to find a way to dislodge the *vehos* from their hole.

As Two Horses waited for Bull Buffalo to get near, he glanced back at the canyon.

Two men appeared at the rim, leading horses. They quickly moved away and were followed by two more. As one man climbed into his saddle, Two Horses recognized the blue uniform and boots.

"Tall Boots!" he said, then shouted and pointed at the riders. "There! There! The *veho* wolves! Shoot! Shoot!"

Tall Boots spurred his horse into a gallop. As its forelegs landed, they met those in the back, and it flowed forward. Tall Boots was flung back by the force of the horse, his pistol swinging over his head. Then he leaned forward and leveled the gun.

Two Horses could count the hoofbeats, each making a distinctive noise as it struck the ground. He heard the gray's breath grow harsher as it fought for air.

The other white men kicked their mounts and slowly caught Tall Boots until the four rode abreast. They seemed to float across the land.

Why didn't the warriors shoot? He tried to bring up his rifle, but his arms refused to budge. Were the whites using some kind of sorcery?

Tall Boots screamed a word.

Two Horses heard it clearly, though he had no idea what it meant. But he saw the spittle fly from the white wolf's mouth, saw the anger in his eyes. It was a war cry, long and drawn out as a coyote's howl.

Tall Boots aimed and a long orange flame jetted

from his pistol. The boom rang hollowly, intertwined with the plodding thud of hooves.

Two Horses saw the bullet emerge from the fire and smoke. He was no longer afraid. He would easily dodge the bullet if it came his way.

The other three fired their weapons, spitting death at the warriors.

Two Horses saw the other bullets, too. He watched his men throw themselves down, drifting to the grass. Why were they afraid? Could they not see *veho's* bullets? The whites were so far away, the sun would set before they got close.

He blinked, and Tall Boots was almost upon him. They locked eyes, and the soldier brought his weapon to bear on the Cheyenne warrior. Two Horses knew that though he could see the bullet, he could not move, and so would watch the instrument of his death as it approached and pierced his flesh.

Yet, Tall Boots held his fire. Perhaps he, too, understood the magic of this moment—this time when the spirits allowed everything to be so clear for Two Horses. Perhaps he respected the young warrior. The feeling was reciprocated, for how could a warrior not respect an enemy who pursued him across the plains?

Tall Boots passed so close to Two Horses, the Cheyenne smelled the gray, felt the sweat flung from Tall Boots's face. He heard both horse's and rider's hearts beating wildly. He could feel the fear and anger.

Then the spell was broken. The whites thundered past, shaking the ground with their passage. Two Horses watched them as his men slowly sat up or stood. They seemed to move as though trapped in water, yet Tall Boots and his companions flew across the prairie.

Bull Buffalo ran among the warriors. "Gather the horses!" he shouted. "Quickly!"

The Cheyenne ran. As he mounted, Two Horses felt someone grab his arm.

"What about the dead?" Moonface asked plaintively.

Two Horses glared at the youth and pulled free. "Stay here if you wish," he said, climbing on the horse's back, "but I have a white man to kill."

They had ridden about five hundred yards when Baldwin glanced over his right shoulder. To his surprise, the Indians milled about. Apparently, the sheer effrontery of the charge had thrown them into chaos.

Good, he thought. *The more confused they are, the more of a lead we get.* "All right, boys," he shouted, "let's bring it down."

The scouts slowed to a trot, holstered their pistols, and moved steadily across the land. Baldwin looked back to see the war party mount up. He wanted to kick the gray back into a gallop, but knew better. If his horse collapsed, he was a dead man.

Within a mile, they began a gentle uphill run. The horses slowed to negotiate the slope. Baldwin checked on his pursuers and saw they had closed the gap appreciably.

After another mile, the pursuers had come closer still, within three hundred yards, but the scouts had the higher ground now. Baldwin reined in.

"Hold up, and unlimber the rifles," he ordered.

The scouts quickly stopped and dismounted, pulling their rifles as they hit the ground. Each wrapped his horse's reins tightly around one hand. Wing dropped to one knee, the Sharps tight against his shoulder. Schmalsle stood beside him, his thin face drawn. Wilson stood next to his horse, rifle against one hip.

Baldwin threw the lever on the Spencer, loading a round in the chamber and cocking the hammer. He raised the rifle, face against the cheek piece, and drew a bead on the largest warrior in the group. Just as he started his squeeze, Wing's Sharps boomed, startling him. He jerked the trigger, sending the shot wide.

Schmalsle and Wilson fired at the same time, and an Indian fell off his horse. Wing fired, and another warrior went down. Schmalsle's Spencer cracked again. A third man pitched forward.

Two Horses reined his mount in hard. The sudden attack by the whites had caught him by surprise.

"Follow me!" Bull Buffalo called, wheeling his chestnut toward a small stand of trees. They offered scant protection, but were better than out in the open. Two Horses heard a cry behind him, then the flat crack of a rifle. Leaning closer to his gray's neck, he willed the animal to fly across the grass.

Once among the trees, he stopped and looked at his men. They all seemed dazed and frightened, except one who almost lay on his horse. Blood ran from a bullet hole just below his left shoulder blade and dripped on his mount.

Two Horses looked at Bull Buffalo who glanced at the wounded wolf and shook his head.

"What do we do now?" Two Horses asked.

A warrior suggested, "Let them go?"

Two Horses rode out of the trees and watched Tall Boots and the others disappear.

"We can leave," he said. "We can go home, and let the whites get away. I will not. Tall Boots has brought the soldiers to us before, and he will again. Now you must choose."

Bull Buffalo rode to Two Horses's side. "He is right," he said. "If these *vehos* live, they will think the Cheyenne weak. There will be stories of how only four men shamed twenty wolves. I will ride with Two Horses." He paused and sneered at the others. "The old women can go home."

"What of Star Man?" Moonface asked.

Two Horses looked at the wounded warrior. "Someone needs to take him home. Perhaps Sparrow—"

"Me?" the thin youth shouted, his voice cracking with strain. "Why me? Is there no other man here who can go?" He pointed at Two Horses. "You don't think I can fight, do you? You think I'm weak! Well, I'm not! I can fight."

Two Horses was dumbfounded. "Uh . . . uh . . ."

"I'll go," another warrior offered. "My horse is old, and so am I. Star Man is family. He's married to one of my cousins, so I'll take him home."

Two Horses nodded. He never imagined that Sparrow would react so violently. He always seemed so reluctant to get into a fight.

Bull Buffalo said, "It is important that we get so close to the soldiers they can't use their rifles. I think we should divide into two groups. One will follow, the other will ride around and attack from the front."

The warriors quickly split into two parties. Bull Buffalo took his men and followed the whites. Two Horses took his, including Moonface and Sparrow, and rode south before swinging back to the east. He sent one warrior to ride along the bluff, to signal when they had passed.

They made their way across the prairie, Two Horses constantly watching his scout for a sign. But the warrior just trotted on the edge of the mesa. Two Horses kicked his mount into a gallop.

He started to believe the enemy had gotten away when he saw his outrider pumping his rifle up and down. Two Horses turned the gray northward and led his men around the base of a hill.

They emerged several hundred yards ahead of the soldiers and charged. The whites reined in sharply, then wheeled their horses when they heard Bull Buffalo begin his attack.

Two Horses felt wonderful. Tall Boots was trapped, surrounded by Cheyenne wolves who would tear him to pieces.

Suddenly, Tall Boots spurred his horse and charged Two Horses. The *veho* wolves followed closely behind. They drew their pistols and shot in every direction.

Two Horses heard three solid thuds. A pair of warriors toppled off their ponies. Panicked, Two Horses pulled his mount to the left out of the way of the attacking soldiers. The four white men thundered past.

What kind of demons are these whites?

Baldwin glanced over his shoulder. The Indians were several hundred yards back, so he slowed to a trot again and holstered his pistol.

"Damn!" Wilson swore. "I thought they had us for sure."

"*Ja*, me, too."

"Well, it's not over yet," Baldwin said. "They've split up again."

"Why the hell don't they just quit?" Wilson asked. "We done kilt eight or ten of 'em."

"We might have to kill eight or ten more," Wing said. "You cain't tell about Injuns. They'll fight you to hell and gone, and then just walk away." He shook his head. "You just cain't never tell."

The scouts rode on, scanning the country around them for some sign of the enemy. Baldwin kept one eye on the sky. It had remained cloudy since daylight, and a cool, wet breeze blew from the north. If nothing else, that would help the horses.

"Lieutenant," Wing called. "We got company."

Baldwin looked behind and saw about a dozen Indians riding their way at a gallop.

"Follow me!" he ordered. "We're heading for the Llano."

He kicked his horse into a lope and turned toward the plains. He saw another group of Indians ahead of them. Apparently they were unaware of Baldwin's sudden change of direction. He drew his pistol and ordered a charge. Like the Four Horsemen of the Apocalypse, Baldwin intended to visit death and mayhem on his enemy.

Two Horses never saw them. He was so busy coordinating the next attack, they were upon him before the first words of warning rang out. This time they had no room to maneuver, and wheeled their horses, running into each other.

The soldiers closed, pistols barking. Two Horses heard someone cry out. Then the soldiers were gone.

Two Horses fought for control of his mount and watched his prey escape again. He was livid. Three times they had charged close enough to touch. Three times they had killed his men and ridden away untouched.

"Bear Killer!" Sparrow cried.

Two Horses twisted around and saw the youth kneeling next to a fallen warrior. He quickly dismounted and ran over.

Moonface lay on his back. He'd been struck by three bullets, twice in the stomach and once in the chest. He was ashen and clearly struggling for breath. Each time he exhaled, his chest wound bubbled, blood dribbling out. Bright pink froth stained his lips. He blinked rapidly, eyes rolling wildly.

"Oh, Bear Killer," Sparrow moaned. "Does it hurt?"

Moonface stared at his friend a moment. A small grin spread on his face. "No," he said, almost a gasp. "No, not really . . . just hard to breathe."

Sparrow put his hands on the wounds. "I need something to stop the bleeding."

Moonface slowly shook his head. "Don't . . . bother." He fixed his gaze on Two Horses. "Tell . . . my father . . . I was brave."

Two Horses drew a deep shuddering breath. His eyes stung and a knot twisted his stomach. "I will, Moon—" He paused. "I will, Bear Killer. Everyone will know."

Moonface looked past Two Horses's shoulder.

"Never mind," he said. "I'll . . . tell him . . . myself. Fath—"

Sparrow slowly stood, his hands covered in Bear Killer's blood, tears streaming down his face. He looked at Two Horses.

"He was only here to impress you," he said dully. Then he looked at the body again. "And I was here because he wanted me to be." He drew a deep breath. "Well, I'm going home. I am going home to bury my friend."

"He's right," a warrior said. "We are cursed. We have angered a spirit or something, and this is our punishment. Let some other Indians kill those white men. I am going home, too."

Other murmured in assent. Two Horses knew they had no fight left. But he did.

"Those of you who wish, go home. I will not until Tall Boots's scalp decorates my lodge pole."

Two Horses walked to the gray and mounted. "Anyone who wants to come with me is welcome. Those of you leaving, gather the dead as you go." With that he turned the horse and rode off after the *veho* wolves.

Soon he heard hoofbeats, and Bull Buffalo pulled alongside. There were a half dozen men behind him.

"You don't think I'd let you go alone and get all the glory, do you?" he said with a smile.

Two Horses grinned back and kicked his pony into a lope.

They had ridden about a thousand yards onto the Llano Estacado when Baldwin first noticed his horse starting to lag. He reined to a halt. They were in the middle of open country with no cover at all. The only saving grace of the situation was that the Indians suffered from the same kind of exposure.

"I hate to say it, boys," he said to the other scouts, "but we have to stop. My horse is done in. If I don't rest him, he'll die for sure."

"Und mine," Schmalsle said, patting the chestnut on the neck. "She is on her last leg."

Wilson sighed. "I reckon they're all pretty done in. What you want to do, Lieutenant?"

Baldwin dismounted and pulled his rifle from its scabbard. "We're going to take a stand. We need rest; the horses need rest. If the Indians want a fight of it, we'll give it to them."

The animals staked out, the scouts sat in a small circle, their backs together. They reloaded the pistols and Spencers. Wing's Sharps was a single-shot, so he laid out a cloth and set a handful of rounds on it. They were as ready as they could be. The rest was up to the enemy.

Baldwin fished his watch out of its pocket. He was convinced they'd fought the Indians all day. He opened the case.

It was 9:00 A.M.

TWENTY-FOUR

The scouts waited quietly under lead-gray clouds that skated across pewter skies. Thunder rumbled across the plains. No lightning flashed, yet the air promised rain.

Baldwin took a deep breath, enjoying the freshness. Then he stared at the dozen Indians sitting astride their ponies fifteen hundred yards to the west. They had shown up shortly after the scouts stopped to rest.

"What you reckon they're thinkin'?" Wilson asked.

"I wish I knew, but if I had to guess, I'd say they were in deep discussion about how to get close to us. They seem to have gained a healthy respect for Ira's Sharps."

Wilson regarded the sky. "Looks like rain," he said; then he sniffed. "Smells like it, too."

Squall lines formed in the distance; sheets of rain moved across the prairie. Occasionally, a bolt of lightning raced to the ground, followed by a low rumble like faraway artillery. The wind freshened and increased in intensity.

A great thunderbolt shot across the heavens, ripping open a cloud's belly. Without preamble, a waterfall cascaded to the earth. The rain instantly soaked the four men and their mounts.

Baldwin shivered as water sluiced off the brim of his hat and down his collar. The wind came harder, from the north, chilling him to the bone. Visibility vanished in the torrent, and he worried the Indians might take advantage of the weather to sneak up on them.

He leaned toward the others. "We need to move on," he shouted above the storm.

Lit by a lightning flash his companions' expressions told him they thought he was mad.

"Listen," he continued. "We cannot see the Indians. What is to prevent them from coming closer?"

They climbed into rain-slick saddles.

"Which way, Lieutenant?" Wilson called.

Baldwin pointed north. "In case the Indians decide to follow. We'll turn east come dark. No matter what happens here, our only real hope is Lyman."

Wilson led off. Schmalsle fell in behind him, then Baldwin, and Wing. They moved slowly, allowing the horses to pick their way across the plain.

As darkness fell, the electrical storm moved on, leaving behind a steady rain. They continued until the night grew so dark they couldn't tell which direction they traveled.

Baldwin called a halt. The scouts staked their horses. Using their saddles for pillows and covering themselves with their thin army blankets and saddle blankets, they turned in.

Baldwin was miserable. The north wind sliced through him. He burrowed inside his uniform coat and turned up the collar for what little protection it afforded. His hands shook, and his bones ached with cold.

Shivering, teeth chattering, and soaked to the skin, Frank Baldwin would have killed for a shot of whiskey.

Baldwin opened one eye and gazed at a still, gray world. The rain had changed to a drizzling fog that painted everything the same color. He looked for the horses and found his gray, almost invisible against the nickel sky. By contrast, Schmalsle's chestnut mare stood out stark as coal in snow.

The plains disappeared just beyond the horses, as though the small plot of land they occupied had been lifted from the earth and deposited in the void.

He felt movement at his back and looked over his shoulder. Wilson lay there, moaning softly and fidgeting. Baldwin wondered what the scout dreamed.

Baldwin sat up, allowing the sodden blankets to fall away. His neck was stiff; hunger gnawed at him. And he was cold. Not just chilled, but the kind of cold that makes a man feel he will never be warm again.

Wilson groaned and slowly sat up.

"My God," he swore. "If I was any stiffer, you could use me for an ax handle."

Schmalsle, sleeping next to Wilson, rolled onto his stomach and moaned. "Mine belly thinks it has been deserted."

"The lack of food doesn't bother me as much as no coffee," Baldwin said. "I'm not worth a damn without it."

"Amen, brother," Wing said, kicking off his blanket and sitting up. "Since there's no coffee, anyone got food?"

Baldwin grabbed his saddlebags. "I brought some bread," he said, opening a bag. He withdrew a lump wrapped in cloth. As he squeezed, the mass compressed, bits of gooey, waterlogged bread pushing past the cloth. "Let me amend that, gentlemen. I brought some dough."

Schmalsle's face wrinkled in disgust. "I am not dat hungry."

"You know," Wing said, "there's some oaks up here, so we got acorns. I seem to recall wild plums, grapes, and such, too. I reckon they'll do until we kill something." He chuckled. "Leastways, we won't go thirsty."

Baldwin laughed and wiped at the moisture on his face. "Let's go. Maybe we'll find Lyman today."

They saddled their mounts and continued east.

"Lem," Baldwin called, "just because we can't see them doesn't mean our Indian friends have gone home. I want you to ride fifty, maybe a hundred yards ahead of us. William, you do the same to the rear." He gazed at Wing. "And you, sir, I want you to keep your powder dry."

Baldwin's hands ached from the cold. He flexed his stiff fingers to relieve some of the pain. He'd stuffed his gloves into his saddlebag after the leather had become waterlogged. They just pumped more chill to his bones.

The skies around them darkened again and a steady rain began. While not the driving torrent of the day before, the water was still cold and soaked Baldwin. Muttering curses, he turned up his uniform collar and hunched his shoulders.

They had been riding about two hours when Wilson signaled for a halt again. Baldwin licked his lips, anticipating another find of grapes or acorns or maybe even meat.

Climbing off his horse, the scout lay down in the tall wet grass and crawled toward a low bluff.

The scout reappeared and walked the roan back.

"I cain't believe it," he said quietly.

"What?"

"Injuns, goddammit. That's what." He pointed back to where he'd stopped. "I spotted a pony grazing in an arroyo right about there." He looked back at Baldwin. "When I got to the top of that ridge, I seen maybe a dozen more. Then I saw the redskins. They're hunkered under a bank that had been hollered out by flood water."

"Was it the ones we been fightin'?" Wing asked.

Wilson stared at him. "How the hell would I know? It wudn't like I was goin' to ask 'em. Damn, Ira, what a fool question."

Wing felt the blush redden his cheeks. "I'm sorry, Lem." He grinned. "I reckon my head's as waterlogged as the rest of me."

"Vhat shall ve do, *Herr Leutnant?*"

Baldwin chewed his lip a moment, then shook his head. "I'm not sure, Schmalsle. I guess we should give those boys a pretty wide berth."

He faced Wilson. "Lem, you ride between us and the Indians. If you see any movement from that arroyo, come running. We've fought our way through them before, we can do it again."

Two Horses huddled under the embankment as close to the fire as he could get. His leggings were soaked through and chill bumps ran the length of his arms.

"I wish I'd brought more clothing," he mumbled unhappily.

Rubbing his hands on his upper arms, Bull Buffalo nodded glumly. "Who would have thought this? Two days ago, I was worried whether there was water to be found. Now I wonder when the snow will start."

"Winter is coming," an older warrior said. He looked at Two Horses. "Soon the sun will be driven away and the earth will die. I do not want to be here when the cold comes to stay. I am ready to go home."

The others gathered under the bank nodded their agreement. Two Horses did not know what to do. He had no intention of quitting the chase.

"Go if you must. I will not. I have no wife, no children. My father is strong and healthy and can provide meat for my mother as he always has. I will follow Tall Boots and the others."

The older warrior who first spoke shifted slightly to face Two Horses. "You have chosen the warrior's road, young man. It's a lonely and dangerous path. Had I no family, I would ride with you. When the sun returns and the grass greens, I will ride at your side again—if you want me."

Two Horses smiled. "You will always be welcome." He gazed at the others. "All of you."

The afternoon passed quietly. The rain slackened to a heavy mist, but the sky grew progressively darker until it looked as though night had fallen. The warriors decided to wait until the next day to leave.

Two Horses and Bull Buffalo sat side by side next to the fire, taking turns tossing twigs into the flames.

"Will you be going home, too?" Two Horses asked.

Bull Buffalo sat a moment, rolling a stick between his fingers. "It is not often that I will get to see a boy become a man," he said, dropping the wood into the fire. He looked at Two Horses and smiled. "I think I will ride a little further and see what other surprises you have."

The sky had grown so dark he had trouble seeing the riders around him. As the rain eased, Baldwin saw they rode alongside a creek.

"I don't know about you men," he said wearily, "but I'm beat. Let's camp here."

The scouts dismounted, loosened their saddles, then sat, back to back, each man holding on to his horse's tether.

Wing nudged Baldwin with his elbow. "You reckon we're anywhere close to Captain Lyman?"

"I don't know, Ira," Baldwin answered glumly.

Schmalsle said, "I hear somzing."

Baldwin heard steps, then a noise he didn't recognize. The men slid their pistols from their holsters.

They heard a grunt, then shuffling.

Baldwin stared at the swirling mist trying to catch a glimpse of anything. He pointed at a shape he saw.

The object was as large as a small horse.

A shape with small horns and wide flaring nostrils emerged.

It was a buffalo. The animal looked at the four men, shook its massive head, and moved away.

Baldwin lowered his pistol. "Thank God for that," he whispered. "It was only a buffalo."

Wing stood, holstered his weapon, and grabbed the Sharps. "It was more'n that, Lieutenant. It was supper."

He handed his reins to Baldwin and quickly disappeared into the mist. A few moments later came the distinctive boom of his rifle. When Wing reemerged from the fog, he carried his gun in the crook of his arm and his hands were full.

"I got us a chunk of the hump," Wing said, grinning. "We'll eat good tonight."

Wilson rose. "I'll see if I can find some tinder and wood."

"Remember vhat happened with ze last fire?"

"Schmalse's right," Baldwin said. "We don't know that those Indians we passed earlier aren't on the move."

Wilson made a face. "Raw? We got to eat it raw?"

Baldwin opened his saddlebags. "I might have some salt or something in here. Hello, what's this?" He pulled a bottle wrapped in paper from the bag. "Well, I'll be damned! Somebody left us a present."

"What is it?" Wing asked.

Baldwin unwrapped the parcel and examined the bottle. He pulled the cork, sniffed, then took a small drink and grinned. "Whiskey!" He handed the vessel to Wing. "Each of you take a drink. We'll pour the rest over the buffalo meat."

"Ain't the same as cookin'," Wilson grumbled.

"True," Baldwin conceded. "But it's better than nothing."

Wilson grunted. "If'n you ask me, it's just a plain waste of good whiskey!"

TWENTY-FIVE

Thin black clouds, fringes edged in tendrils of white, scudded across the uniformly ashen sky, pushed by a keen northern wind that sliced into Two Horses like an obsidian blade. He shivered as he gazed at the white disk of sun peeking through thinner layers of cloud. The orb offered little light and no warmth.

The members of the scouting party roused and quickly prepared to leave. Conversation was scarce, the camp's mood bleak and uncomfortable. Two Horses could think of nothing to say to lift the warriors' spirits.

Mounted and eager to be home, the wolves waved and offered hearty farewells to Two Horses and Bull Buffalo as they left. They soon disappeared into haze.

"I see no reason to wait any longer," Two Horses said. "Do you?"

Bull Buffalo shook his head.

"What will we do?" Two Horses asked as he picked up his rifle, quiver, and bow case.

"Find the wagon trail. The rain has probably washed away all hoofprints except those made today, so if we find four sets of prints, we can be sure it's the soldiers we've been chasing."

Two Horses pulled the loops of the quiver and bow case over one shoulder. He picked up his robe and left the shelter of the embankment and walked to where they'd staked the horses.

He quickly climbed on the gray's back. He pulled the quiver and bow case loops down to his waist, allowing the carriers to rest on the horse's behind. The rifle lay in the crook of his arm. Prepared to ride, he glanced over at Bull Buffalo. The older warrior was ready as well. Two Horses nudged his horse into a walk.

Baldwin looked into the sky and let the rain pelt him in the face. Someone watching him might think he was enjoying the shower, but it was his way of giving in—like a drowning man who suddenly takes a deep breath of water.

The morning had started cloudy, but relatively dry. He had a stiff neck from using his saddle as a pillow, and his joints ached. His tongue was covered with a thick film, and he still tasted the bitter, coppery combination of whiskey and raw meat.

They'd ridden for less than an hour when the rain started again. It seemed every turn they made, an obstacle stood in the way. Sometimes he felt as if he were destined to ride the plains forever, never to see his wife and child again.

The wind still blew from the north with a razor edge. They were nearing the head of the Washita River when the rain stopped, as suddenly as it had started.

"Let's ride to the crest of that ridge," Baldwin said, pointing to the east. "I want to get a better lay of the land before we move on."

The ridge was not tall, but it was the highest point in sight. From its back, the scouts had a commanding view for miles around.

The surrounding landscape was flat and featureless. The weak sunlight precluded shadows to show differences in elevation or where the land was cut by arroyos and gullies.

They saw squalls still raging in the distance, and the Washita ran below them, its banks filled.

"Say, Lieutenant," Wilson said, "lookit over yonder, way to the east."

Baldwin saw nothing but ground shrouded in haze. "What am I looking for?"

Wilson pointed to a narrow valley. "See where the land's cut? You can make out hills on either side, and a low spot in the middle."

Baldwin's gaze followed the landscape until he found the area Wilson described. He still saw nothing remarkable, until he noticed objects paler than the surrounding haze. Concentrating, he realized they were arranged in neat rows.

"Well, I'll be damned," he murmured. "Tents." Then louder. "Tents! Is that what you see, Lem?"

"I reckon."

"How about the rest of you? What do you see?"

Schmalsle squinted. "*Ja*, maybe so. Is it Lyman?"

"Has to be," Wing said. "They's the only soldiers out here besides us."

Baldwin took off down the slope at a trot. The others caught up at the riverbank. They forded the stream quickly, ignoring the water that once again drenched them and their weapons.

They moved across the plains smoothly, conversation animated by the anticipation of finding Lyman and his wagon train. Soon they reached the foothills that would eventually open into the small valley where they saw the tents. The rain started again as they climbed the gentle slope, but it didn't dampen their spirits.

Baldwin spotted a lone figure silhouetted against the sky to the south.

Odd, he thought. *Why would they post a sentry way out here?*

He then looked to the south and saw another guard. "I wonder if they've had some Indian trouble."

"Why do you say that?" Wilson asked, suddenly nervous.

Baldwin pointed at the first man. "They've got sentries posted there"—he indicated the second—"and there."

"Well, hell," Wing complained, "I knew it was too damn good to be true."

The scouts rode into an arroyo, up its other side, and continued until they crested a hillock. The valley stretched out before them. It was narrow, and the hills surrounding it were steeper than Baldwin had first thought. Groups of the tents they'd seen formed neat circles with their openings to the east. Horses were staked outside the tents. Smoke came from the open tops, curling around tall poles.

"Sweet Mother of Jesus," Wilson whispered. "Tipis."

Baldwin couldn't speak. What they had thought was Lyman's camp was actually a large Indian village. He estimated at least fifty tipis. He quickly looked for the guards he'd seen earlier. Neither was in sight. Had they been seen? Were the lookouts already racing to the village to gather the warriors?

"We could try ridin' hell-bent through the middle of 'em," Wing suggested. "It worked before."

That had worked before, but it was against a small group of Indians—not an entire village. "I don't think so," Baldwin said. "There's too many of them, and we'd have to travel too far. By the time we were halfway through, they'd all know we were there, and we'd be dead."

He looked for a possible avenue of escape, and spotted a deep narrow gorge that led to the north. "Let's head in here. We'll walk the horses and circle the area. Maybe we won't be seen."

"I vould not count on it," Schmalsle said glumly.

Once they were at the bottom of the ravine, Baldwin sent Wilson ahead. The scout immediately rode back to the top, reasoning that he could see more and offer better warning.

Fifteen minutes later, the scout was back.

"There's a buck riding down a arroyo that's fixin' to join up to this one. He's herdin' some colts. I figure they're strays. He wasn't carrying a gun, but I did see a bow."

"Then ve must kill him," Schmalsle said. "Ve cannot allow him to varn ze others."

"We cain't shoot him," Wilson argued. "That'll bring all of 'em down on our heads."

"True," Baldwin said. "Another thing to consider is when they find the body. We have no way of knowing how or when this arroyo ends." He paused and took a deep breath. "We'll have to capture him."

"What?" Wing exclaimed. "Are you outta your everlovin' mind?"

"Look, if we take him alive, the others might think he is still off hunting those horses. And, he might be of some use."

"Like what?"

"Hell, I don't know, Ira. Just quit arguing. We're taking him prisoner, and that's it."

Wilson sighed. "All right, I'll do it. Ira, you and Bill come with me. Lieutenant, you mind holding the horses?"

Wing and Schmalsle dismounted and handed Baldwin their reins. The three scouts jogged down the arroyo to disappear around a bend. Baldwin followed. As he rounded the corner, he saw Wilson perched high on the wall behind a large rock. Wing and Schmalsle crouched on the ground near the junction where the two gorges met.

Three colts trotted into view, closely followed by the Indian. As he approached Wilson's position, the scout slowly rose. He took two quick steps and launched himself at the Indian. They collided with a loud smack and quickly went over the horse and onto the ground. Wilson grabbed the Indian by the neck and throttled him into silence.

Guns drawn, Wing and Schmalsle ran from their hiding positions. They grabbed the Indian and stripped off his bow, knife, and tomahawk. Once he was unarmed, Wilson released him. Gasping for air, the captive sat up and stared wild-eyed at the men.

Baldwin rode up at a trot. The Indian stared at him and the lieutenant was startled to see green eyes. The Indian's hair was red, and freckles showed under his deep tan.

"He's white," Baldwin declared.

"Yup," Wilson said, still breathing hard. "I saw that. Most likely he was took as a child, but make no mistake, sir, he's a Injun."

"Me Tehan," the Indian said. "Me good Comanche. Me friend."

"He's just a boy," Wing said. "Leastways, if'n he was still white, he'd be a boy." He addressed the prisoner. "You still savvy English, boy?"

Tehan nodded slowly, cautiously. "Me *good* Comanche."

"Yeah," Wing said dryly. "You said that." He looked at Baldwin. "What now?"

"We'll tie him to his horse and continue on."

They bound Tehan's hands, and placed him back on the paint. The scouts tied a rope to one foot, passed it under the horse's belly, and tied it to Tehan's other foot. They looped a lariat over his neck and drew it tight. Wing held the other end of the rope. The three scouts mounted up, and the party got under way again.

"I wonder where this arroyo lets out," Baldwin said. "Do you think he knows?"

Wing shrugged. "Let's ask him." He leaned close to Tehan. "You hear the lieutenant, boy? You know where we're going?"

Tehan glanced from Wing to Baldwin and back and shrugged. "Me Tehan. Me—"

"Yeah, yeah, I know," Wing interrupted. "You *good* Comanche."

Tehan smiled and nodded.

"I don't know, Lieutenant," Wing said to Baldwin while still watching the Indian. "Could be he don't understand. Could be he don't know, though I cain't imagine that." He looked at Baldwin. "Most likely, though, he's just tellin' us to kiss his ass while he waits for a chance to get away."

The weather worsened, hard rain interlaced with hail showers. The scouts pulled out their soggy army blankets, tied them around their waists, and draped them over their heads. Tehan was left to suffer without cover, but it didn't seem to bother him.

The arroyo twisted and turned until Baldwin had no idea which way they were headed. The pouring rain prevented any normal navigation by the sun. They continued to ride until they rounded a sharp corner.

Wilson, riding ahead a few yards, looked back. "I see an opening," he called, stopping.

Baldwin and the others pulled alongside him and peered through the rain. Less than a quarter mile away was the Indian village. They could see the tipis clearly, could hear the horses nicker, and smell the smoke of cook fires.

"Someone's bound to have seen us," Baldwin said. "So we have to go on." He looked at Tehan. The boy grinned back. "I don't know if you remember enough English," he said, drawing his pistol, "but if you try to escape, we'll shoot you."

The boy's smile faded, and he nodded solemnly.

"Good." He addressed the others. "We're going through the Indian camp at a trot. Keep the blankets over your heads. I want Wilson and Schmalsle to keep their pistols trained on our young friend here. If he does anything suspicious, kill him."

They broke into a trot, the horses splashing through mud puddles. The village was like a ghost town. They saw tipis, horses, even an occasional dog, but no people. Baldwin was relieved. He was thankful the cold rain and northern winds had kept the Indians inside.

Near the edge of the village he spotted two women gathering firewood. Neither paid them the slightest attention, apparently just wishing to complete the chore and get back in the lodge. He glanced at the prisoner; the youth seemed content to ride along quietly.

As they rode out of the village, Baldwin finally released the breath he'd been holding. Under different circumstances, he would have shouted for joy.

The scouts hurried to the Washita, flowing behind the camp, and rode into the timber lining its banks. They followed the river's course until it stopped abruptly at a bluff.

Baldwin looked around them, but saw no easy avenue. "Well, we can swim the river or ride out in the open."

"I ain't leavin' these here trees," Wilson announced. "I can swim, and so can my horse. Go on if you want. I'll meet you downstream."

"Lem's right," Wing said. "It'd be a damn fool thing to do, riding back out on the plains. If this boy's family spots us, they'll hunt us to hell and gone to get him back."

"All right," Baldwin conceded. "We'll stick to the trees and the river."

He walked the gray into the water, allowing the horse to take its time. When he reached the deepest part of the river, he slid off the horse's back and, hanging on to the pommel, swam alongside. When the stallion got a purchase near the opposite bank, Baldwin climbed back on. Dripping, he surveyed the trees around him, then waved the others forward.

Schmalsle went first, crossing without mishap. Wing and Tehan went next, the Indian's expertise with a horse showing as he forded the river with ease. Wilson was the last man across, his big strawberry roan swimming strongly.

Over the next hour they were forced to make four more crossings to avoid obstacles. As Wing and Tehan cleared the water, Wing's mare collapsed, dumping the scout into the mud.

"Goddammit!" he shouted. "Son-of-a-whore horse."

He jumped to his feet and spun toward the animal. Then he saw it wasn't going to get up.

"Christ Almighty! Ain't this a lovely picture? Shit!" He walked over to Tehan and cut the ropes holding him on his horse. "Come on, Injun, climb down."

Tehan glanced from face to face, then slid off his horse. Wing pulled the tomahawk from his belt and handed it to the youth.

"Kill it," he ordered. "And make it quick."

Tehan stared at the weapon a moment; then he regarded Wing and the others. He sighed and nodded. He crossed to the downed mare and struck it several times in the head and neck until it quit moving. Covered in the horse's blood, he walked back into the river to wash.

Wing stared at the Indian a moment, then looked at Baldwin. "Ain't no way we can make any time dragging that boy along. I aim to take to his horse, which leaves him afoot. We cain't make no time like that."

"What do you propose?" Baldwin asked.

"We kill him outright, here and now. I can slit his throat, and we'll be back in saddle in no time."

Baldwin took a deep breath and slowly let it out. The same thoughts had crossed his mind after seeing Wing's horse go down. Yet the boy could do them no harm—and he was white.

"I sure as hell don't care for the notion of it," Wilson said, "but Ira's right. We cain't afford to be slowed up."

Tehan looked at the men and suddenly understood the implications of their argument. He rushed to Baldwin and grabbed the lieutenant's leg. "Me good Comanche. Me good Comanche." He turned and faced the others, tears mixing with the rainwater on his face. "Me good Comanche!" he cried. "Me friend." He fell to his knees sobbing.

The Indian's action left Baldwin distraught. He'd expected anger, defiance unto death, all those things Indians were supposed to show when captured. Yet the prisoner was little more than a boy, and he wasn't born into the life. Seeing him there in the mud, face buried in his hands, Baldwin knew he couldn't do it, knew he wouldn't do it.

He cleared his throat. "We're taking him with us."

"What?" Wing exploded.

"He's my prisoner. If I kill him now, it would be murder."

"Who the hell's gonna know?"

Baldwin drew himself erect in the saddle. "Mr. Wing, I am an officer in the United States Army. Part of my duties is to faithfully and accurately record the details of the missions I am assigned. Rest assured that I will report our activities on this trip." He looked at Tehan.

"Now, this man is in my care and your charge. You will act accordingly."

Wing stared at Baldwin openmouthed. Then he glared. "Goddammit! No-good, stinkin', son-of-a-bitchin', crybaby, red nigger's gonna get us all kilt." He pointed at Baldwin. "And you're gonna help him." He stumped to his dead horse, loosened the saddle, and jerked it off the animal.

"Mark my words," he muttered, dragging the mud-covered saddle to the Indian's paint. "Just you mark my words."

Wing flung the saddle on the paint and cinched it up. Grabbing the horsehair reins the Indians preferred, he mounted, then pulled on the rope. Tehan grabbed the lariat as it tightened on his neck, and clambered to his feet, coughing.

"I'll tell you one thing, Lieutenant, that boy's gonna keep pace with us, or I'm gonna drag his sorry ass all the way to Supply."

Two Horses and Bull Buffalo had found a partial set of tracks just before the storm hit. They kept riding the same direction looking for small clues that showed their quarry's passage before the rain could wash them away.

That afternoon, the rain stopped again, and they stood atop a ridge and looked at an Indian camp below. Bull Buffalo said he was sure they were Kiowa.

"Surely they didn't go there," Two Horses said.

Bull Buffalo chuckled. "Not on purpose." He looked at the gullies around them. "Let's ride in some of these. Maybe they snuck by."

The third arroyo showed signs of travel. Finding marks on the stone left by horseshoes, the warriors were convinced they'd found the trail again.

They came upon three colts standing near the junction of two ravines. A new set of unshod tracks joined the others and continued down the gorge.

Two Horses and Bull Buffalo paused at the mouth of the arroyo. Before them lay, mostly washed away, the trail of the five white men. The tracks lead straight toward the Kiowa village that Two Horses's man had seen from the hilltop.

"We might as well go home," the older warrior said.

"Why?"

"Because it's obvious to me they are prisoners of the Kiowa." Bull Buffalo stretched. "Besides, I miss my wife, and I've had enough rain and wind and cold."

"We don't *know* they've been captured."

They rode among the lodges and asked to speak to a chief. They were escorted to the tipi of an older man who sat on a buffalo robe in front of his door smoking a pipe.

The Cheyenne introduced themselves and were invited to share the chief's robe and pipe. After the ritual smoking, they got down to business.

"What is it my Cheyenne brothers wish of Poor Buffalo?"

"We are seeking a small group of men," Two Horses said. "They are *veho*, whites."

Poor Buffalo nodded slowly. "No such men have passed here." He smiled. "Or they would not have passed."

Bull Buffalo cleared his throat. "We have found their trail, and it leads here. We rode through a big storm on the way. Maybe they passed then."

"Hmm." Poor Buffalo signaled a warrior near him. "Go through the village. See if anyone has seen any strangers."

While they waited, the three men talked about the current situation with the whites, what was happening at the Kiowa Indian Agency, and the Cheyenne battle

with the soldiers. Presently, the warrior returned trailed
by a woman.

"What have you seen?" Poor Buffalo asked.

"I was gathering wood during the big storm when
the ice fell from the sky. Five riders came by. One of
them was that white boy with the red hair that Mamanti
adopted."

"Were the others white, too?"

The woman shrugged. "They had blankets over their
heads. I thought they were just boys out playing in the
storm."

Poor Buffalo turned his attention to his visitors.
"There is your answer, much to my embarrassment.
Had they been soldiers, we would have been slaugh-
tered in our warm, dry homes."

Two Horses looked at the woman. "Do you know
which way they rode?"

She pointed toward the Washita. "That way. To the
river and into the trees."

The Cheyenne thanked Poor Buffalo for his hospi-
tality and left. They rode to the edge of the village and
stopped, regarding the tree line in the distance.

Two Horses thought of how he and Bear Tooth had
managed to sneak into the soldiers' camp and steal his
horses. How strange it was that Tall Boots had done
almost the same thing to the Kiowa. Even *veho* knew
how to hide in plain sight.

"They've gotten away," Bull Buffalo said. "We will
never find the trail down there." He laughed. "So now
we go home with many stories and a good one on the
Kiowa." He glanced at Two Horses. "Maybe I'll let you
tell that one to Crow Woman."

Two Horses stared to the east at the mist-covered
plains. "You tell her, my friend. I am not going back."

"What will you do?" Bull Buffalo asked quietly.

Two Horses looked at the older warrior. "You don't sound surprised."

"I'm not. Let me guess. You have chosen the warrior's road. You will not take a wife. You will not hunt or participate in village life until your quest is fulfilled."

Two Horses nodded. "I will not return until I have faced Tall Boots."

Bull Buffalo held out his hand. Two Horses gripped his forearm tightly.

"Good luck, Two Horses. May the Great Spirit ride with you."

"Thank you. I hope you have a safe journey home."

Releasing Bull Buffalo's arm, Two Horses kicked his mount into a lope, heading for the river.

Bull Buffalo watched the young man until he disappeared among the trees. He slowly turned his horse around and started home.

The scouts forded the river eleven more times in fifteen miles. Their captive had no choice but to swim when the others crossed. As the current would start to carry him away, Wing pulled him out of the water by the rope around his neck. Sputtering, he'd climb up the bank and cry, "Me good Comanche. Me good Comanche." Baldwin and the others thought the whole matter rather humorous, laughing each time Tehan was dragged through the river.

Night approached quickly as the men made their way downstream. In the fading light, Baldwin spotted the wagon trail where it intersected the river. Turning back to the north, the scouts crossed the divide between the Washita and Canadian Rivers in the dark.

Long after midnight, they saw fires in the distance. They rode closer cautiously, until they heard the familiar sounds of an army camp. Grinning, Baldwin arranged them in pairs with Tehan following. They made their way straight to the camp.

"Halt! Who goes there?"

Baldwin peered into the darkness, but couldn't see the sentry. The man had a good hiding place. "I'm First Lieutenant Frank Baldwin, Fifth Infantry, riding dispatches for General Miles. These men with me are couriers as well."

"Advance and be recognized."

As they approached, a figure stepped from the shadows. He scrutinized Baldwin and the others, paying close attention to Tehan.

"He's a prisoner, son," Baldwin said, anxious to move on.

The sentry saluted. "Go on in, sir."

"Thank you," Baldwin replied, with a casual wave of his hand.

When the scouts rode into the light of the campfires, all conversation stopped. The collection of soldiers and teamsters stared at the five men as though they were ghosts. Finally, an officer walked forward. Baldwin recognized Captain Lyman.

"My God, Baldwin," the Fifth Infantry officer exclaimed. "You look awful."

"Thank you, sir. It's a pleasure to see you, too."

Lyman grinned. "Come, come, dismount." He waved at the others. "You men as well." As he helped Baldwin off his horse, he felt the other's clothing. "You're positively soaked!" He saw his first sergeant. "Sergeant, I want dry clothing, food, and coffee with a healthy dose of whiskey for these men. Immediately."

Baldwin nodded at the Indian. "We caught this fellow near one of our old campsites. Claims to be a Comanche named Tehan. I'd like you to take him to the general for questioning."

"Certainly, old man." He pointed at a couple of soldiers. "You two take this prisoner and find a secure place for him."

Wing tossed the rope to one of them, and they led Tehan away. Unencumbered, the scout made his way to the nearest fire. "Any you boys got a snort? Last whiskey I had tasted like buffalo."

Wilson and Schmalsle soon located men they knew and followed Wing, leaving Baldwin alone with Lyman. An orderly brought dry clothing. By the time Baldwin had changed, a plateful of roast antelope and beans and a steaming cup of coffee, reeking of whiskey, were ready. He took the plate and sat with his men. Lyman joined them.

"I've got a thousand questions, but I'll let you eat a bit first."

"I appreciate it," Baldwin replied around a mouthful of beans.

Up on the bluffs, Two Horses watched Tall Boots and his men. His hunch had paid off. Never finding a good trail among the trees, he'd ridden cross-country until he came upon the wagon trail. It led across the river. On the other side, he found the hoofprints of the five men he'd been seeking.

They'd made no effort to conceal their tracks, and he'd followed them until he saw the campfires. Moving up into the rocks above the soldiers' campground, he waited until, finally, Tall Boots and his wolves rode in.

Two Horses felt good.

TWENTY-SIX

Two Horses awoke shivering to a cold, drizzly dawn. The sky looked the same as the day before. Though the land had not changed, this day was different. Today he would at last meet his enemy.

His enemy. That was how he thought about Tall Boots. He had chased this man for three days. Tall Boots was his and his alone.

He wanted to hate the *veho* wolf who had first pursued him across the plains, then led him here. Tall Boots brought the soldiers to the People. He fought against them, and had killed more warriors in the last several days than had been killed in the big fight on the Red River.

Two Horses had been wrong about Tall Boots at the stream where Porcupine died. He'd thought the soldier soft and a weak warrior. He'd also been wrong about Bull Buffalo. What else had he made up his mind about, only to learn the truth later?

He lay at the top of the ridge and observed the camp below. Soldiers moved about eating breakfast or brushing their horses. There were many more wagons than he remembered seeing at the camp near the bluffs.

A man walked through the camp, and Two Horses recognized the blue coat and boots.

"Good morning, Tall Boots," he said to himself. "Are you—"

He cut the question short as another Tall Boots stood up at one of the campfires. He saw still another talking to several soldiers. And still another just putting on his coat. Then another—no, that man had marks on his arms.

Suddenly Two Horses didn't know who was who. Was Tall Boots still there? Had he slipped away during the night? Dread knotted his stomach at the thought of his quarry already gone.

Three men mounted horses and rode from the camp. One was a soldier wearing tall black boots and riding a gray stallion.

Two Horses heaved a sigh of relief. He hurried to his horse and threw the buffalo robe across its back. Climbing on, he urged the animal forward. Topping the ridge, he paralleled the path the men rode.

Baldwin felt wonderful. Though he'd had less than four hours' sleep, he was rested. More importantly, he'd gone almost thirty days without a drop of liquor. He was clear-eyed, leaner, tougher, more sure of himself. The past three days of adventure had done nothing but assure him he could cope without alcohol.

Now, he was on his way to Camp Supply to deliver the general's messages. From there he was to go to Fort Leavenworth and deliver Miles's personal plea for help. Even the wet morning couldn't dampen his spirits.

"Hey, Lieutenant," Wilson called, "take a look at that ridge yonder."

An Indian rode along the bluffs. He made no effort to conceal himself.

"You reckon he's one of them redskins that's been doggin' our trail?" Wing asked.

"I can't imagine how," Baldwin remarked.

Wilson peered at the lone warrior. "I wonder what he wants."

Suddenly the old fear gripped Baldwin. Maybe this fellow was just a scout for the rest of his war party. They could be lying in wait anywhere along the trail. He shook his head angrily.

"Damn it, leave us alone!" he shouted at the Indian. Feeling foolish, he grinned at the scouts. "Sorry, boys, but I've had about all the adventure I want. Ignore the bastard. He's only one man. Now let's ride."

"Wait a minute," Wing said, reining in. "He's doing something."

Baldwin stopped his horse to watch.

Two Horses stopped at the edge of the cliff. An eagle flew in the distance, and he knew he would follow no farther. The prey had escaped the lands of the hunter, but this prey was like no other. He was a warrior, and like all true warriors, he would return.

Two Horses raised his rifle in salute and called, "Ride in safety, Tall Boots. Come back again to my land. Bring your wolves. I will be waiting."

The words were faint but distinct as they floated across the valley. He didn't understand what the Indian was saying, but Baldwin thought he understood the meaning. The gauntlet, the challenge of individual combat for the sake of honor. It gripped his warrior spirit, but only momentarily. There would be another time, another place, another fight, but not today.

Frank Baldwin pulled himself erect in the saddle and crisply saluted his enemy.

EPILOGUE

Miles's campaign was the first of what would be called the Red River War or Buffalo War. Officially, it was named the Indian Campaign on the Staked Plains, 1874–1875.

Miles indeed heard from Lyman—and came running. He continued to lead his troops through an autumn as wet as the summer had been dry. The Indians referred to this time as the Wrinkled-Hand Chase.

Winter shut down all operations on the plains, and Miles took the opportunity to refit and prepare for his second campaign against the Plains Indians in the spring of 1875.

The story of Frank Baldwin's journey with William Schmalsle, Ira Wing, and Lem Wilson became known as Baldwin's Ride or Baldwin's Run. It made all of the big newspapers in the country, and Baldwin's name was on everyone's lips. But for all his celebrity, Baldwin, a soldier's soldier, was back at the front in less than two weeks.

The Cheyenne managed to escape another major encounter with the army throughout the rest of 1874, though some Cheyenne were in Palo Duro Canyon during Mackenzie's raid. In the spring of 1875, they were hounded by Miles, Buell, and Davidson. Though deaths were minimal on both sides, the constant harassment by the military deprived the Plains Indians of their natural lifestyle. Faced with starvation and slow annihilation, the Cheyenne chiefs surrendered their peoples in the summer of 1875.

Western Adventures
From Pinnacle

__Requiem At Dawn__
   by Sheldon Russell   0-7860-1103-3 $5.99US/$7.99CAN
They called it Fort Supply, the last outpost of the U.S. Army on the
boundary of Oklahoma Territory—home to the damned, the dis-
graced, and the dispirited. Now, Doc McReynolds has been ordered
to establish a redoubt at Cimarron Crossing. But while McReynolds
leads his company to Deep Hole Creek, a past he'd like to forget
dogs his every step.

__Apache Ambush__
   by Austin Olsen   0-7860-1148-3 $5.99US/$7.99CAN
For a military man it was the farthest you could fall: the command
of a troop of Buffalo Soldiers in the Ninth Colored Cavalry Regiment.
For Lieutenant William Northey, managing misfits was all that he
was good for. Amidst the dying and the valor, a bitter, defeated army
man would find a woman to love, soldiers to be proud of, and the
warrior that still lived in his heart. . . .

Western Adventures
From F.M. Parker

__Blood Debt
          0-7860-1093-2   **$5.99**US/**$7.99**CAN

They thundered across the Rio Grande as one of the most powerful fighting forces in the world. But disease, ambushes, and the relentless heat turned America's fighting forces into a wounded and desperate army. By the time General Winfield Scott reached Mexico City, some of his men had become heroes, others outlaws.

__Blood And Dust
          0-7860-1152-1   **$5.99**US/**$7.99**CAN

Grant had smashed Vicksburg and cut open the heart of the Confederate States. Still, the war raged on. But the fighting was over for Captain Evan Payson, a wounded Union Army surgeon, and John Davis, a Confederate prisoner of the Union Army. Now, two desperate soldiers have struck a deal: in exchange for his freedom, Davis will carry Payson home to die in Texas.

Call toll free **1-888-345-BOOK** to order by phone or use this coupon to order by mail.

Name_____

Address _____

City_____ State _____ Zip _____

Please send me the books I have checked above.

I am enclosing $_____

Plus postage and handling* $_____

Sales tax (in NY and TN) $_____

Total amount enclosed $_____

*Add $2.50 for the first book and $.50 for each additional book.

Send check or money order (no cash or CODs) to: **Kensington Publishing Corp., Dept. C.O., 850 Third Avenue, 16th Floor, New York, NY 10022**

Prices and numbers subject to change without notice. All orders subject to availability.

Check out our website at **www.kensingtonbooks.com**.

William W. Johnstone
The *Last Gunfighter*
Series